BEYOND THE BLACK GATE

By Mark JF Hudson

Beyond the Black Gate
Published by The Conrad Press Ltd. in the United Kingdom 2025

Tel: +44(0)1227 472 874
www.theconradpress.com
info@theconradpress.com

ISBN: 978-1-917673-21-1

Typesetting by: James Sadlier, jamessadlier@me.com
The Conrad Press logo was designed by Maria Priestley.

Printed and bound in Great Britain by Clays Ltd, Elcograf S.p.A

It is only with the heart that one can see rightly;
what is essential is invisible to the eye
ANTOINE DE SAINT-EXUPÉRY

The truth will set you free
JOHN 8:32

About The Author

After Oxford University, Mark Hudson worked as an editor in the Economist Intelligence Unit before later co-founding a digital-government research and conferencing company. After this, he co-founded several charities and mentored people coming out of prison. Married and living in Dorset, Mark is a sculptor in stone. *Beyond the Black Gate* is his first novel.

Contents

····· Nehtan's Journey

Kilometres 0 — 250
Miles 0 — 125

Hadrian's Wall · Colud
Start · VINDOLANDA

EBURACUM
York

Mare Germanicum

Britannia

CORINIUM
Cirencester
LONDINIUM
London

COLONIA AGRIPPINA
Cologne/Koln

R. Rhine

Lemma Magna

PORTUS DUBRAE
Dover
BONONIA Boulogne

MEDIOMATRICUM
Metz

MOGUNTIACUM
Mainz

DURNOVARIA
Dorchester

Alan Camp

REMORUM
Rheims/Reims

TREVERORUM
Trier

LUTETIA Paris

R. Moselle

R. Rhine

Gaul End

Bonadeni

LUGDUNUM
Lyons

MEDIOLANUM Milan

BURDIGALA
Bordeaux

R. Rhône

TOLOSA Toulouse

Via Domitia
Tarusco

MASSILIA Marseilles

Enserune
ARELATE Arles

NARBO Narbonne

ROMAN BRITANNIA AND GAUL IN AD 409

6

Principal Characters

BELLATOR:
the Biarchus (sergeant) in the cavalry escort for the delegation from Britannia.

BRIGOMALLA:
wife of the Christian presbyter (priest) Vigilantius.

CLARA:
the wife of Paulinus of Pella.

CRISPUS:
leader of the delegation from Britannia, travelling to the Emperor Honorius in Italia.

FROMUS:
one of three delegates from Britannia, travelling to the Emperor Honorius in Italia.

GERONTIUS (HISTORICAL FIGURE):
senior General (or Comes), rebelling against the usurper Constantinus III. A cousin of Fromus.

GOAR (HISTORICAL FIGURE):
prince or chieftain of a tribe of Alans, seeking a homeland in Gaul.

MESSOR:
an experienced soldier, part of the cavalry escort for the Britannic delegation.

NEHTAN:
young enslaved woman, bought by Centurion Marcellinus, to look after his son, Vitalis.

NOVATELI:
officer commanding the small cavalry escort for the delegates from Britannia.

PAULINUS OF PELLA (HISTORICAL FIGURE):
a wealthy and literary Patrician.

PHILUS:
a veteran cavalryman, part of the cavalry escort for the Britannic delegation.

URSACIUS:
a wealthy grain supplier and one of the three delegates from Britannia, travelling to the Emperor Honorius in Italia.

VIGILANTIUS (HISTORICAL FIGURE):
unconventional Christian presbyter (priest) and theologian.

YOCHANAN BEN ZAKAI:
Jewish merchant, selling spices and fine clothes.

CHAPTER ONE

LATE AUTUMN 409, INSIDE A ROMAN ARMY CAMP IN NORTHERN GAUL.

Not now, not yet, but one day she would be free. The top of the beech sapling swayed at the back of the yard, fluttering above a pile of rotting planks. The tree had survived because Master Marcellinus had protected it. Next year it would be tall enough for its seedlings to be blown over the ramparts. They would fly with the wind, and she would go with them.

Nehtan ducked out of the master's hut. Dirty army tents lined the track on both sides. No one in sight. By Heaven, her arms ached from the first trip with the water pitcher. She'd have to skirt past wolfish soldiers to fetch the week's provisions. But she could bear it; the Lord was at her side, and, one day, she would find a way back to the north of Britannia, to her family and the village.

Strands of hair flopped across her face as she walked: no rain, only a breath of wind. Squawks came from a mud-caked raven, tethered on a pole next to the quartermaster's cabin. A dog leapt and the raven shot off its perch, its leg fastened by a gristly rope. Wings beating, a feather fell and was pounced into the mud, the dog biting and barking. Nehtan shivered as the raven settled back onto its perch, squawking a loud 'krrruk', one wing arched above its back.

Twenty paces round the corner, a knot of legionaries lounged across the track. One of them was the tall man who liked to force his hand under women's cloaks. She turned back; best to go the long way, past the latrines.

A shout: 'Hey, girl, we need our share.'

She couldn't stop herself looking back.

'Yeah,' said the tall soldier, slouching on a post-rail, 'we know where you live. Make it easy on yourself.'

Agritia said it was best to pretend you hadn't heard them, but the soldiers weren't interested in a wizened old herb-cook like Agritia.

Shifting the pitcher in her arms, Nehtan flexed her calves. She wanted to run, her stomach tightening at the memory of what had nearly happened before. It was sport for them, but they wouldn't get away with treating her like an animal, like they did with the others. She belonged in Colud, free-born; she was not what the Romans said.

Turning to face them, she shouted. "Stick with the goats. You've got nothing they'll notice.'

The legionaries guffawed, but the tall one yelled. 'Who do you think you are? Come here, you fucking slave.' He started after her, yelling over his shoulder. 'We can't let her get away with it.'

She ran, clutching the pitcher. The Master would be furious if it broke, but the soldier was catching up with her. She flung the pitcher aside.

Something was coming out of a tent - too late, she ran into a burly man with bushy eyebrows. For a moment, they clutched each other, scrabbling not to fall over.

'Hold there, my pretty.' It was the Quartermaster, a friend of the Master. 'What's up with you?' His big arm was around her.

'Nothing sir, sorry. It's...'

Her forehead brushed against his stubbly chin as he held her tight. He smelt of beer. Looking back: the tall legionary was striding fast back to his mates.

The Quartermaster shouted over her shoulder. 'Hey, you, what are you up to? I recognize you, you'll be on report.'

'No point bothering with him.' The Quartermaster released Nehtan, his finger brushing her chin. 'I know his type. As for you, you'd best find another water-pitcher.'

She looked down at the shards in the mud. The man's voice softened. 'I'll tell Centurion Marcellinus what happened. Now, be on your way.'

His hand reached behind her. A moment's hesitation, then he picked a scrap of mud off her cloak.

'Thank-you, sir.' Forcing a smile, she nodded.

Tension lessening with each step, she walked back to the hut through a slush of grey water. There was a spare pitcher at home, but its handle was broken, making it difficult to carry. It would be aching work, but by the late afternoon she could rest out of sight, tending the fire in the master's billet. Worries would drain away, leaving only a drift of smoke and the distant sound of the baker's boy pounding grain into flour.

The peace would not last. Vitalis would burst into the hut, hungry from playing with his friends. Barely eleven, she had looked after him since he was five, and now he liked to boss her around. Pray God that he was in a good mood and would not make her go out at dusk. The tall soldier could be anywhere.

May the Lord God's mantle be about me, she prayed, and may it be different in the new camp when we get there.

* * *

Days later, Nehtan was the lone female, perched high on a baggage cart amidst a grumble of red-cloaked soldiers, trudging south through all the waking hours. A scattering of chestnut and lime trees dotted the edge of the road. In the distance, a cloak of forest covered a hillside.

She shivered and huddled down in the army cart, thankful that the boy Vitalis was asleep. He didn't seem to notice the jolts from the deep ruts in the road.

The field they were passing reeked of rotting cabbage; the villagers must have fled. Poor Gauls; the stony track had echoed for centuries to the thump of Roman sandal-boots. Now they also had barbarian raids to fear.

Damn the army! It was forcing her south, away from beloved Colud, nestled in the river valley, well beyond the Wall. But she would not let the soldiers see how miserable she felt, nor would she join in their marching chants like she used to. Nowadays they never stayed long anywhere, each camp more threadbare than the last.

The carter kept looking to the right and left, peering into the scrub.

After some hours, she heard the master call a halt. His voice carried as he sent two soldiers to scout the steep-sided valley ahead. The singing stopped, and the twenty legionaries at the front stood at attention. Nehtan wanted to jump off the cart and stretch her legs, but she saw the men scanning the bushes and trees. Even the soldier on the water-pitcher cart stayed put.

Tossing back her black hair, Nehtan smoothed her hands over her forehead. Serve them right if they were ambushed: she would run into the scrub as quick as a rabbit. These Romans thought she was no more than a savage, with no right to bite and scratch when they put their hands on her. The sooner their empire crumbled, the better.

A relaxed shout from the front, and the column resumed marching. The carter cracked his whip on the ox; two pigeons flying towards the column veered away. She drew her cloak close. It was cold sitting on the baggage cart, but at least she didn't have to tramp like the legionaries.

The ox-cart trundled past a collapsed hut at the edge of a weed-filled field. It would have been home to a family, before their world had been crushed. Perhaps their bones lay nearby, picked clean by foxes and badgers. The Romans didn't care, wouldn't notice.

She remembered a grove of yews on the hillside above her village, north of the Wall. Before going into their hut, she always turned to look at it. Inside, she had sat with mother-nymayr and father-atir, watching the flames dance in the hearth, smoke swirling above, warm voices all around. All that had been wrenched away when those men captured her. Why had atir let her go out? The feeling of how it had been was almost out of reach, and there were things she didn't want to know. The one good thing that had happened since then was the risen Lord Christ, where there was no 'us' and 'them', no place for fear. She tensed, imagining how nymayr would scorn and think her a fool, a little girl who used to run to her grandmother and now ran to the Roman god.

A sharp pain flashed in her ribs. The little master was grinning as a lock of hair flopped about his forehead. She glared at Vitalis and pushed his foot away. Was it a game, or was he reminding her that she was his father's slave and he could do as he liked?

The boy clutched his throat, grunting fake coughs as he lifted an imaginary pot to his lips. Getting him a drink would mean jumping down from the high cart and running to the water-wagon. Anything could happen, and the oxen were bad-tempered brutes whose hooves could crush a foot. She forced herself to smile.

'Tell you what, let's roll a dice. You win, and I go for the water. You lose, and we wait until the next stop.'

'I could *make* you go.' Vitalis puffed out his thin, brown-cloaked chest. 'I should.'

'You want the soldiers to see that you need a woman to get your water?' She hesitated to call herself a woman, though she was six years older than the boy and old enough to be wed - or traded.

'You would say that.' Vitalis flicked her shoulder with the back of his hand. 'Father told you ... all right, where's the dice?'

They rolled and Nehtan won. She suppressed a smile and stroked her round cheek. Looking up, she checked the sky for birds: a flock of starlings darted over the tree-tops. Lucky them.

High clouds streaked the sky. These soldiers thought they were tough, but nowadays they were fuss-pots, anxious about every bit of news and gossip. She lay back, letting her nose fill with the musty dampness of the woollen cover. There was a familiar stinging in her scalp, but she didn't have the energy to scratch. Better to lie quiet, nestled down below the cart-sides, out of sight of the legionaries. They were all new to her, except the master. High God, she prayed, I give you thanks for the protection of Master Marcellinus – and may the Lord bring me home.

Vitalis huddled up to her, and she put her arm round him. 'Do you remember when we first met, near the Wall in Britannia?'

'Weren't you always there?'

She shifted to lie sideways, looking at the boy's freckled cheeks and broad forehead. 'Don't you remember your mother?'

13

Vitalis was silent, looking up at her with wide eyes. He shook his head.

'Never mind. I'm sure she was a good woman.'

'Father says she was the best.'

They lay still, with the boy close. He was so much nicer like this. Something jutted into her hip, a hard stem from one of the vegetable sacks under them. She didn't want to move and wake the boy from his reverie. Her belly adjusted to the pressure sticking into her side as she felt the warmth from the boy.

Minutes later, Vitalis grimaced and nudged her with his bony elbow. 'These sacks stink. Let's have a wrestling match.'

'I can't, not now.' The boy was too old for that sort of thing, especially out here.

Another push from Vitalis. 'Come on, Nehtan, like we did at home.'

'That was ages ago; it's different here. Look at the soldiers behind: which one's the best marcher?' Vitalis's lips curled, so she pointed ahead. 'The master's at the front. Try to spot him.'

'I've done that hundreds of times,' he huffed. 'Father said you'd keep me happy, but you're not.'

She knew she shouldn't, but she reached and tickled Vitalis in his armpit.

'Don't, that's not fair.'

His kicking thrust the rug off her legs. 'I'll stop, if you promise to behave.'

'All right, I surrender.'

As soon as she removed her hand, Vitalis pulled her hair, making her shout. 'Ouch! Don't do that!'

The carter turned and leered over his bulbous nose. He was about to say something when the oxen lurched towards a reed bed down the side of the road.

Vitalis called, 'Watch out!'

'Another time, another place,' the driver growled as he wrenched the ox-reins, 'and you'd know what's for.'

'Father said you had to be careful.' Vitalis sat up straight. 'You got stuck yesterday and it took hours to get out.'

'By Hell's rim, you little cur.' The carter half-rose from his seat, then glanced forwards to the column of soldiers. 'I wouldn't be here if I had my way, none of us would.'

Nehtan motioned to Vitalis with her finger on her lips. She made herself smile at the man. 'We'll be all right with Centurion Marcellinus. Wait till we get to the new place. He'll get us the pick of the rations.'

One of the six legionaries striding behind winked with his mouth open. Sweat trickled from under his helmet. She raised her eyebrows, then quickly looked away to the stumps of bush and tree at the side. The soldier would be like all the rest.

Vitalis heaved himself up, peering forwards over the oxen. Nehtan slumped on a sack and shut her eyes. Pulling her cloak-hood tight, she let the pinpricks of tiredness soften.

She was not a slave – not like old Agritia, who could think of no life other than cooking for the centurions. In the eyes of the Lord, everyone was equal. More than that, through him, who was all in all, everything was part of one eternal root, far beyond Emperors, soldiers - and the old gods.

Even so, fear crowded the edges of everything. In Colud, father always told Eothar and her to be quick, not to waste time. What was his voice like? She couldn't bring it back; only the sound of murmurings and a rising wail when Grandmother had been banished.

Nehtan hunched her knees and rocked. Grandmother had been the best person to snuggle up to, never too busy.

Now, out here in the wilderness of Gaul, everything was slipping away, like sand. What was it that the master's poet said? Something about each sea wave pursuing the next one, and the crest is only there for a moment, and each moment happens afresh every time. It was like forgiveness – the chance to start anew and rise above the soldiers' taunts, the master's coldness, and what they had done to her in Colud.

* * *

Suddenly, a loud cawing burst over her, like a huge flock of crows taking off. Her eyes snapped open. The boy's nostrils were flared, his eyes wild. He jerked his head to the front. She froze: ahead of them, scores of horsemen were crashing through the marching Roman line. A long-haired warrior smashed his sword down on the head of a collapsing legionary. Another Roman crumpled, screaming as a horseman's lance pierced his back. Cold sweat cut through her.

'Father!' Vitalis yelled.

The cart-driver jumped down and ran into the scrub. The other drivers and the soldiers at the back raced after him.

Her mouth was dry and her stomach clenched. 'Mother of God, save us.'

From the front, the harsh voice of Centurion Marcellinus rang out amidst the raw screams of the attacking riders. 'Stand firm, form a square.'

She grabbed Vitalis. 'Get down!'

The boy was digging into the bundles beneath where they had been sitting. A cook's knife flashed in his hand as he jumped down.

Leaping after him, she grasped his shoulders. 'What are you doing?'

16

'Let me go! I'm going to help Father.'

Fear seized her as Vitalis pointed the knife at her belly. She slammed his arm against the wheel and the knife dropped from his hand.

'You're a barbarian, like them!' Skinny arms flailed at her chest. 'Let me fight. I'm going to find Father.'

'No, you're not, you're coming with me.'

She dragged Vitalis round the back of the cart. The sound of thundering hooves, a horseman lunging towards them in a ragged brown tunic, sword pointed skyward. She shoved the boy hard into the bushes.

Whooping shouts, the rider was nearly upon her. Running, jumping across a ditch. A heavy thump, her head twisting sideways. Then – nothing.

* * *

Mud, a ditch next to a straggly wood of larch and alder. She spat and tried to focus. Blood on a rock beside her hand. Her skull ached. Above, the road ran straight as a javelin through twilight-grey trees.

Squelching her hand into the earth to keep her balance, she wobbled to her feet. The top of her cloak was matted with blood. A baggage cart lay on its side. Further off, dark shapes stained the road.

Holy Lord! Bodies.

Not Vitalis. If you have taken the master, then leave Vitalis. Almighty Father, let me find him. He's all I have.

A dead horse lay with its rear legs splayed, a crust of froth curdled on its lips.

'Vitalis,' she shouted, 'where are you?'

At the coast, the soldiers had been talking about Vandals

17

and Alans rampaging through Germania, but they were not meant to be here.

Further off, more bodies, all with the cropped hair and shaven faces of Romans. She thought of the braggart who had winked at her – but he had run away.

Heavy Roman spears lay sprawled on the ground. The pale chest of a half-naked soldier was drenched in blood. His neck was slashed and two black-red spear-holes were punched through his belly. A javelin stuck up out of the chest of the legionary next to him. The Romans would have done the same if they had won, though they would not have left any weapons behind. Praise the saints that she had fallen into the ditch.

No sign of the master. She couldn't bear to look further. Vitalis must have escaped to a village.

It was getting dark as she found her way back to where the road snaked out of the wood. She clutched her head, then stumbled against something. A body! No, a sack of cabbages.

Wandering on, she struggled to keep her balance. What to do? A thought flickered through the gloom. She went back to the capsized cart, found the sack, and dumped the cabbages. Skull pounding, she squeezed down inside the leather sack, clenching her knees, trying to ignore the wet patch above her ear. Exhaustion gave way to fitful sleep, swords cutting through red-cloaked flesh, metal flashing into Marcellinus's jellied face.

* * *

Dawn and a pale, bitter brightness. Grasping her head, she almost yelped.

Hold to the one true light; she would not die in this wretched wood.

18

A sudden rush. By the blood of the martyrs, she was free! The wind blows where it will, and a great gust had come her way. Marcellinus was a good Christian, a decent master, but one of his friends had been urging him to sell her while she was ripe. Soon Vitalis would not need her, or would want her in a different way.

Crouching inside the sack, holding her head, she concentrated on that silent place where everything was held:

> *Many are the branches of the one tree*
> *Our mighty trunk from earth to sky.*
> *Many are the arms of the great oak,*
> *We are one in Christ.*

Voices? But it was the cawing of crows. She stumbled out of the sack. Five crows hopped away from a mess of innards spilt from the side of a cloaked legionary. One bird remained, tugging at long piece of gut.

'Go away!' She threw a stone. The crow flapped, but kept its hold.

In the distance, two foxes were ripping at flesh.

God forgive her, she would not look for Master Marcellinus. But she had to find Vitalis, see that he was safe. She would make her way to the coast, but not back to the camp, never again would Romans command her. There had to be a way. By her faith alone: everything else had been taken from her. They would see, they who ruled the world, that she was her own person.

Flat-topped, moulding mushrooms glistened atop the ditch. Agritia would have known if they were safe.

A screech from the trees ahead. *Mudebroth*! A spirit, a dead-soldier spirit, angry at not being buried. Or a bird, frightened by someone in the thicket? She reached for the

19

amulet hanging around her neck and rubbed the Chi-Rho three times.

Another screech. A crow swooped out. She ran down the road, then stopped: the Lord would protect her from the ancient ones. She looped back across boggy ground.

Damn Vitalis. She crossed herself. If he had not run away, she wouldn't be alone. A sparrow flitted by – a sign? She must speak to break the spell.

'I'm coming, I'm coming, whatever you are.'

Clutching the amulet, she tramped across puddles to reach the clutch of hawthorn and elder from where the crow had flown.

'Vitalis, Vitalis?'

Thorns tore her leg as she picked her way in, using a stick to bash the brambles. Her head seared with pain. Then, in amongst the decaying greenery, she glimpsed a blue tunic.

He was face down. A faint, acrid smell of blood and urine. She knelt, sobbing, stroking the dark brown hair and freckled cheek. The belt was gone, as was the thick cloak with its silver fastener.

His body was flat, as if it had been emptied. She had seen dead people, but not like this, not little Vitalis. His body should be anointed; it had to be done on the first day.

So tired, lying down, facing away from him, she winced as she moved off a thorn. No villagers for at least several day's march. What about the barbarians? Too much to think about. Listen to the blackbirds and thrushes, their ordinary twitter. At church, they sang about the many light-beams from the one light, everything given life, all creation bursting into song. But what about Vitalis? Full of life, then, suddenly, everything gone, nothing there. Was it her fault?

Holding her ears, eyes closed, she sank into a cold oblivion.

* * *

Aching. The blood-patch on her scalp throbbed. Brushing ants off Vitalis, she heaved him up, his head lolling backwards. The blood on his back was dry. The ground was too hard to bury him with her hands.

She remembered Vitalis's thin, sharp voice proclaiming what he would do when he grew up. Now, he would never join the army or own two horses.

If she left him, he would be eaten by animals. Dragging him up, her arms under his shoulders, she lugged him back towards the road. Brambles caught round her foot, and she fell. Vitalis's head hit the ground with a thud, but nothing came out. His soul must have left his body. Away from the gloom of the thicket, in the daylight his face looked older. Two blade slits stained the back of his tunic. A week ago she had rubbed herb balm on his chest and neck when he had come back bruised from fighting bigger boys.

'Vitalis,' she groaned, 'my little man, forgive me.'

She pushed him back into the fading briers and nettle stalks, and lay on her back. A faint orange light bathed the branches above. She thought of the friendly gatherings to which she had gone each week, with the master and Vitalis, in the wooden oratory in Bononia. She loved the long services, standing side by side with everyone, no one telling her what to do. The singing was spirited and there was something else – a glimpse of peace, like a drop of water falling into a still pond, rippling and settling back.

Fog drifted from the treetops down to the track. A tawny owl sounded; the first she had heard since leaving Britannia.

Thuds. The pounding of hooves from the track off to the right. Barbarians? But they wouldn't be coming back to the same place. If they were Romans, she wouldn't tell them who she was. Heart racing, she pushed through a broad patch of brambles, tearing her hand. The thud of horse hooves was already receding.

A glimpse of a cloaked rider disappearing in the evening mist. 'Sir!' she shouted. 'For the love of God.'

'Heia!' The horse stopped. Looking back over the rump of his animal, a clean-shaven young man pulled his hood back. No army insignia, and his cloak was finely woven.

'The dead men,' he demanded. 'Who did it?'

'Barbarians.' She edged forwards, hand over head-gash. 'They killed everyone.'

'Get up behind.' The man was peering into the dark of the trees. 'Come on, jump up.'

'I can't leave Vitalis.' Stepping back, she slipped in the mud.

More beasts appeared out of the vapour beyond the rider. A cavalryman in a red, mud-rimmed cloak nudged his horse forwards. 'Sir, the Decurion says we're to keep moving.'

Nehtan was picking herself up. A laugh came from a thick-set rider. 'Look at the state of her.'

'Fromus,' a harsh army voice broke through, 'I must ask you to get back in line.'

The soldiers turned their horses, the heavy saddles straining, hooves thumping. Within seconds they had gone, even the one called Fromus.

'Don't leave me!' she yelled at the vanishing shadows.

Glooming night. Rustling sounds. She darted behind a bush and crouched. Silence. Scrabbling in the undergrowth, looking for a stick, but there were too many nettles. Rubbing her hands in dock leaves, sniffing the scent of rotting leaves floating in the mist.

Then, heavy clops and the rider returned, the man Fromus. He held his hand out, long face and young eyes shining, a gold ring on his finger.

'I can take you if you're quick.'

'Vitalis is in the bushes.' She stumbled up. The rider was a master, but there was no help for it. 'I can't leave him.'

'By all the saints,' he said, 'tell him to come out. I can take you both until we reach the others.'

'You don't understand, sir, he's dead. I can't leave him.'

'There's no time. Woman, this is it. Get up.'

'I can't, sir, I've looked after him half his life.'

The rider jumped down and seized her, hands shoving her up onto the saddle, the animal jerking forwards. She did not resist. Then, they were away, trotting past a soldier corpse, his arms bent back, a gaping hole in his belly, empty eye sockets and peck marks on his face. She shut her eyes. Only the sound of creaking leather, her fingers too cold to tie the neck-cord on her cloak. Had she made a mistake?

They caught up with the others and rode on. A chafing soreness spread along her thighs, her head throbbing, but it did not matter. The arms of the man in the fine cloak were around her waist, holding the reins in front of her. His warmth was good. If only it could go on like this, suspended above the ground, moving without making any effort.

Hours later, they stopped for the night. Her rider walked into the gloom with the cavalry officer and two civilians. Their voices carried.

Someone spoke the name Novateli. He answered, his voice sounding like he was the stiff, plume-helmeted officer. He wanted to leave her: she would slow them down. Another man agreed; someone else called this man Ursacius; perhaps he was the bearded one. The urgent voice Fromus, her rescuer, saying that they must bring her with them, it was their duty. Then an old man spoke, sounding too important to be out here in the wastelands. His voice was muffled. She couldn't hear any more.

The cavalrymen were feeding handfuls of oats to the horses. In another world, she remembered nymayr boiling oats with water and barley for the evening meal.

Fromus came back, ahead of the others, his face beaming.

'You can come with me, until we reach Remorum. You must tell us what happened.'

The grey-haired civilian pushed in front and glared at her. 'Why are you here?'

She did not usually talk to high masters such as these, let alone look in their eyes, but she had to make herself do it. 'We were on our way to new quarters when barbarians attacked. One of them slashed me, and they must have thought I was dead.'

The one called Ursacius stroked his pointed beard.

'Are you sure you are the only one to survive? You don't sound Gaulish.'

'Sir, I'm from Britannia.' Her people were cattle traders who knew how to deal with Romans. She glanced at Fromus. 'By the good Lord, I beg you, I'm Christian. Look, I've got a Chi-Rho on my amulet.'

That seemed to satisfy them. A soldier called, the officer walked away, and the others moved to the fire.

CHAPTER TWO

Fromus woke with first light. Yellow birch leaves drifted down in the chilly breeze. Dampness tinged everything.

The young woman Nehtan was up. Short-legged, high cheek-bones, almost defiant. He watched as she swept back her black hair and felt her head wound. He wanted to grasp that lithe, curving body.

The others could go to Hell; he would keep her as long as he wanted. Besides, Crispus needed him and should know it. The man treated Fromus like a distasteful acquaintance, not as a fellow patrician who had hosted him at the family home in Lemma Magna. A little friendliness was all Fromus asked, and he'd be damned if he'd explain why he had picked up the girl. Let them ask, if they dare.

Soon, they were leaving. A pack mule could carry her, but there was a problem.

'You see, sir,' said the barrel-chested Biarchus Bellator, 'we'll have to shift up the load, and these here mules will make a right braying. Likely, she'll find it hard to stay on.'

'She can come with me.'

'As long as you're of a mind, sir,' Bellator grinned. The Biarchus arranged a blanket behind Fromus's four-horned saddle. The girl stood still, eyes twinkling in her round face. There was a firmness about her.

'Tell me,' Fromus said, when she was up behind him, 'were you born a Roman?'

'Sir, I lived with Centurion Marcellinus. He adopted me after our village was attacked, and I looked after his son.' A pause. 'Sir, it's not right that I left Vitalis unburied: foxes were at the dead soldiers.'

'It would have taken too long.' Fromus stopped. She should be grateful. Didn't she realise who he was?

The flat land on both sides of the track was deserted, overrun by thistles. A cavalryman grunted as he pushed his horse past them.

Many nights lay ahead, and the girl was in his charge. Fromus shifted in the saddle. 'It's a long way to Remorum. You can hold on to me instead of the saddle horns.'

'That's all right, sir, there's no need.'

'If that's what you prefer. What brought your father -?'

'Centurion Marcellinus.'

This was direct; a plebeian shouldn't interrupt him. He felt the heat of her behind him. He could forgive her lack of training.

'Well, what brought Marcellinus to Gaul? Was he part of Constantinus's army when he invaded?'

'No sir, he was on guard duty. He wanted to retire back to Britannia. He was a proper Christian, and he helped me.' Her voice trailed off.

'How?'

Something was distracting her. He glanced back. The square-set, dark-eyed cavalryman behind them was staring at Nehtan's exposed calf.

'You see, sir,' her voice was quiet, 'I learnt to read and write with Vitalis, and I joined the Christian services. I was a catechumen, but now I'm baptised.'

'Do you like that?'

'What do you mean, sir?'

The horse stumbled over a root. Her arms clutched around him. He hesitated, then he put his palm on her hands. They felt small as she eased them free. Father would not approve –

all the more reason.

They were passing through a tunnel of overhanging trees. Branches with black and red berries crowded the edge of the road. Brown leaves dotted the ground.

'Sir, may I ask where you are going?'

'We're on our way to Italy to see the Emperor,' He paused, but the young woman said nothing. The words should have had more effect. 'You said that you come from Britannia, but you don't look like a Briton.'

'My mother came from a Sarmatian who served on the Wall.'

Fromus twisted round: her eyes were the colour and almost the shape of the almonds from Hispania that Mother liked.

'I thought that was long ago?'

'It was, I suppose. But we – I mean they – they kept apart, or some did, and had their own religion. That's what Grandmother said.'

'What, even now?'

'No sir, not any more. Everyone was suspicious of Grandmother being a stranger, and they didn't like us naming the eldest son Eothar; it was too foreign for them. They said that Grandmother had the evil eye.'

'Was she a priestess of your religion?'

'I'm a Christian, now.'

'I meant, your grandmother.'

'No, she couldn't. Only men are elders.'

An image flashed of the black-haired woman dancing naked in the moonlight around a burning oak tree. There was something hidden and enticing about her, something he wanted to taste. For now, he must build a bridge.

'You know,' he said, pushing a low-hanging branch out of the way, 'since you are half-Sarmatian and half-Votadinian, and you're a Christian, brought up in the army, you are a modern Roman – a bit of everything.'

'As you say, sir, but it's not special to me. I look after Vitalis – or I used to. There wasn't much else, except, I did love singing in the services.'

'You mean the Sacramentum?'

'Yes, sir.'

'There's no need to call me "sir" - out here. Call me Fromus, like I call you Nehtan.'

A grunt. One minute she was calling him 'sir' and the next she barely answered. She should know her place. He urged his horse through a large puddle. Not much later, she asked if she could hold him around the waist, as she was tired of holding on to the pommels. He felt the twin pressure of breasts pressing, and her cheek leaning on his back.

He remembered Silviola, a few years ago at home in Britannia. She was a new servant-girl, slow moving, with fair hair and a snub nose. For several weeks, he had pursued her with his eyes, smiling whenever they met, while she giggled. One day, when no one else was about, he had come across her carrying an urn at the rear of the house. He put his arms around her from the back, and, when she didn't say anything, he fondled her breasts through her tunic. She squeaked and he kissed her neck and told her how pretty she was. She broke away, but in the small hours of the morning she crept into his bed. It had been bliss every night for a month, until Mother found out. Silviola was dismissed, and he was heartbroken, for weeks. He endured a sharp lecture from Mother, who cut him to the quick by asking if his prayers were a sham, and didn't he care what happened to the girl? Father barked that he was setting a bad example and that it was not right to take advantage; he had let the family down. Fromus squirmed at the memory: yet again, he had confirmed Father's low opinion of him. He had kept his hands off the servants after that–though everyone else did it, and there was the slave brothel in Corinium where most of his friends went, and he with them.

It felt different out here in Gaul with Nehtan riding behind him – at least, so far.

In time, the sun was high, the horses were sweating. Fromus's legs ached and his thighs were sore, yet Nehtan made no complaint. If his sister Barita had been with them, she would have insisted on having her own horse and an elaborate arrangement of blankets and cloaks.

They passed under beech trees, dappled-bronze leaves, glistening. The air was good. Gaul was better than he had thought. He was on his own, far from Father, one of only three delegates from the whole of Britannia. And the young woman was with him.

Nothing was fixed; he didn't have to follow the rigid ways of old men. Thinking was clearer, away from home. Back in Corinium, this woman would barely have spoken to him, and he would not have been interested in her, except for what she was paid to do.

'What was it like,' he asked, 'being in army camps all the time?'

'It was my life. I'm used to it.'

'Yes, but soldiers everywhere. Not many women in the camp.'

'I did my best, sir, I defended myself. And Marcellinus was there. He protected me.'

Her life was barely imaginable. Far removed even from the life of the household servants back home, though at least she had escaped working in a house of Venus.

'With Marcellinus gone, is there anyone you can live with?'

'No, sir – I mean, Fromus. But don't worry about me, I'll be all right. There are friends back in Bononia.'

He pulled his hood back and sensed her supple form close behind. She would never get to Bononia - not a single woman like her, travelling alone - quite apart from the fact that they were heading in the opposite direction. No point in telling her. Strange, this meeting. He had never been so near to a non-patrician for such a long time, talking almost as if they were equal. What would it be like to be someone like her? Thank God, he'd never know. Impossible, where did such a thought come from?

Then again, was it so far away? If the barbarian invaders went unchecked, everything would be destroyed, even the lives of the servants and field-workers. The delegates' mission had to succeed, for everyone's sake.

CHAPTER THREE

THREE MONTHS EARLIER, SUMMER 409, OUTSIDE THE VILLA OF LEMMA MAGNA, IN SOUTH-WEST BRITANNIA

Messor was standing in the shade of two chestnuts, a javelin's throw from a couple of round huts. He felt for the pommel of his spatha-sword. Mithras! He should be in uniform. If it were not for the spatha, someone might mistake him for a field peasant.

Grabbing a foxglove stalk, he broke it off. In the distance, hefty men pushed a cart while a boy heaved from the front.

What a dump. His troop had careered like a fox on fire down half the length of Britannia merely to escort Tribune Treverius to an 'important' meeting at this southern villa. Time was, the cavalry was the elite, fought the hardest, had respect. Now, they were reduced to a single, bare-bones troop and had to act as bodyguards to arseholes like the Tribune.

There was nothing at this villa with the fancy name, Lemma Magna, at least not for the soldiers – without whom there would be no empire. The men were squashed into abandoned huts and had to make do with watery millet. Even the escort officer was only in the foreman's house, where they said the food was no better. No wonder the army was falling apart.

The land was dreary, stuffed with clodhoppers who stuck as close together as a virgin's arse whenever they saw soldiers. They must have tasted the edge of the blade. Likely, it was what they were used to, up to their eyes in debt and made

31

to do whatever their master wanted. Theirs was no life, not like that of a cavalryman, free of land-toil and ready for the next blood-quickening fight – but not down here, not in the choking depths of country-cousin land. It was the peak of the northern raiding season up at the Wall, and they were in the wrong place. It had been good roaming across the hills in the last active cavalry troop in Britannia. They grabbed whatever they wanted from scrappy settlements, slipping up the thighs of any girls they caught in the open. The few times they had come across Pictish raiders, his troop had sliced them up quick. Picts were blue animals on two legs.

Messor brushed flies off his short-cropped hair and grimaced in the direction of the Biarchus. Bellator was always smiling. He was sitting under a large oak tree, waiting to play dice with anyone foolish enough to try their luck with him.

Hay-top Philus, the other senior cavalryman in the troop, threw a coin in front of Bellator, laughing as he squatted in the dusty space between two huts. What did they know? A couple of old boozers, sitting there, bragging of their shared Brigantian background.

Philus threw and two dice bounced against the headboard of a water trough. Bellator stood, pretending to be unsteady on his feet as he scooped them up. Messor felt like telling the peasants what was going on - but why should he?

The big man chuckled towards two villagers who had stopped to watch. 'That's a fair belting, Philus. Mind how a real cavalry pro does it.' Bellator's head swooped round, fat cheeks bulging. 'Trooper Messor, coming to join us?'

'No.'

'A man of few words.' Bellator nodded at a young farmer with sunburnt cheeks and thick-set ears. The Biarchus raised his eyebrows as he looked back at Messor. 'I tell you, if you want to see cavalry go to work on a pack of yelling Picts, heed that man.'

Messor jerked his head and was minded to walk away. Killing was serious work, not to be shared with a rag-tag of bumbling peasants.

The Biarchus paused and appeared to be ruminating before he continued, speaking as if he were telling a tale around a late-night fire.

'Not more than a month ago we came across raiders up near the Wall. Trooper Messor launched on his own into a thicket of blue tattoos and axes. Fair split them in two, he did, crashed his horse right through and left us to mop up the leftovers. Saw him take out two Picts in quick succession, the last one a fat bastard with a heavy shield. Trooper Messor stabbed him in the neck, quicker than a viper on a lamb's heel.'

The villagers gawped at Messor. 'That true?'

Messor's eyes narrowed as he glared at Bellator, busy shaking the dice above his head. The big man threw them across hard earth and a die bounced off a log.

So predictable. Philus raised his eyebrows in triumph and Bellator squeezed his heavy chin, promising revenge, but lost again. The villagers watched, mesmerised: it must have been the most excitement they had had in weeks. In the distance, dogs barked.

Bellator grinned at the growing circle of onlookers. 'Hold. Do you see what I'll throw next? The Immortals are with me.'

'*Mehercle.*' Philus scratched his pinched cheeks and picked up the dice. 'You wait; you won't like what's coming.'

'Take a double, that's the kind of man I am.'

'You old ones, your bones need woollen beds.' Philus snorted as he threw the dice. 'There, look at that.'

'Try all you might, you can't make a hill from a sewer.' Bellator winked at a scrawny woman who stood behind a couple of admiring youths.

'Skill – skill and patience mark the long game.' Philus held his chin as he peered at the dice, laughing. 'See that.'

'Pure luck. Now watch this.' The Biarchus threw the dice. Messor's eye dropped; nothing else to do but watch this peasants' circus.

'Happen, this is the moment.' Philus bent to pick up the cubes. He rolled and let out a loud laugh. 'The saints are with me.'

'I'm out of patience with this man.' Bellator handed a coin to Philus before turning to the pushy youth who had been at his elbow. 'Hold there, youngster, do you dare throw against an old soldier?'

Messor had had enough. One idiot taking money off another. He stalked through the crowd of farmers and labourers. Nervous glances made him relish the weight of the sword slapping on his thigh.

The only duty coming up, though it was hardly that, was a game of hipposandal against the yokel team in the evening, and that was hours away. The villagers claimed they had run out of beer and the local swamp-rot they called wine, so there would be no joy there.

Messor headed down a dusty lane, regretting the orders to rest their horses. Even so, walking was better than seeing Bellator's smirk after he had cleaned out the few spare coins in the village.

A mass of wildflowers hogged the edge of the track. Anyone could see that the black soil was good, which was why they had ripped up all the trees. Long strips of spelt wheat, millet and barley were interspersed with smaller plots of beans and white goosefoot. Thatched huts were dotted about, and in the distance tall oaks loomed. A cart appeared, pulled by a mule.

Messor walked in the centre of the track, his hand on his spatha hilt. Raising his hand slowly, he stopped the cart and squinted at the women. Nothing but bags of old bones. He let them pass.

The sun beat down. He came to an overgrown wall, and turned off the main track. The path was lined with alder and blackthorn on one side and a tall fence of willow-hurdles on the other – another rich prick's villa.

Peering through cracks between the hurdle-stakes, he spied round huts and pigs rootling under apple trees. He could smash the fence and take what he wanted.

No one in sight, but he was not hungry and he could do with a rest. He walked on until the path broadened to reveal a wide green bank between the path and the hurdle-wall. After flattening a mass of goosegrass and comfrey, he flopped down in the shade of the fence.

In the distance, a girl was calling her animals to feed. Her voice was cheeky, brazen, reminding him of his first time. He had been about twelve, tagging along with a couple of big lads. They had held the slave-slut down, but, when it was his turn, she had laughed at him.

What was that? Something rummaging in his bag. Messor whipped out his belt-knife. Growling, a black dog leapt back, lost its hind footing and fell into a pool of brackish water. The cur scrambled up the bank onto the path. It had a bony forehead and liverish-brown eyes. There was something wrong with its left leg.

Messor laughed and peered into his leather food-bag. The mutt had failed to get anything. The crippled cur would not last long, and there were welt marks on its rump. It was odd for a dog to dare to steal from a man. His chest tingled as the dog held his stare.

Could it be a spirit of Canis Minor, a sign from the bull-killing god, Mithras, angry that the miserable Christians were persecuting his devotees?

Messor sliced a piece of hard cheese and threw it to the mutt. It sniffed the offering.

'I don't blame you.' he grinned, 'it's wretched, the scrapings from last year. But if you want better, you'll have to come to me.'

He squatted and held out a piece of stringy meat. The dog shuffled forward, retreated and came back, reaching its neck out to grab the meat. Soon he had the mutt on his lap, nuzzling the leather pouch under his arm. They played together as the sun burnt its way across the summer sky. The dog snarled when Messor brushed flies away from the red welts on its back.

He held the dog's jaw and muzzle and gazed into brown-flecked eyes. The mutt barked and tried to back away, but Messor stroked the black-brown patch above its nose. It was good having a dog, but perhaps there was more to this mongrel? The day before, an old man had made the secret sign of Mithras from the roadside as they rode past.

A growl, then jaws opened and teeth clenched on Messor's hand.

'What's up, Lefty? You'll have to do more than that to set me off. I won't hit yer.'

The heat of the dog's bite warmed his knuckles, which blanched with the crude hardness of the teeth. The pain was familiar, a throbbing rather than an agony. He almost liked it. It spread up his arm. There was a powerful surge in his lower limbs, a growing numbness, then a torrent of energy breaking into his belly. A scintillating light soaked through; all was luminous in a vast black expanse. Something soft and livid pulsed, power held in readiness, a bittersweet taste. Then, from behind a furry, canine nose, he was looking into the dark-set eyes of his own weathered face. Dog and man, he was both - but there was no urgency, nothing unusual; simply washing through them, a kind of sticky peace. And something else, looming above, a vast presence.

As quick as it had come, it went. Messor dropped back into familiar skin and bones. The dog loosened its grip and sniffed Messor's fingers. He held his hand out to let the mongrel lick the smear of blood on his palm.

Nothing like this had happened before, not in all his years of chanting the Mithraic mysteries in gloomy temples, amid smouldering pinecones, black masks and dancing light. He stroked the animal's head. Dogs had a special significance for Mithras. What did the god mean?

The mutt's breath reeked of rotten meat. Many a human smelt worse, especially when they had shat themselves on the end of his blade. He could take Lefty with him and get his wound sorted. Let others mock; they were fools who were forever snickering. In time, he would know what Mithras wanted.

A high-pitched, insistent woman's voice came from behind the wooden wall.

'... the two of you is like peas in a pod, you don't say nothing. I could be dying of the plague and you wouldn't tell till it was too late.'

The voices came nearer. Messor held the bony mongrel close to his chest, playing with a loose scruff of its hair.

The woman persisted. 'If you was to pass word via

Riocatus, tell our son Silvius to come home for the worst of the winter. He'd make the journey, you know he would.'

'That's as may be, but he's taken the coin and it's up to the master.'

'They can't do the regular work when it's frozen. Besides, what about the holy day of the Lord's birth? There's going to be a big feast in the villa.'

'So they say, but I'll have nothing to do with that scum Riocatus. By heaven' - it was a quavering old man's voice - 'he cheats rich and poor alike, and folk don't realise. The worst of it is that everyone buys his lentils at market.'

'That's how it is. You know what the good book says: the sun rises on the evil as on the good, and so too it rains on the just and the unjust.'

Messor glared at the fence. How could anyone believe such a lying coward's creed? Curse their Christianity. It was the likes of these priest-struck peasants who had destroyed the sacred temples of Mithras in Londinium. The bitch should shut the fuck up. She would soon shrivel if he slit her man's throat.

The dog was edging away. Messor bent down and tried to coax it back but it was no good; the spell was broken. The mongrel loped off.

From behind the fence, the woman's voice was rabbiting on.

'... and another thing, when are you going to fix the hen-hut? The fox will get them all. If our boy Silvius were here, he'd do it. We should never have let him go.'

The ring-bag would not let up, and she had driven Lefty away.

Messor lurched towards the fence with one hand on the hilt of his sword.

'Shut up. Fuck off to Hades.'

Silence.

Shouting, then the old man rushed to the fence. 'What's that, who are you? You've no right.'

'Let it be.' the woman cried. 'Husband, come away.'

Grey wisps of beard and angry eyes peered through gaps in the wooden frame. Messor unsheathed his sword. He could skewer him through the fence if he was quick about it.

Is that what Mithras wanted? But Messor felt no rage, and he couldn't have another row with the officer, not so soon after the last one. He lowered his spatha.

The old peasant was shouting at his woman. 'Run, quick as you can, get our brothers and nephews, go! I'll not put up with this.'

'No, husband, come away, be gone. He's got a sword; he's one of them soldiers. Holy Mary protect us, don't let him do this.'

The old man pointed his staff at Messor, no more than a sharpened stick. 'You can't be fouling our name with your filth. You don't belong in these parts, you're no good.'

'Piss off.' Messor growled. 'Bring your whole rickety family – I'd like that – and your daughters too.'

They were nothing. But what of the dog and that strange mingling? It had left him shaking; his mouth dry, the taste of ash and bone. He could get rid of it if he hurt them – but it was too late, the dog had gone. The place was a scab heap.

He walked away, clattering the sword along the wooden fence. The tip was a biting tooth, a receding presence. Its echoing sound drowned everything – the old man's shouts, the green path, the warm dog and the bright sun. There was only rat-trat, rat-trat, trat-rat, trat-rat...

CHAPTER FOUR
THE SAME DAY, AUGUST 409.

Father had made it clear that to Fromus that he had to attend the feast in their villa at Lemma Magna. He would miss a long planned day out in Corinium with his friends.

Mother's meticulous preparations had been annoying, but he saw that she had transformed their dusty old villa. Even Father, the Honourable Matugenus, had noticed. Flowers had brought the oratory back to life, and the main hall had been painted blue to frame the wall hangings and frescoes. From the garden courtyard, the guests would step down four marble steps to the dining chamber, their eyes drawn to the repaired floor mosaic of Christ with his Chi-Rho, in front of a semi-circle of interlocking couches.

Heaven above, it would be a boring lunch. Most of the guests would be the same old patricians: Crispus, Father's closest ally, but unfriendly to Fromus; bulky and bald-headed Aquilinus; and Fastidius, an ancient neighbour. Father said that the most important man would be Tribune Treverius, an outsider who came from the city of Eburacum in the far north. There were four other guests, including the bumptious new City Councillor, Neso. It was a mystery as to why Father had invited him, a man whom Father could not stand and who would not fit in. He must want a favour from him. With any luck, Neso would make a spectacle of himself and provide some discrete entertainment.

At midday, Fromus stood with Father and Mother in the cool courtyard of Lemma Magna greeting the guests. Mother, the Lady Aula, sparkled like a golden kingfisher: pendant earrings and long gold chains shimmered on her cross-layered, dyed-silk dress. Then Barita entered. Her thick, curly hair was done up in the latest fashion. A coiling gold thread twisted around her waist, enhancing the firmness of her breasts. All the men turned. Her jewellery came from her future husband's family; the man was handsome enough, but had no substance. Barita didn't seem to care that there was still no word of him since he had gone to join the army in Gaul.

Fromus winced as Aquilinus caressed his hand down Barita's arm, before beckoning her aside. She broke into a nervous peal of laughter. Fromus moved nearer, looking down at his wine-glass.

'My dear young woman' - the old fatty simpered - 'did you hear about that wedding in Corinium, the one your father refused to attend? It was positively the most glamorous occasion we've had since they opened the new temple of pleasure. The statues and servants came from a certain equestrian whom we all know.' Aquilinus bent forward, but his voice was loud and clear. 'Between you and me, their silver saved our friend from selling his villa.'

Barita: all she had to do was stand there. Fromus could see that she was purposely keeping her back to him: she was in a huff about being excluded from the luncheon feast. Fromus turned aside to talk about the weather with an old neighbour. He wished he had the nerve to ask Neso what he thought of the family villa, but the town trader was deep in a private conversation in the corner. Crispus was holding forth to Father.

After a while, Mother and Barita left. It was a relief when everyone took their places on the large semi-circle of couches. Fromus grimaced when he ended up next to Crispus. After exchanging a few conventional remarks on the glittering dining chamber, Crispus turned and devoted himself to the man on his other side, Aquilinus.

Fromus drained his glass. Instead of this ordeal, he could have been out with his friends - if Titus were still alive. Titus never said the wrong thing, ever the dutiful eldest son, at least in front of Mother and Father. At other times, when no one was listening, Fromus remembered his brother, his sacred brother, reminding him that he would always be unimportant, a useless second son. Well, now it was different. Titus's death had meant many things, and one of them was that he had taken over Titus's membership of the Corinium Council - and his place at this feast. But the Council hadn't been like he had thought: they never discussed important things, like the Scotti raids or the civil war in Gaul.

Even the big things in Corinium were small. Toying with his glass, Fromus remembered lingering with his mother after church services. He had become friendly with a hunched man with a broken nose and a foxy face called Macarius, a tanner, who had let slip a joke about customs weights. Fromus probed, and it came out that there was a swindle in the marketplace that everyone knew about – everyone except the members of the Corinium Council Chamber. This snippet had enabled Fromus to make his mark, but nothing had changed. Corinium was such a backwater.

The chamber doors re-opened and a procession of servants brought in the first course on four huge Samian dishes, decorated with swirling blue and green animal patterns. The plates were filled with grilled carp and perch, marinated in a paste of cumin, coriander and the last of Mother's peppercorns. Fromus had known this dish was coming and had been looking forward to it.

After an awkward pause, as if everyone were waiting

for a signal, the men settled down to feast. The fish course was followed by beef and chicken dishes, glazed and spiced in a technique particular to their head chef – a Gaulish acquisition from the last slave market three years ago. There was also smoked hare, shredded in a garnish of rock samphire and pigweed. Fromus's nostrils twitched as he savoured the aroma wafting from the chicken dish: was that a hint of the ridiculously expensive saffron that Mother had bought?

Father had said to mix the red Biturica wine lightly with water, instead of the usual half-and-half. The white wine came from their own vineyards, spiced with chamomile.

To Fromus's surprise, the guests drank sparingly and conversation was muted. He hung back from finishing off his third glass of wine. On his left, ghastly Crispus was still engrossed in hushed conversation with the heavy-set Aquilinus. Once or twice, Crispus turned to Fromus to compliment him on his household's food, but somehow Fromus never managed to get a hold on the man's attention.

It would almost be better to be Barita, fuming in her room, than sitting with everyone and being ignored. What was the point of the feast?

After the main meal, fruits and desserts arrived. Fromus took a large helping of dewberries and wild strawberries, soaked in a resin of honey and elderflower juice. Crispus did the same and grinned over his arched eyebrows before turning back to Aquilinus. It was a relief when Father called the major domo to usher the servants out of the dining chamber. No one would notice if Fromus nodded off during the speeches.

Aquilinus waddled to the front of the semi-circle of couches, adjusting his toga like a great bird about to flap its wings.

Great God, let him not ramble on forever.

'My friends, I must start by thanking our host for a superb luncheon.' Several guests thumped their couches. Fromus sighed heavily. His eyelids drooped. 'We will hear from Matugenus in a minute.' Aquilinus cleared his throat and reached for a spotted glass tumbler. For a moment, the man's fingers fumbled and the glass teetered on the edge of the table. Fromus grinned, hoping it would smash down, but Aquilinus caught the tumbler. At least Mother wouldn't have to fuss around trying to find a replacement.

'We are all on our most sacred oaths,' continued Aquilinus, 'to keep what is said here today absolutely confidential. You know what is at stake.'

Fromus's ears perked. What was this? Father had told him nothing.

'We are cut off from Rome and we're crippled by taxes.' Aquilinus's bald head glinted. 'We know why: Constantinus's war in Gaul has gone on far too long, and he has been allowed to get away with declaring himself a junior Emperor. Meanwhile, I trust you will allow me to say plainly that the Emperor Honorius is as slippery as an eel and daren't poke his nose out of Ravenna. In a word, the Imperium is rudderless, and we have to do something about it.'

Fromus sat up straight. Real politics, though it would end up with a minor adjustment, getting rid of an official and putting in their own man. Nevertheless, it was like breathing sharp air after being stuck in a cave. Aquilinus was a dry old stick, but now Fromus was on the inside track, ahead of his friends. The rasping old man's hands hovered over his glass and then swept out with a flourish.

'But what move should we make? Britannia has backed usurpers like Constantinus before – and who loses? Each time they fail. It is we, the great men of the diocese. *We* are the ones who pay – and it is we who are persecuted when things go wrong. Britannia has twice been the victim of rebellions in living memory, and each time we are trapped between Scylla and Charybdis.' Neso wouldn't know what the old fart Aquilinus was going on about, thought Fromus. It always came down to taxes, disguised as loyalty.

Aquilinus was droning on. 'If we do not support the new power, our land and houses are confiscated. If we do support the usurper, then we face the horrors of Imperial revenge when Rome gets back in charge.' Aquilinus leant forward and rapped the table, his eyes shining. 'And there is a new factor, a change in the position of Constantinus's right-hand man, Comes Gerontius; I'll leave our host to tell you about it. Matugenus, I hand over to you.'

What was this? Father staggered up and peered around the room. He rummaged in the pocket of his robe and brought out a parchment with a broken blue seal. Fromus scanned the faces of the guests. They looked patient.

'I have here a letter from Comes Gerontius.' Fromus blinked in astonishment. Had Father had been in contact with his cousin? Even mention of Gerontius's name was forbidden at home.

'He has proved to be the best of the British commanders, and it was his armies which subdued Hispania. You know that I strongly disapproved of Constantinus's revolt. I still regret it, but what's done is done, and he has been recognised as the legitimate Caesar by Honorius.'

The usual waffle. Fromus groaned inwardly: don't let him embarrass me. Father shuffled across the mosaic floor so that he stood with his back to a large wall-hanging that portrayed a pack of dogs bringing down a stag.

'As you know, when he raised his usurper's standard in

Britannia, Constantinus claimed that the purpose of his revolt was to rescue Gaul from the barbarians – but he's lost control.' Fromus stared down at his hands as his father puffed and paused before plunging on. 'And now he has decided on treachery. This is what the letter from my cousin says, and through me he is speaking to you.'

There was a slight gluck in Father's voice when he used the words 'my cousin'. He had said nothing to Fromus, not the smallest hint.

Matugenus waved the letter above his head, speaking fast. 'Gerontius writes that Constantinus has dismissed him as the commander in Hispania, appointing his son instead, by all accounts a vicious young man. Much more serious is the news that Constantinus intends to seize the Imperial throne. This is exactly what I feared – once disobedience is rewarded, order collapses and greedy hands reach out.'

Matugenus stopped abruptly. Was that it?

A brief silence, and then everyone turned to his neighbour and started talking - everyone except Fromus, who drained his glass and re-arranged his toga folds. It didn't mean anything to be here if Father treated him like this. He almost felt like walking out, right in front of Father.

The hubbub grew louder as each man lamented the evil times and the weakness of Emperor Honorius. Tribune Treverius, looking like a typical 'big man', with his imposing forehead and fat arms, raised his grating voice.

'I've always said that Constantinus was not to be trusted. His fine speeches didn't fool me; the man is a jumped-up centurion and his seniority was never confirmed. Now he has shown himself to be unworthy of command. We have to do something about this.'

Fromus grinned. One by one their facades were falling.

They thought they were high and mighty, but they were as jealous about their status as old washer-maids.

The Tribune was followed by the rich merchant Ursacius, who stood up, waving his arms. His trimmed rectangular beard was a Gallic fashion that was frowned on in Corinium. Ursacius was not an equestrian, and somehow it showed in everything he did. The man stood there, smoothing the hairs at the end of his chin with his finger, turning his head from side to side, and gradually everyone stopped talking. Ursacius's money had helped to fund Constantinus.

'My friends, this is not all. A month ago, Scotti pirates attacked one of my estates. They burnt the villa, killed some of my labourers and enslaved the rest.' Not that the weasel cared a jot about his people, thought Fromus, but his pocket had been picked, and that he didn't like. 'They even took the son of the local deacon. The Saxons are doing the same on the east coast. These barbarians return to their hovels and slake their appetites on whomever they have seized. How long do we have to put up with this? We don't have enough troops to defend ourselves, let alone to carry out raids to destroy these animals in their lairs.'

'It's as bad in the north,' Treverius broke in. Fromus saw momentary annoyance at the Tribune's interruption on Ursacius's face, but the weasel controlled himself, stroked his beard and sat down.

Treverius continued, oblivious. 'The Picts lost their fear of us when the field army was withdrawn to Gaul. They pillage at will. In the last few months they've sacked two *oppida* well to the south of the Wall.'

The men in this room were meant to be his people, but Fromus felt nothing for them.

Crispus rose. His nasal voice commanded silence. 'Yet it's

our money which is being used to pay for Constantinus's war in Gaul – and now he's gambling everything on taking the throne for himself. Even more importantly, despite our taxes, we're not getting any protection from these vile marauders.'

Voices echoed around the room. Fromus turned to Crispus, glad to have something to say. 'You're right. Both Father and I are on the Council, and we had to give up three barns of wheat last year to make up the tax shortfall. Things can't go on like this.'

'Indeed, as bad as that?' Crispus raised his bushy eyebrows.

Fromus frowned. What a hypocrite the man was. The room felt small and cramped. The noisy guests were pushing the couches apart and yelling over each other.

'*Honestiores*.' Father raised his arm but the clamour continued. Fromus drummed his hand on the couch. This was their house and people should be respectful; Father was virtually shouting. 'All this is true; this is why we are here. Let me continue.'

The guests went back to their seats. 'The fact is,' Matugenus took a deep breath, 'I can tell you that Gerontius has broken with Constantinus. He no longer serves the usurper and is intent on making peace with the Emperor.'

Roars of approval. Someone waved a cloth. An elderly man – it was Fastidius – cupped his hand to his ear. 'Speak up, I can't hear you.'

Fromus reached for a flagon and refilled his glass. This was what it was all about. Father knew all along. He had said nothing, but he would have told Titus, his 'faithful eldest', if he was still alive. Well, he wasn't.

'It took months for this letter to reach me.' Matugenus's voice strained to be heard. 'Gerontius wants Honorius's and our blessing. He must bring his army to Britannia, but first he has to deal with Constantinus.'

Matugenus clasped his hands and paused. Ruddy-cheeked, portly Neso rose. Fromus remembered that when they first met, outside the Corinium Council Chamber; he had been pleased at the friendly way in which Neso had spoken to him. However, Father told that the man was insincere and dangerous. He was a dominant force in the luxury goods market, and several minor traders who had stood in his way had disappeared. But at least Neso knew what he stood for.

'*Honestiores, honestiores.*' There was a hint of irony in the slow way in which Neso enunciated his words, with a pronounced local accent. Neso squinted at a well-padded guest, who stopped talking.

'The cattle have been let out of the pen and each man is claiming them as his own. We should do the same. After all, you can only possess what you can protect. We must think about our goods and our land, not about how things used to be.' Neso patted his side. 'Lalbertus Aurelianus Matugenus, you are a respected equestrian with friends in high places, but many of us depend entirely on our business in Corinium. Trade is suffering and we can't wait for your cousin to bring his army back here. We need help now.'

Neso broke off. Fromus saw that he was expecting finger-clicking approval or laughter, but there was silence. What effrontery. Fromus clutched a cushion. Should he stand and object to the man's tone? Father was grave-faced, and the others were guarded. If it came to a real confrontation, how would the men in the room divide? He wasn't sure of any of them.

Neso continued. 'Besides, we don't know if Comes Gerontius *will* come back. The sea-raiders may be the least of our troubles. They say that Londinium is hiring Saxon guards, and they're putting the property of anyone who's not a local under what they call protective custody.'

The man was rambling. What did this have to do with Gerontius? Fromus squirmed and clenched his fist. But Neso had a point: Corinium was defenceless without soldiers.

The red-cheeked trader seized a knife and held it upright, like a military staff.

'I say that this situation is something we've got to deal with. The Empire has had its day and it's time we looked after what is ours. Why do we need Rome? It can't protect itself, let alone us.'

What was this? The faces around the chamber were shocked.

'Neso,' Father spoke deliberately, 'my fellow Council member, we all agree that we have got to do something, but you forget yourself: we are Romans. You have been granted the dignity of the Corinium Council toga. Surely, you are not suggesting that we forget the Roman way?'

'Yes, I am,' Neso shot back. 'With all due respect, I don't give a fig for the toga. What's the point of being in the Empire if Scotti and Picts lord it over us? We need to show everyone that we are people to be reckoned with ... without Rome if need be.'

Uproar. Bodies leapt from their seats. Fromus followed suit, looking for a wine flagon, but none was near. A side-table was knocked over, dishes smashing to the floor.

'That's impossible!'

'What on earth is he talking about?'

Aquilinus bellowed, 'Who is this man?'

Father's face was blank. Flailing arms and raised voices swarmed around Neso, but he pushed through and crooked his finger at a short, fat man – Fromus remembered that he was called Mogontius – and the two made their way to the doors in front of the apse. Ursacius drew Treverius and Aquilinus to the other side of the room, where they huddled together.

Fromus stood alone, his mouth dry with excitement. What Neso had suggested was treason, not just to the Emperor but to the very idea of Empire. No one – neither Gerontius nor Constantinus – had dreamt of acting without ultimately seeking approval from the Imperial centre. If they were not careful, men like Neso might seize power in Britannia. His family would be swept aside. Fromus glanced at the colourful tapestry with its calm vistas beyond the stag and hounds. They could lose everything.

Neso stepped back into the centre of the mosaic, feet planted firmly on the Chi-Ro. His voice cut through the hubbub.

'Aquilinus asked us to be frank, and I have been, so please, let me finish.' A slow traverse from his piggy eyes quieted the room. Fromus sensed resentment that this plebeian held the floor.

'What I'm saying is that we should stake out our territory, it stands to reason. These barbarian raids are just the beginning, you wait and see; worse will follow if we don't stand up for ourselves. We've got to look after what is ours.' Neso lowered his chin. 'Besides, Aurelianus Matugenus, you are a believer. Surely you don't want to hang on to old Rome and its pagan ways?'

Tense silence. While some were genuine believers, Fromus knew that many remained pagan at heart, though forced by law to genuflect to Christianity.

Matugenus's voice quavered. 'I–I don't think that ... that is helpful. We've reached a *modus vivendi* in matters to do with our religion; we've had enough of persecution.'

Aquilinus broke in. 'Let's not get distracted. Our host hasn't finished. Thank you, Neso, we will come back to your suggestion later.'

Neso hesitated, then sidled back to his couch. Fromus had to admire Aquilinus's adroit control.

Father scowled and gestured to Aquilinus. 'I leave it to you.'

The large equestrian took the floor. 'Reinforcements from the east are coming to the aid of the Emperor. The situation is fluid – the usurper Constantinus's day will soon be over. In short, we need to decide if we should withdraw our support from him now, in good time.'

Neso barked across the room, 'That's as may be, but you're talking high politics while our homes are being attacked. Honorius isn't going to send troops here – Gaul is in flames and his precious Italy is full of Goths.'

Ursacius broke in, speaking from his couch. 'Neso has a point. If we declare against Constantinus, we cannot wait for a year to find out if Imperial troops are coming to wipe out these brigands. Moreover – my friend Matugenus will forgive me – who knows if Gerontius will survive? It seems to me that in order to defend ourselves we need to raise our own troops.'

This set the chamber alight; the room buzzed like an erupting hornet's nest. No one was against Ursacius's proposal – not even Father, thank God, judging by his resigned expression. Bony-headed Crispus was speaking to Aquilinus; Fromus was squashed between a side table and Crispus. The old man flapped his arms, emitting a salty stench. Fromus pushed past and hurried across the room to join Father under the apse.

'Is this what you thought would happen?' he asked. 'Can

we do this?'

Father nodded in the direction of Treverius. 'It's up to the army – better him than the rabble.'

Aquilinus clapped his hands. 'Thank you, thank you. This is a matter of the utmost importance. I beg you all to sit down.' There was a ruffle of togas and the scratching of broken glass being trodden underfoot. 'I – that is, *we* – propose that this diocese nullifies the administration of the usurper Constantinus. Furthermore, we propose that the three leading city councils of Britannia send a delegation to profess loyalty and to ask the Emperor Honorius for permission to raise militia for defence against barbarian raiders – and against the usurper. In the meantime, command of all military forces in the diocese will fall under, ah, a suitable local commander.'

The words felt prepared. Aquilinus's bald head tilted towards Tribune Treverius. Fromus shuddered. How distasteful that this man was to be the new supremo. The Tribune was silent as he held their gaze. Neso jumped in.

'That's what we're here for … yes, yes, let's do it.'

'Agreed.'

'Here too.'

'By the true God, so be it.'

Everyone looked to the Tribune, who acknowledged his incipient power with a slight bow and a flourish of his arm towards the nine civilians. Fromus's eyes sparkled as he looked round the room. At last he knew what was going on.

Treverius raised his chin. 'I support this loyal action.' The pate of his lined forehead shone. 'And I am mindful of the great trust which you have placed in me. There is much to do.'

Fromus picked up a glass and put it down. What if the Emperor did not agree to the raising of local forces? Could the old order survive, and his family's power? Best not to say anything; it would only lead to more pointless arguing. What would it be like to live under the rule of Treverius? One thing was certain: these decisions changed everything. Britannia was different already – and Corinium.

Fromus drank the nearest glass of wine and pressed his thumbs against the oak rim of the couch. Lemony scents wafted from a vase in the corner brimming with white roses and blue gladioli. Mother had taken an age to decide what to put there.

An urgent clamour swept round the room. They were doing something, these men, something momentous. Fromus was tied to them, whether he liked it or not. It felt like they were standing alone on a hilltop, heroes from the old stories, surrounded by raging barbarians.

He pulled his toga about him and felt his head rise to full stretch. The Tribune sat down on a broad chair as Ursacius raised his arm.

'What shall we do about Constantinus's officials? As soon as he hears about this, he'll want our heads.'

Treverius leant back. 'I can deliver the troops in Britannia, if you gentlemen promise to pay them, including their back pay.'

Neso smirked. The man was distasteful but one had to admire his forceful cunning. 'You are right about that, Tribune. If the boys in Corinium are anything to go by, the soldiers will see that the right thing to do is to go where the money is. Not that they are all like that, of course. Your troops, for instance – they take their line from their commander; they're your men.'

It was good to watch Neso squirm. Treverius was sound. The disciplined swords at his disposal, though wretchedly few, made all the difference.

Ursacius fingered his beard and bowed his head in the direction of the Tribune, ignoring Neso. 'I'm sure that money can be found for the troops of my esteemed friend, at least for this year's back payments. The harvest is good, though the value of the coin is much diminished and there's no new supply, but we'll manage once we have control of the Praetorium in Londinium.'

Neso rose again. 'We can't wait for Honorius's reply. We should get moving before Constantinus works out what's happening. We've got to get him first.'

Several men murmured and a sharp-faced man next to Neso tugged the lapels of his toga. Neso's eyes swivelled around the room. He was about to continue, but he sat down with a thump. Fromus's lips puckered as he recoiled from another waft of bitter sweat. Father reached for a tumbler of water; Crispus smiled. Fromus imagined him intoning that it was 'important to get the principles right before rushing into the details'.

Aquilinus cleared his throat and raised his big head before he spoke.

'Make no mistake; our necks are on the block if we don't act quickly. There is no going back.' He thrust his broad chin forwards. 'We must be sure. I will ask each of you, starting with you, Matugenus. Do you agree to the proposal?'

'Most assuredly; I am glad it has come to this.'

'Mogontius?'

'I'm with you and the Tribune.'

'Crispus?'

'As you say, this is essential, and we must be united.'

'Bononus?'

'We have to do this. The people will follow us.'

'Neso?'

'Yes, yes, let's get going.'

'Ursacius?'

'You and the Tribune have my support. Constantinus will crumble.'

'Tribune?'

'Yes, I agree; it shall be done.'

'Fastidius?'

'I support this – and I think that the diocese is with us. Our citizens are sick of Constantinus and his taxes.'

'Fromus?'

'I agree.'

Fromus gulped from another tumbler; the wine had no taste. Men were striding across the room. Moments later, everyone was raising their glasses in an eerie, silent toast. Neso hugged sharp-faced Bononus, their faces beaming in the candlelight. The door from the servants' hall half-opened and shut. Matugenus proposed a toast to the success of the delegation and there was another round of cheers.

His glass empty, Fromus found himself raising his voice and waving his hand. '*Honestiores*, everyone, Aquilinus, may I speak?'

Aquilinus flourished both hands downwards. 'Surely, young man. You have the floor.'

'I was thinking, if this is what we're doing, it'll be a long time before a new Vicarius gets here.' A wall of fleshy faces and dark eyes levelled on him. 'And that means that we will be taking our own decisions – we'll be independent, at least for a while.'

Neso laughed. 'Well, Aurelianus Matugenus, it seems you have raised a dangerous one after all. He is looking straight past a Senator's purple gown to the green centre of this land.'

'That is not what he meant,' barked Aquilinus. 'We are part of the Empire, and if we speculate about anything else, we will give an excuse to some double-dealing traitor who wants to make an impression on Honorius.'

This was not what he meant to say. Fromus raised his hand but no one noticed. It was too late to ask what would happen if Honorius never sent any troops.

Aquilinus swivelled his bulging head around the room. 'We must stick together; Honorius is hardly going to object when we detain Constantinus. He will see reason in our militia, but we have to get his signed Rescript, even if it is afterwards. We cannot rely on messengers. We need to send trustworthy men to bring back the Emperor's considered response.'

'Absolutely,' shouted red-faced Fastidius.

'I should think so,' said Mogontius, sitting next to Fromus.

Fromus was surprised when Aquilinus turned to him, grinning. 'As for you, perhaps you should be part of the delegation. What do you say, Matugenus, can your son go to Ravenna as the delegate from Corinium?'

Father's hazel-brown eyes flicked from side to side and he bit his upper lip. He brought his hands up and clasped them, nodding his head. There he stood – an overweight, old-fashioned patrician, whose whole world was crumbling – calculating if he could trust his own son.

'Yes, well … yes, I suppose Fromus could do that. Most of Gaul is safe, so the journey to Italy is possible, though it won't be easy.'

* * *

Things moved fast after that. Treverius left next morning

with his troop to expel Constantinus's Vicarius from Londinium. Aquilinus was to take over as the temporary Vicarius-designate, awaiting a new man from the Emperor. Crispus travelled north to Eburacum, where he had once lived, to persuade the city council to send him as its delegate.

Ursacius had been reluctant to be part of the embassy to Ravenna, though he was the obvious choice to be the delegate from Londinium. Eventually he agreed, Father said later, because the man wanted to secure the Imperial contract to supply grain to loyal troops in Gaul.

The next day, Matugenus gave Barita and his youngest daughter, Sida, an outline of what was happening, and the momentous fact that Fromus was to be part of the delegation to Ravenna. Barita jerked her head up.

'That's ridiculous; my brother is going to the Emperor to ask permission for this little island to arm itself. What about my husband-to-be? He could go, he's already in Gaul.'

Father had cut her short. Fromus was to be treated with a new respect - at least by his siblings.

* * *

Later, on the terrace at Lemma Magna, Father grasped Fromus's arm.

'I'm proud of you, my boy; you did well.'

'Thank-you, Father, but why didn't you say anything before?'

'I'm sorry, but it wasn't possible.' Father stepped back and clasped his hands. He paused and Fromus looked away from his piercing brown eyes. 'Never mind about that. I am going to give you a sealed parchment scroll, which you are to give to our cousin, Aurelianus Gerontius. You must find him in Gaul and deliver the scroll in person, and in private. It's highly confidential, no one else must know, not even Crispus.'

'Why, what's in it?'

'It must remain a secret, even to you. You will find out when you meet Gerontius. Do you remember him?'

'Maybe. No, not really.'

'He was fond of you. I must emphasise that it's imperative that you deliver the letter to Gerontius, even more important than the delegation to the Emperor.' Father's hand reached out, and Fromus was forced to hold it. Awkward. 'In fact, if you need to leave the embassy in order to reach Gerontius - and I think this is not improbable - you *must* do so. Fortune favours the brave and I know you will not let me down. I can't tell you how crucial this is.'

'But surely, you should tell me what's in the letter?' Fromus took his hand back. 'You're asking too much.'

'Fromus, my son, my only son, you know how dear you are to me. You will be safer not knowing. Trust me, it is better that way. With this letter, the future of our family will rest on you. I will say no more, you have your duty.'

They parted. There was no one to whom Fromus could talk. Father said his role must remain hidden for as long as possible. Why was everything always like this? Mother was fussing about the journey. Barita refused to talk, simmering with anger that she had been excluded, though that was normal, as she was a woman.

It was a long way to Ravenna. What would the Emperor's court be like, and Honorius himself? Not to mention the great city, filled with marble-clad walls, sly men and jewelled, wanton women. Fromus had heard tell of silver trays of wine and strange fruit floating down long corridors, borne by an army of obsequious servants. Exotic barbarian guards outside every room, with outlandish breastplates and long trailing hair, menacing all but the most powerful with their long, curved swords. Silk-robed bishops waiting in alcoves, whispering, impatient for an audience with the Emperor – a difficult master, people said, clever but secretive. Schemers surrounded Honorius, and Father said that the palace was rife with faction-fighting: ancient families desperate to know which way the wind was blowing; eunuchs wielding unknown power; and Tribunes fearful of leaving for their legions in case they were accused of treachery. How would the delegation navigate this?

Pray the Christ Jesus that their mission would return with the precious Rescript from Honorius. Everything would be different when he got back.

CHAPTER FIVE

THREE MONTHS LATER, LATE AUTUMN 409, ON THE ROAD TO REMORUM, NORTHERN GAUL.

Nehtan shook her cape, damp from rain. Sitting up on the horse, she could see across the field to an old badger set in the far bank. There was a sense of power when you looked from this height, the world at your command - and horses were faster than army carts. No wonder Romans loved these animals.

It had stopped raining but the trees were still dripping. She put out her tongue. The water tasted good, woody. She cupped her hand, smoothing strands of hair away and slowly feeling around her head-wound. It stung, and the throbbing continued, but the tree-essence was good.

Fromus had made them change positions. Now, she was wedged in front of the young master, his arms pressing her belly to hold the reins. She couldn't relax like she could on the cart with Vitalis. Her shoulders tensed as she remembered Vitalis's corpse in the brambles. Anything could happen, whether you were a slave or not. She had been spared for a reason.

But she was still in the hands of Romans. Fromus hadn't tried to take advantage, at least not yet. He was oblivious of her unless it suited him to talk, and there didn't seem to be anyone else he liked to speak with.

'What will you do,' Fromus spoke quietly, 'when we get to the next city?'

No one would make her their servant. She raised her chin. 'I'll find an army person, someone who knows about my master. Marcellinus was well-liked.'

'I'm not so sure that there will be anyone. It's not how it used to be. Everything is being destroyed.'

'There'll be someone, I know there will. The Lord will help me.'

'That's as may be, Nehtan.' She flushed slightly. This was the first time Fromus had used her name in this way. 'But you've got to be realistic. You need protection.'

'I can manage, sir. I've had to do it all my life.' Anyway, Fromus didn't seem to carry much weight. 'But you're kind to think of me.'

The horse threaded its way round a fallen tree. Nehtan shifted her weight. Fromus was not like Master Marcellinus, who was always doing something, sure of himself and only quiet when he was exhausted. Marcellinus noticed everything, good or bad, and could read his men as if their emotions were blazoned on their helmets. This man, Delegate Fromus, didn't see the soldiers leering at her whenever the high-ups were not looking. One man – a short, dark-haired soldier – looked angrily away whenever their eyes crossed.

She felt Fromus's head come close to the back of her neck. His finger played for a moment with a knot in her hair. How brutal could he be?

The young Roman behind her patted the side of the horse's neck, making his arm squeeze Nehtan slightly.

'He's called Papiteddo.'

There was a pause. He wanted her to say something. 'Yes, I see.'

'He's my best animal. Can outrun any of the others back home. And he can keep going, never gets lame.'

'That's good, sir.'

The horse snorted and threw its head, forcing her back into the warm body behind her. She let herself relax, her shoulders drooping for the first time in hours. The smell of the leather was pleasant and the rasping sound of the saddle was soothing. Fromus wasn't greedy, putting his hands where they shouldn't go. But he was taking her further and further away from Britannia. Was this a sign that her future was not back home?

Short prayers reach heaven: God of the high mountain, keep me by your side.

'What would you have done,' Fromus asked, 'if we had not come along?'

'I don't know, sir. I'd have found a village and hoped for the best.'

'Do you have no one, that is, no one left alive?'

'There were only three of us.' She was grateful to him, but no more than that. 'We have friends back in Bononia. Everyone knows us. We have things there, our possessions.'

'Well, we're going south, away from the coast. It's a new world, and we don't know what's coming next.' He laughed. 'For now, you'll have to make do with me.'

'I'm honoured... I didn't mean to sound ...'

'That's all right. Nothing's like it used to be.'

That evening, they found shelter in a straggly wood, away from the road and up a shallow hill. She stood where Fromus had left her, under the canopy of a vast oak. It was better on the far side of the tree, out of sight of the men. She sat on a huge root that elbowed its way across the earth before disappearing underground. The wood was ridged and pitted with small knots, and felt worn, like the hand of an ancient. Her fingertips tingled in the supple oak furrows.

Dusk fell. The calls and commands of the soldiers receded. In Colud, an oak like this might be worshipped. She wanted to sink into its knobbly immenseness, to forget being a lone woman, and be allowed to creak silently from root to tip in the breeze. Surely, the Christ would allow such thoughts.

'I know you, don't I?' It was the square-faced soldier, grabbing her from behind. 'I seen you in Londinium.'

'Get off! Let go.' She pushed her shoulder back but he held her fast. 'What are you doing?'

Dark, pitted eyes peered into her face. 'You listened.' His hand on her chin, her head forced back. 'I laid my mark on you.'

'Get away.' She pushed hard and the man fell backwards. Snatching himself up, he snarled like a wild dog, his hand pulling on his sword hilt.

Another trooper appeared. 'Hey, Messor.'

'Fuck off. I got my own business here. She knows what it's all about, don't you?'

He reached across to grab her arm, but Nehtan smacked his hand away and ran to the other men around the fire. If the trooper was that man in Londinium, then he knew who she was. But she wasn't sure. Shaking, her hand on her neck, she searched for him in the shifting twilight, but he had gone.

Chapter Six

Fromus shaded his eyes as they struggled along a track traversing a bare hillside. It was better than being in the forest, but the mud was slowing them down. Nehtan was behind him, full of promise, but she wouldn't say more than a few words at a time.

Harsh sounds, yelling, coming from suddenly visible black and green banners at the top of the hill opposite. Horsemen, galloping down. Black sticks, no, lances pointing at them. A line of horses in a confused jangle, their riders, not Roman. It couldn't be.

His stomach clenching, mouth dry, Fromus wrenched on the reins. The horsemen were getting bigger, so fast. His mouth open, he felt for his spatha, dreading. He wasn't any good with it.

Decurion Novateli was shouting, 'By Hades. Too many – we've got to run for it. Follow me.'

Novateli should have known. Fromus turned Papiteddo downhill, squeezing his knees hard. His animal would get them away, he must.

'Poitus,' a loud bellow, 'turn those mules.'

The cavalryman struggled. Novateli kicked his horse up the side of the bank. 'It's no good.' He looked at Bellator. 'Biarchus, take the delegates. Get into the trees. The rest of you, follow me.'

Young trooper faces showed the whites of their eyes. The cavalrymen galloped away, unsheathing swords as they rode.

Bellator whacked the rump of his horse. Fromus glimpsed over his shoulder as he followed down the track. Nehtan's dark hair was streaming, her eyes fixed ahead, high cheekbones hardened.

Bellator careered downhill and jumped his horse across a small stream into a wood. Hurtling under branches, ducking low, Fromus followed, kicking Papiteddo's flanks as hard as he could, Nehtan's arms gripping his chest so tight he wanted to ease her back, but there was no time. Could barely see the horse in front, a flash of brown twisting past a tree. Mustn't fall off. A branch whacked into his face, he couldn't see out of one eye, must keep going.

Then it was light, no more trees, and Papiteddo shot out into a clearing Bellator was to the right, sitting up sharply, his horse rearing at the edge of a deep ditch. Fromus yanked Papiteddo's head to the left, forcing the animal's head back, feeling the weight of Nehtan pushing into him. The other Romans raced into the clearing, bunching up behind Fromus, horses squashing rider legs.

'What do you think, Biarchus?' Crispus panted. 'Are they ours?'

'Not army.' Bellator was leaning forward. 'Keep going.'

But there were shouts, men on small horses coming from the topside of the clearing. Pale faces, too white, sunlight flashing from patchwork metal. They were charging down the side of the ditch.

Ursacius kneed his mount and raced back into the wood. Papiteddo's front hooves were on the edge of the ditch. Fromus wrenched the horse's head, but Bellator shouted, 'It's no use, stick together.'

The wild horsemen were almost on them, long hair flying, a jangle of colour, lances pointing to the sky.

Suddenly, their horses slowed to a walking pace, swords sheathing. The leading barbarian advanced, showing empty hands. 'No danger, friend, no danger.'

'*Mudebroth*, it's them.' Nehtan's voice, hard, like a pebble hitting his ear. 'The ones who attacked us.'

'Are you sure?'

His hand went to his sword pommel, but they were already surrounded.

Tall men on little horses, bones hanging from their saddles, incised markings on their faces. A warrior stared, his hair bushing out from a conical helmet. He shook a long spear and shouted to the rider behind him, pointing at Nehtan. Fromus felt himself bristling.

Their leader spoke jagged sounds. Three horsemen sped into the wood where Ursacius had gone.

Fromus put his hand on Nehtan's thigh. 'It's all right.' It was all he could do. 'We'll get through this.'

A brown-bearded warrior peered into Nehtan's face. A stink of burnt fat. He heard her spit, and spun round, horrified. But the rider guffawed and rode off.

'They murdered Vitalis,' she whispered, gripping tight around his waist.

Fromus pulled her arm off. He must control her.

The barbarians beckoned the Romans to follow and soon they joined a larger group of riders. God be praised, Novateli and the other cavalrymen were there – and with their weapons.

The Decurion urged his horse towards them. 'It is all right. These men say that they are friends of Rome'

Novateli rode closer and leant forwards. 'Crispus Natalius, I had no choice. They're Alans and they serve a Prince Goar. The leader of this troop is called Dorgolel. He says we must go with him. I don't think it was them who attacked our soldiers on the road.'

Fromus jolted upright. He could not remember anything about the Alans, except that they were part of the horde that had been devastating Gaul.

Nehtan stayed clinging to him. He wanted to hide her inside his cloak, or for them both to disappear. Looking quickly from warrior to warrior, he didn't want to catch their eyes. What sign of violence would they give?

But the Alans were chatting to each other unconcernedly, as if capturing Roman soldiers were no more significant than winning a game of dice.

Surely, they would make their intentions clear? But there was nothing, no explanation. After a few short exchanges between the barbarians, the head man led them off. They pushed on at a fast pace, and soon Papiteddo was frothing. Yet the Alan horses were prancing, brimming with energy. Nehtan groaned.

'Don't worry.' He leant back against her. 'You heard what the Decurion said.'

'What will they do with us?'

'Well find out soon enough.' He patted Papiteddo as they crested a ridge. His favourite animal, the only solid piece of Lemma Magna that he possessed. They would not take the beast from him – though there was nothing he could do to stop them. Everything was coming into sharp focus.

A whiff of pinecones rose from the track as they came out of a tunnel of close-packed fir trees. Large stones pitted the way ahead, interspersed with clumps of maple, sycamore and hawthorn. Below them, far off, a plume of smoke climbed from dense forest.

'Pray to God and Holy Mary,' Nehtan's voice was tight, 'that these are not the ones who killed Marcellinus and Vitalis. Could you?' She stopped.

'What?'

'Could you pray with me?'

'If that is what you want.'

He began to say the Our Father with her. One of the nearby Roman soldiers joined, in a low voice. The old words burned afresh.

'Thy Kingdom come, thy will be done, on earth, as it is in Heaven...'

If it was true, Heaven had to be now, riding with spears on all sides, and Nehtan breathing into his ear. He felt a swilling of warmth through his body. They might be killed at any point; it wouldn't be difficult for these muscled, alert warriors, who massively outnumbered them.

And yet, and yet, at the same time, it was as if his whole past was being sloughed off. A new world, all washed away except the reins in front and the woman behind. Everything was vivid, uncertain. He shifted uncomfortably, smoothing his hand down the fine leather tracings on the saddle front. His horse, so much better than anyone else's. He always had the best, but it was no good out here. Nehtan, he had to keep her.

'Forgive us our trespasses, as we forgive those who trespass against us.'

The words were fresh, he saw what they meant: not a plea for reward in return for good behaviour, but telling how things truly are; wholeness coming exactly as suffering is let go. Even what he felt about Father.

He remembered the chanting in the church back home, losing himself in the Sacramentum, no longer hearing his own voice but only the *Te Deum Laudamus*, the words swelling within him and obliterating the recognition he deserved and the hounds he was not allowed. It was not that they were united in praise of the Creator, but that there was nothing else. Hard to say what that presence was, if it was Christ, or all life – or if there was any difference. Rather, he reflected, it was not having to think, the relief of not-being-Fromus and of allowing the many-stranded voice to be all that there was. In those moments, there was no looking forwards or dwelling on the past, no likes or dislikes, only the flowing river that was the core of being.

But he could never sustain it. Most of the time, he was looking out for a pretty girl, listing his parents' faults, planning a tavern outing or – when stirred by the preaching – resolving to reduce his visits to the House of Venus. In any case, he could not see how what the bishop said fitted with being a patrician who was expected to do things the Roman way, where love did not come into it.

Britannia seemed like ancient history. Just as well. The others had ignored him when they left Londinium, before they crossed to Gaul. They were coming out of the southern gate when they were surrounded by a mob of beggars. Someone reached for Papiteddo's mane, a desperate-looking fellow with a bald patch and filthy rags. A small, freckled girl gripped the man's cloak. Above her pinched cheeks, her eyes had an almost adult appeal. He had reached into his cloak for a small coin. Crispus shouted at him to push 'the guttersnipe' away and kneed his horse forwards. The hard-faced cavalryman in front wheeled his horse into the tall beggar, knocking him over. The column rode past the man, sprawled on the ground. The red-faced child shouted something fierce, her stony eyes fixed on Fromus as he twisted back to look at her.

With Nehtan, it would be different.

With a shock, he realised that the prayer had ended and the

soldier was staring at him. He nodded. The man had fair hair, pinched cheeks and alert eyes.

'You're Philus, aren't you?'

'Yes sir.' The trooper glanced at the barbarian banner floating from a spear tip just ahead of them, then lowered his voice. 'As I live, I don't like being in the hands of these long-beards. I've had dealings with Alans. They worship their spears and horses and nowt else, but they keep their word, I will give them that.'

Fromus's shoulders softened. The soldier had experience; he lived in the real world where what you knew is how you survived. Fromus scrutinised the straight-backed warrior with the banner; the man had proud, dancing, green eyes. He might as easily stab his lance into a Roman as rush into a brawl to save the same man. He too had no privilege to back him up.

It was different with the delegation. They called it 'thinking ahead', but it was about how to stay up amongst the elite. Crispus only supported the Emperor because that was how he would get back into power in Britannia. Ursacius wanted an army supply contract. Even Father, old stick in the mud that he was, had twice swapped sides. At least the leader of these Alans, Dorgolel, knew who his chief was, and his chief knew him.

He nudged Nehtan. 'Who do you support?' Too late, he grimaced at the crassness of the question.

'Me, Sir? All I know is, I'm with you.'

He felt her shift in the saddle.

'But,' she whispered, 'perhaps the Alans will keep us and then I'll belong to them.'

He flicked his head round. She wasn't smiling.

A rasping command came from the front and everyone

stopped. The Alans hopped off their horses and led them
to patches of grass, chatting and laughing. If only he could
understand what they were saying.

The column had come down from a ridgetop and was back
amongst clumps of larch and pine. An Alan rode up, leading
a dishevelled Ursacius on his horse. The warrior let go of the
reins and gestured towards Crispus and Novateli. A pity: they
were better off without him.

'The bastards hit me.' Ursacius was scowling. 'Couldn't
you hold them off longer? I might have found troops to rescue
us. Now we're their prisoners.'

Fromus saw Crispus struggling to keep his temper.
'Perhaps, Ursacius, perhaps. But keep your voice down. Gaul
is more dangerous than we thought, and we're fortunate that
these Alans are our allies.'

'I might have been killed. This mission is a disaster.'

'Let's not jump to conclusions.' But the man had a point.
'We need to find out what's going on, and see if they'll let us
go south.'

'You're still thinking of that?' Fromus followed Ursacius's
glance towards two Alans who were pointing at the Roman
horses. 'Out here, there is no Empire.'

* * *

After that, the Alans made them ride hard, stopping only
to eat and sleep, hardly noticing the forested hills and mucky
tracks. At night, Fromus huddled close to Nehtan, squeezing
close behind, his breath on her hair. It was too cold for
anything else.

They passed through burnt-out villages, nettles pushing
through fences, brambles sprawling over broken hut walls.

Occasionally, they came across people working the fields.

One man was resting his hands on a hoe. His expression was blank, even as his head swivelled and Fromus caught his eye. Who knows, the man was the sort of person who might have been Nehtan's father. Were peasants a different type of human being, he wondered? Did they have the same emotions as he did? Nehtan seemed to. And hadn't Jesus been a peasant? Or were these people somehow different, their life so grim that the ups and downs of invasion, death and devastation didn't mean the same as it would to him? Did they live at a lower level of thinking and feeling, not fully human? Perhaps they deserved it for things they had done, or for things done by their fathers. But that didn't make sense, as that would mean that he deserved his life of privilege - but he hadn't done anything particularly good, or bad. If there was no difference in essence between the peasant with the hoe and himself, then why was he so lucky? How could the Lord allow such injustice?

He glanced at the gold ring on his hand. He could have thrown it to the peasant. But it was nothing, a drop in the ocean. There were countless others like him. Jesus said the poor are always with us. Surely, he didn't mean that they didn't matter?

When Fromus got back home - if he did - he would ask the bishop about this. But it might be too late, pointless – the time of the patricians was passing. Fromus itched his head. This chaos could come to Britannia: dead soldiers left to rot, barbarians roaming freely, villas torched, no one in charge. His family would not last. Father wouldn't cope, could only give orders. Mother – she would sooner die than forget her *Romanitas*. Barita – she would never find her husband-to-be, lost somewhere in Gaul. If it all fell apart – when it did - how would he face it? Would he become like the man with the hoe?

CHAPTER SEVEN

M essor wrenched his horse aside.

Nehtan was riding with dung-hole Fromus practically wrapped around her. What had the patrician known but slaves handing him honey on a silver tray? Out here, away from Imperial control, the weakling was no one. A sword was the only power that counted.

The girl belonged to him. She could soothe the black ball burning inside.

'Messor, Messor, can't you hear me?'

The cavalryman glared at the new recruit. After three months, Poitus was no better than a chicken on horseback. He could be chopped down in seconds.

Poitus spoke in a rush. 'Biarchus Bellator says that you are to ride with the Alan scouts.'

'Why?'

'I don't know, sorry. You'd better ask the Biarchus.'

Another louse – what was he on about, 'the Biarchus'? The kid thought that fat fool Bellator was someone to admire. The scouting must be Novateli's idea. Prick-head officer, too precious to give the order direct to a trooper.

Messor pulled his horse out of line and trotted towards the Alans at the front. As soon as he got close, they set off at a canter, their horses rushing through the woods like a winter wind. After ten minutes of furious riding, sweat trickled into Messor's eyes. Another ten minutes and he was panting.

Something ahead, a dark line across the track. He squeezed his horse to jump a fallen log and caught up with the rear Alan. If there were more room, he could overtake him. It was what he was made for. He and the Alans were like fire blazing through the forest, nothing standing in their way.

The horses in front abruptly slowed to a walking pace. Messor dug his heels in and gripped hard. Even so, his animal bumped into the beast in front and it was all he could do to stay on.

Mithras! His horse could have broken its leg.

The Alan horsemen were laughing, weaving in and out of the trees. They faded into the forest, melting into the dripping brown bushes and dappled tree trunks. Their swords and spears looked like sticks, and one had a bow, a puny thing. His hair was ridiculous, long and plaited like a woman's. Little bits of bone. They were a rag-tag mess compared with proper Roman cavalrymen, but they rode as if they were part of their horses, he had to give them that. As for fighting, they'd be showy, like all barbarians, but fast.

One spoke faltering words. '*Bonum? Vis?*'

'I don't fucking like ...' He moderated his voice. 'This sort of riding.'

The Alans resumed a walking pace.

'You crazy men. ' He pointed at the man who had spoken. '*Quid est tibi nomen?*'

'Sangiban. *Tu?*'

'Messor.'

The Alan laughed.

'What's so funny?'

'No.' Sangiban flicked his reins, speaking over his shoulder. 'You name, different in Alan, not you.'

Messor took a slow breath. Sangiban had noticed his anger. They might act like street urchins, but these savages had quick little minds.

They rode on through the damp, bristling forest. It

reminded him of Londinium and a dangerous area of slouching thickets beyond his childhood home in the slum outside the walls. You could run out from a hidden spot, stick someone with a blade and flee back into the shadows. Sometimes, he wished that he had spiked a knife into Da's ribs, not to kill him but to hurt him, to have him helpless on the ground. Da never let up, making him beg in front of his whore. That was worse than the beatings.

* * *

He remembered being a boy, quivering in their Londinium shack, missing the small black pup that he had brought home, against Da's wishes. Da had lost patience and had left with the dog yelping, dangling by its rear legs, swearing it would never be seen again. Messor had known not to protest, but he had been torn apart. Was the pup lying twisted amongst a heap of broken pots, or had it been washed down the river? He had raced around the muddy lanes, asking everyone he knew.

By dawn, Da had not returned from serving in the tavern. His prostitute girlfriend had come back stone-drunk. Thin streaks of light cut through the splintered edges of broken window slats. The whore was snoring, her clothes strewn about the earthen floor. Messor crept around the edge of the bed to the food jar below the windowsill. Beneath the mouldy grain, his fingers found the coins. He was going to join the army, however long it took him to persuade them.

The woman's legs were bare up to the buttocks. Russet hair spread from her big-boned head, her thin tunic was rucked up, a mass of curls between her thighs. A rush of unbearable desire: he would have her, fierce and hard, like Da did, but this time it would be him on top. She had often winked at him.

Prick straining, he plonked down, feeling between her legs, pushing up. Rumbles, but no resistance. He rammed in.

Her eyes opened. 'Steady.' Her lips barely open. 'It's you, is it? About time.'

She pulled her under-tunic above her belly. His face was dragged onto sagging breasts. He tried to push away, grabbing her wrists while he thrust. With easy strength, she raised her arms, making him let go. Half the pleasure drained, but he kept going. She watched with eyes half open. Then she smirked and everything in him tightened.

He finished and collapsed, his toes reaching her shins. She stroked his head and reached for a beaker. A sob rose in his throat. Her warm arms could hug him, and suddenly he was almost overwhelmed by a desperate wish for a comforting arm, the arm of a mother. Then he remembered her drunken guffaws the night before, when Da had made him fetch the mutton with his mouth. She had jabbed him with her finger. Damn the bitch to Hades. He leapt off her and snatched a pot of water. In one bound, he was back at the bedside, smashing the pot on her crumpling face, her mouth open and her eyes black dots of fear. That was his leaving gift to Da, the bastard who had killed his dog.

The army had taken him, shaking off the cold ash of his boyhood.

* * *

The Alans whipped through the woods on their short, stringy horses. What would it be like to be one of them? They must get to fuck all the women they captured. Maybe not. There were many things that barbarians would not do unless it was according to their customs.

They came to a track and slowed. The Alans prattled on, ignoring him. He was stuck on this half-arsed journey, a prisoner in the middle of nowhere, everything pointless – except the girl.

Without warning, the Alans resumed a fast trot. They drew their swords. Messor reached for his spatha hilt, but his horse stumbled and he had to grab its mane to stay on.

They swept round a curving bend through pine and birch, into a village of flimsy huts. The Alans whooped as they careered around the muddy lanes. Messor glimpsed scruffy peasants running into huts or trees. It was a small settlement, pinned to the side of the forest. Joy surged as he unsheathed his blade.

They rode through a litter of brown piglets, wounding a couple – a waste of food, but they would get them afterwards. He followed the five Alan riders around sharp corners as they came back to the main forest track and wheeled. Messor ground his teeth. Quick words passed between the Alans. A rush of extreme excitement – this was it; they were going to waste the forest fuckers. He would find that ripe-looking woman who had ducked into a rickety hut.

Something was wrong. The Alans sheathed their blades and walked their horses back through the village. The idiots. They were like rats waiting at the miller's door. What were they playing at?

'Sangiban, Sangiban!' Messor spurred his animal forwards, pushing an Alan warrior out of the way, forcing the barbarian's horse to knock down a fence.

'What are we doing, why don't we attack?'

'Food. You help.'

'Kill first, food later.'

Messor waved his sword and struck a wattled door. A

woman shrieked.

The six riders came into an open space in the centre of the village. Two Alans dismounted, walked to the biggest hut and rapped on the door.

'Break it down,' shouted Messor. They hammered and a bony old man opened the door. He pointed a wooden rake at the nearest warrior. Sangiban gestured at Messor.

'Ask food.'

'Give us everything you've got.' Messor pointed his sword at the old man. 'We'll slit your throat if a feast isn't piled up in front of us, sharpish.'

'You're Roman,' croaked the old man in Latin.

'What of it? Get your people out. Everyone – women and children.'

'We can't, we've nothing left. This is the third time, and winter's coming.'

Messor jumped off his horse and strode into the hut. The skinny old man backed away, dropping his rake. It was dark, but in seconds the tip of Messor's blade was scraping a scrawny throat.

'Give us what we want or you'll die in agony. I'll roast you in your shitting hovel.'

Shuffling at the far end of the hut.

'What's this?' Weak light. A slight thing, a girl, scurrying on all fours out of a hole.

He turned on the old man and was about to carve his throat when a strong arm grabbed his wrist from behind. He spun around. A tall Alan shouted and yanked him out of the hut, almost making Messor drop his spatha. It was bright outside. Messor got both hands on his sword hilt.

Sangiban barked from his horse. 'What you do?'

It was madness. He could not take the Alan crows on his

own. That girl, she would do.

'These people.' Why did he have to explain anything? 'Bad, not give food, we punish.'

Wasting time. Kill the men, rape the women, torch the village. Standard procedure.

Sangiban spoke to the other Alans. Two warriors thundered back into the hut and emerged, leading the old man and a shrivelled woman. Sangiban glared at Messor.

'Why you do this? These your people.'

'They're not mine. I wouldn't give a turd for them.'

Sangiban spoke to the old man. '*Cibum*. Food.'

Messor was tired of this. Stomping across to the old woman, he jerked her head up. The stubbornness of centuries flashed in her scrunched-up, steely eyes.

'Listen old man.' He held the eyes of the flint-faced woman. 'Your hag's blood will mix in pig piss if you don't get your people out, now, with all your food.'

'Give us time, we will do it, I swear. Let her go.'

'Be quick or I'll test my blade on your rat-bag.' Messor laughed. 'She doesn't look like she's got much blood in her.' A surge of warmth pulsed through him as he thought of what he'd like to do to their daughters. 'Make the women bring the food.'

The scruffy couple sat hugging each other on the ground while the old man shouted for help. Eventually, four lean men appeared and scurried back and forth, dumping a pile of nuts, berries, bones, bark bread and mushy vegetables on top of torn pieces of old clothing. Three dead piglets were laid on the side. It was nothing, and they had not sent their women.

'They have pigs – big ones, we saw them. For fuck's sake, where are they? Let's kill the old cow. That'll make them pull their fingers out.'

The withered woman spat and growled; her husband held her tight. A mangy black and white dog hopped out of a hut.

The bastards. Look how they starved the old mutt. Messor stroked the scarred top of the mongrel's head and scooped a bone from the pile. He gave it to the dog, which ran off, bobbing its head up and down.

'What you done that for?' asked the old man.

'You take care of him, you better, or we'll be back.'

In the shadows of a small hut, a young woman with big eyes and open mouth stood with a baby straddling her hip, its head clamped to her pert breast. He could nip in and take her. By Saturn, why shouldn't he? He had as much right as the fucking Alans, more – these people were Roman, his people. He started towards her and the girl vanished.

'Messor' – a bellow from Sangiban – 'we go.'

He turned. Sangiban and the other Alans were on horseback. The bundles of food would slow their sword arms, but there were too many of them.

'I'm coming.' Sheathing his spatha, he sprang into the saddle. Another time, another place, and they'd know who he was.

CHAPTER EIGHT

Nehtan's arms ached from holding on to Fromus. It was near the end of the third day of riding, and at last they had reached a sprawling circle of wagons, the Alan camp. The carts had wooden walls, with coverings made from twisted sticks and bark. Proud boys marshalled groups of horses; subdued men in rough-hide cloaks tended cows that were tough and small, like donkeys.

The Romans were silent, mostly looking at the ground.

Nehtan hunched tight to Fromus. At least he was Christian, and his attention was pleasing, though he didn't notice the contempt he excited. There was something rigid about him; he thought highly of himself. He would not survive if the Alans kept them as slaves – not unless she helped him. She would cope better with the Alans than mere Romans.

Armed men on horseback shouted greetings. No one appeared surprised by the sight of the Romans. They passed a woman struggling to carry a pile of wood.

Dorgolel led them to a clearing in front of a large square tent which was bright with swirling blue and red patterns that looked like prancing bulls.

'Here, Prince Goar.'

The Alan warrior made a tiny bow at the entrance to the tent and disappeared inside.

Nehtan slid down from Papiteddo. It was good to see the Romans powerless.

The cavalrymen started to take the bundles off the backs of their horses, but the Alans stopped them. Novateli shouted to his men to let them take what they wanted. The cavalrymen dismounted and edged close to each other, perching in a morass of mud.

She knew what it felt like. They could disappear and no one would know. The Romans called everyone else barbarians, but their knives had the same edge, and they treated their slaves like dogs. If it wasn't for their walls and writings, the Romans wouldn't be any different. The Christ had been born in their Empire, but they had crucified him.

More Alans came. Bristle-bearded young men on horseback, proud of their ribbed gashes and gold bangles. Women with amber necklaces, ignoring the wild-haired children running amongst them at full pelt. Others carried bundles, picking their way around the riders.

An old woman approached, supported by two girls. Ritual cuts on her face crinkled, but her eyes were searching and warm. Nehtan flinched as the old lady came straight up to her and laid a hand on her cheek, then down to her belly. The Alan girls on either side of her beamed, and the old lady starting speaking in her native tongue, not looking at her, her head raised to the clouds.

A sudden surge of emotion, and Nehtan found her mouth puckering, though she could not understand what was being said. The old woman wiped the tears away.

Dorgolel appeared. 'She says part of you touches the Alans, and you will bear a great warrior. She is shaman. You are not of Rome, the ancient one says. You must live with us, be at home in the woods and the wind.'

Fromus was looking intently at her from the edge of the small group of delegates. The old woman was smiling, as were the girls either side of her, drawing her in.

But no, not a warrior, not back to being buried in the

woods, nor anything like that. Nehtan dropped her head in a small bow towards the old Alan shaman. 'Tell her, I thank her. I don't know what to say. I am honoured' – she felt for her Chi-Rho amulet - 'but I am Christian, and I want to go back to my people in Britannia.'

The old lady gazed while Dorgolel translated Nehtan's reply. The ancient Alan crooked her finger, beckoning, no longer smiling as she heaved a great breath. Nehtan shivered down the centre of her spine, sensing the blood of her village god, Donn. She grit her teeth, staring into the old woman's dark eyes, feeling herself on the brink of falling into a pit. It would be easy... but she held on, teetering, then glanced at Fromus, and saw his face entreating her. Enough.

'No!'she hissed.

The old lady raised her eyes to the sky, turned and trudged away through mud and puddles, leaning on the arms of the two girls. None of the three looked back.

Fromus strode across and asked, 'What did she want?'

'She wanted me to stay with them. But I don't want that. I haven't come this far... They're pagan.'

What did her prophecy mean? There was something powerful and deep within the earth about the old woman. If she stayed with the Alans, it would be a new way of living, and she would be above the rest. But Donn would be there, in different shape, dragging her down, making her screech with terror, like it had been with the Colud elders.

It came flooding back: her village beyond the Wall, women joshing each other while they milked impatient cows, the men on the hillside counting bullocks. It was where she used to belong: nymayr-mother cooking in the hut, atir-father swinging her onto his shoulders as he strode off to check their cattle. That time had gone, but she would not be moulded to the old Alan woman's will. The Lord was with her, and in him she would fine peace.

The Alans drifted away as evening drizzle fell. Nehtan longed to sit down, but they had to stand. She was stuck on a small island of mud, poised between the soldiers and the delegates. Her nose was cold and she shivered beneath her cloak.

Novateli raised his head. 'It's good that they've left us alone. They can't be worried about us.'

'We're hardly honoured guests,' Ursacius snorted. 'We have been waiting for hours, no food, and we have lost our horses. Let's face it, we're prisoners: the gods alone know what happens next.'

'We have no choice,' said Crispus. 'We must remember that we are Romans. We're not many, but these Alans are inside the Empire and they realise that sooner or later there will be a reckoning.'

Nehtan boiled inside. If the Alans enslaved them, she would love to see Crispus and Novateli grovel in the dirt. Then, she shuddered at the thought of being passed from warrior to warrior like a cup of wine, though that would not happen if she served the old lady.

'They don't care about us,' Fromus was saying to Crispus. 'But our mission might interest them.'

Crispus frowned down his long nose. 'When we go in, let me do the talking, is that clear?'

Rebellion flashed in Fromus's eyes. Nehtan willed him to respond, but he kept silent. The flaps of the large tent opened and a man beckoned.

Nehtan felt her arm being tugged by Fromus. 'You're coming with me.'

For a moment she wanted him to put his arm around her.

Inside, a fire from a Roman brazier gave out a hazy light amidst billowing streaks of smoke. Her eyes watered. The tent stank of burning animal fat. Colourful, intricate woollen rugs covered the ground. Bearded warriors reclined on piles of cushions, and an oval-eyed woman with silver earrings was kneeling next to a man, combing his long hair. In one corner, there was a crude wooden carving of an animal with wings and a scaly tail, painted in vivid red and gold.

Two men stood with spears at the far end of the tent. In between them sat an imposing man, with bare arms and high cheekbones. He sat on a tall chair, patting an enormous hunting dog with a fleshy, dangerous mouth. A warrior was speaking to him. Women carried urns, pouring a strong-smelling liquid into shiny beakers.

It took her back to Colud, though they never had anything like this. It was marvellous to see a power that owed nothing to Rome – no stone walls to shut out the sun and rain; no contempt for the streams and ribs of earth that rippled over the land.

Dorgolel spoke to the man in the high-backed chair and turned to Crispus, speaking in Latin.

'Roman, I bring you to Prince Goar, dread of his enemies, slayer of Huns and leader of our people. Let your name be known to him.'

Crispus saluted with his arm upright in the traditional way.

'*Ave atque vale*, Prince Goar. My name is Quintus Natalius Crispus, delegate from the city of Eburacum in the Diocese of Britannia.' Crispus nodded his head. 'May I introduce Calpornius Ursacius, of the City of Londinium; and Manius Aurelianus Fromus, Council member of the City of Corinium. This is Cornelius Novateli, Decurion of Horse in the Decima Gemina.' Goar raised his eyebrows. 'We wish you good health, the blessings of the Emperor and the wisdom of the Great God Christ.'

Nehtan tensed her shoulders. Such long-winded names the Romans gave themselves. That pompous creep Crispus would learn what life was like if he had to clean shit from an old Alan's arse.

The black-haired Alan leader replied, in good Latin.

'*Ave*, it shall be unto you as you wish to me. Welcome to my tent, Romans. My man Dorgolel found you on the road to Remorum. You were prudent not to resist.'

The Alan leader let out a chuckle. Nehtan saw Crispus flush, unable to stop himself from glancing round, then raising his hand in a feeble salute.

After a pause, Goar continued, speaking in a measured drawl.

'You have travelled far in troubled lands. These are new days and the iron might of Rome is not feared as it once was. Tell me, what brings you to Gaul?'

'Prince Goar, I see that you speak with directness' – Crispus puffed out his chest – 'so I will be plain: we are a delegation from Britannia on our way to Italy, and we ask for hospitality and safe conduct. As a confederate of Rome, I know that we can trust in your friendship.'

These Romans, thought Nehtan, still trying to play the all-powerful. Only death would cut them down.

'Natalius Crispus,' the Alan calmly regarded the Roman opposite him. 'We two, elders of our peoples, were born in simpler times. It grieves my heart that a man can no longer greet another and know to whose word he is sworn. We find Romans who support the Emperor Honorius; others who are allied to the usurper Constantinus; and yet others who are with Comes Gerontius ... who until recently was the right-hand man of Constantinus.' Goar's tone remained even. 'And there are Romans whose oaths are not known, riding before the wind. Which are you?'

'We – we are a neutral party, bound for the Emperor Honorius. We have no wish to take part in civil disorder; we bear no ill will towards Constantinus nor Gerontius. They are concerned with Gaul, whereas our delegation must present itself to the Emperor.'

'These are fair words, but your inward thought lies beneath the bark. It may be that you are uncertain where you stand and to which camp you belong.' Prince Goar paused and tapped the side of his chair. His eyes flashed across the small crowd in front of him, his dark hair cascading onto his shoulders. What would he be like? Nehtan wondered.

Goar tapped again. 'Tell me, why do you travel at such a dangerous time as this? We hear that the Emperor does not move from the great sea-city of Ravenna.'

Crispus shifted and gestured with his hand. He glanced at Ursacius, and Nehtan saw the tiredness in his eyes. Goar must also have noticed.

'You have been riding since dawn.' The prince gestured and an attendant brought a tall stool. Crispus perched on the edge, and Nehtan grinned as she saw that he found it difficult to keep his balance.

Crispus clasped his long fingers together. 'Thank you, I am most appreciative of the generosity of Prince Goar. Our delegation is an official one from the cities of Britannia. We have been charged with taking a message of loyalty to the Emperor.'

Goar smiled at an older Alan nearby. Was he an elder or a priest?

'Your journey will not be easy,' the prince said, 'even when you reach Italy. I ask if you are aware that Alaric and his Goths are camped outside Rome?'

Nehtan's mouth opened.

Crispus jerked his head. 'We knew that the Goths were in Italy, but not this.' He paused. 'Rome's walls have stood for a thousand years. The history of the Empire shows that in the end, the Imperial throne will prevail. This business of Alaric and the Goths does not change our purpose. You say that the Emperor is at Ravenna; then, that is where we will go.'

Crispus's assurance was depressing. Nehtan lost track of what the long-winded men were saying. If barbarians were outside the gates of the great City, would that make it easier to get back to Colud? She tensed as she tried to recall how nymayr and atir spoke. She could hear nymayr's voice, but she could not remember the language. She was cut off from her people. And there was something else, a grinding dread about which her parents never spoke.

Prince Goar threw out his right hand.

'... it is not given to us to know why the wind blows. Princes and peoples rise and fall, and yet the Emperor remains, an eagle in his mountain nest. Ravens fight with crows, but the king of the birds bides his time.'

'You speak with wisdom, Prince Goar,' said Crispus. 'Cicero tells us that a nation can survive its fools, and even the ambitious, but it cannot survive treason from within. Even so, the Empire has endured many times such as these. Indeed, worse, when I think of the civil wars before Diocletian.'

'This is so. Even amongst the Alans, we have divisions. I have separated from the Alan host, which is in thrall to the Vandals. This disunity is a disease spreading across the world.' Goar held his chin. 'Would I be right to conclude that Constantinus is no longer master of Britannia?'

'It is as you say. Britannia has expelled his officials and I represent the loyal citizens of Britannia. We – that is, this small delegation – ask you, Prince Goar, for your protection whilst we are in your territory.'

'Your position is a delicate one.' Goar gazed one by one into the faces of the Romans. Nehtan could not help dropping her head. 'If he knew about your mission, Constantinus would do all he could to stop you. I drank the cup of peace with his ambassador, Comes Gerontius. But this man has now set aside his oath to Constantinus. This breaks the chain of loyalty between Constantinus and myself. Allegiances are shifting like the wind, and words are separate from hearts.' Goar raised his finger. Nehtan found herself standing straight with her head up, straining to hear what he would say next.

'Constantinus's nearest soldiers are three or four days south of here. They are puny and poorly led.'

A shove on her shoulder and a warrior started to push past. For a moment, two black eyes bore into her, then he was in front of her. She made out a red animal face on the back of the warrior's cloak. It looked like the horned god Cernunnos, the cattle guardian whom atir favoured.

At Goar's gesture, the warrior advanced and spoke in a low voice. The prince eyed Crispus.

'I beg that you will excuse me. I must attend to this.'

Nehtan looked at the back of Fromus's head – dirty neck, scraggly hair, already longer than the usual patrician cut. He was less nervous than the other two delegates, perhaps because he was ignorant of the ways of the world, despite what he thought. She had seen the fickleness of apparent indifference in army camps, when a Briton was brought in for questioning. It didn't seem like much until the Briton thought he was safe, and maybe he smiled. Then the soldiers would start to beat him. Maybe the Alans would do the same with these fine Romans. She shivered: they shouldn't touch Fromus.

After some minutes, the Alan warrior left and Goar nodded at Crispus.

'We were speaking of loyalty. I have read the words of Roman history. In my boyhood, I was a hostage at the court of Emperor Theodosius. I learnt Latin and observed your ways. You have many paths, almost as many as there are men. With you, it is not as it is with us, where a man is bound to his chief by ties of blood which mere choice cannot undo.'

How could he say this if he had broken ranks with the other Alans? Nehtan shifted her feet. Men said what they wanted others to hear. Their words did not chain her. She would be free; the Spirit would guide her.

Goar waited while an Alan girl with long black hair brought two cups filled with a dark liquid, which she gave to Goar and Crispus. Nehtan admired her straight back as she walked slowly through a crowd of men. Goar smiled at the girl, and touched her hand. Was she a favourite concubine, or perhaps a daughter?

Prince Goar drummed the edge of his chair and sniffed.

'After war between Roman and Roman, the great river of the heartland breaks back through the weed which would choke it, and opens new channels. Perhaps a usurper becomes legitimate, perhaps not. The strength of the Empire comes from its ability to supply fresh troops and food from its heartland provinces. Whoever is ruler of those regions is eventually accepted as the Emperor of the West. Because of this, my people seek a homeland within your Empire. I will speak my oath for Emperor Honorius. We are as one, and thus I will grant you safe conduct.'

Smiling, Crispus shuffled his hands on his knees.

Nehtan scowled. All these bristling men. What would it be like to live with the Alans, as the wife of a warrior? They were at home in the forest and the river-lands, beholden to no one except their chiefs, their honour and their rites. It could be worse, though there would be no one to celebrate the Lord's Day. She would slide back into Donn's power, the vile god of Colud for whom her family had suffered. She felt him, prowling somewhere out there, on the edges. Fromus, she must hold to him.

Crispus stood.

'I am most grateful, Prince Goar, and I am happy that we are bound by our loyalty to the Empire.'

'It is some time since I sent word to Ravenna.' The prince's eyes flickered. 'We have had no reply. We have offered our fiercest warriors, serving until death. All we ask is for a land of wide valleys and slow rivers. It would be well if you were to tell the Emperor of our desire for friendship and federation.'

'I will speak to the Emperor of your noble allegiance and the strength of your people.'

Goar nodded to Dorgolel before looking back to Crispus.

'Now, you must rest. Food will be brought to your tents. Tomorrow, we will feast and you will meet a Roman who is our guest.'

Crispus stiffened. 'We shall be pleased to meet this man. May I trespass a little longer on your time? Winter is drawing in and I would ask, Prince Goar, that my party continue swiftly onwards. We have far to go.'

'Do not be concerned, Natalius Crispus; our eyes travel to the same place. As for the man of whom I spoke, you will do me a service to take him and his woman with you.'

'We will of course oblige, Prince Goar. May I enquire about these Romans? How might they be here? Are they simple folk?'

'The man is what you call an equestrian. He was travelling when my men came across him. Now he must go back with you.'

Nehtan saw that this parting request – more in the nature of a command – put Crispus on edge. As they left the tent, Fromus nodded at her, and his eyes blinked as he smiled.

They trudged over muddy paths, past Alan fires and ragged, patchwork tents. Eventually, Dorgolel stopped and pointed at three large tents and a small one.

'Here – food, sleep.'

Decurion Novateli addressed Crispus, who was panting and worrying the folds of his cloak.

'If it is all right with you, Crispus Natalius, I would recommend that my soldiers take the small tent and one other, leaving the two largest tents for your delegation and, if I may be so bold, myself.'

Fromus stepped forward. 'But what about Nehtan? She can't go in with the soldiers.'

Nehtan clasped her hands tight.

'That girl has been trouble from the start.' Ursacius raised his voice. 'If she hadn't delayed us, we wouldn't be here now. We should leave her behind.' Ursacius gave a gruff laugh and gestured to Fromus. 'I can see why you want her, but she's in the way and the soldiers don't like you having her.'

Fromus snarled back. 'What do you mean, and what's it got to do with them? They do as they are told. Besides, she's a citizen; doesn't that mean anything to you?'

'She brought us bad luck.'

Nehtan wanted to shrink into the shadows.

Fromus's fists were half-raised as Crispus stepped between the two men. 'Hold on, *Honestiores*, let us not forget who we are. We are in this together, we have to make the best of it and we need to set an example. We have our duty – even to this girl.'

Ursacius grunted and fiddled with his beard.

'So you say. I suppose the young man might as well have his way, but it won't be for long.' He grinned and threw his head up. 'Why don't the three of us take the biggest tent while Fromus shares the small one with the girl? The soldiers can use the other two.'

'That is not what I meant.' Fromus's voice rose. 'We promised her, I didn't mean ...'

'Ursacius has made a sensible suggestion.' The old Roman reached his hand out to Fromus. Nehtan was surprised to see Fromus shrink back. 'It is up to you how you treat it; we're all tired.'

The pointy-beard weasel, Ursacius, wrinkled his nose and walked away.

Alan voices broke the uneasy silence. A man was leading a horse pulling a cart laden with the Roman mule-packs. Women trudged behind, carrying animal skins, food and flagons of water. Nehtan moved forwards to help, but they waved her away.

The delegation gathered to eat in a muddy space between tents. It seemed best to hang back, but Fromus waved her forward emphatically. She barely tasted the rough chunks of meat and vegetables. Water helped to swill it down.

The air was becoming sharp.

Ursacius gulped and belched. 'I hope we get something better tomorrow. This is inedible.'

'I wouldn't expect much.' She saw Novateli grinning in the

firelight. He didn't stay down for long. 'I've had many a meal with federates. If they do the cooking, it always ends up like this; they boil or mash everything, sometimes both. No salt, no herbs, just knobs of food fit for swine.'

The Decurion laughed, and she was about to join in, when he glanced at her, his nose twitching slightly. 'And after,' the man kept his eyes on her, 'there's nothing sweet to follow.'

CHAPTER NINE

Fromus eyed Nehtan waiting outside the tents, half-hidden in the moonlight shadows. She was like a captive fox, poised and ready to leap away. His blood tingled: she would need careful coaxing.

His hand went to her shoulder, but she shrank back, retreating into the tent. He stooped inside, sensing her warmth.

'It was best to settle things this way.' He wanted to see her eyes, but it was too dark. 'I mean, the tents and who goes where ...'

'I understand.'

It was his right, everyone knew. He had rescued her, and she was a homeless plebeian, pressed against him on Papiteddo for hours, her breasts against his back. It was only natural. Yes, they had prayed together, but that was all.

He hunched next to the tent-pole in the centre, trying to control his breathing. Fur-skins and cloaks rustled as she laid their bedding down. The light had dwindled to a thin haze where shapes were more confusing than the pure dark.

The sound of Nehtan's steady breathing in the darkness. His feet caught; he fell and bumped his head on a fleshy hardness. Her thigh.

'Damn, sorry, I can't see. Did I hurt you?'

'It's all right.' A small voice. 'It's nothing.'

He crept alongside her. The warmth of her breath, tension, which way would she spring? Stroking her hair and forehead, his hand found a bump, her wound. He leant across, kissed her cheek, and brushed her lips with his. She had the freshness of a young calf.

Soldiers' voices broke in from the tent next door.

'Sir, I don't know,' he could hardly hear her, 'I'm not sure.'

It was about to happen; he needed her. Pulling back the fur cover, smoothing her belly, the outline of her breasts. Nuzzling her lips. No response.

'You're delicious.' Wrong words.

'I'm not ready, I mean, if you must ...'

Something drained and he shifted. An edge jutting into him – the belt with the letter. He took it off, and his tunic. He nestled back down under the fur-skins, sliding across to her.

'Nehtan, it is all right, we'll be careful.' He felt for her shoulder. 'Don't you like me?'

'It's not that ... I'm Christian... it should be more.' Silence. He dropped his hand from her shoulder. Then she spoke in a rush. 'I don't want to do it, and, when you've had enough, you'll pass me on to someone else.'

'I'm not like that.'

'It's what happens.' Suddenly, this fierce voice. 'It's easy for a man like you.'

'Why are you saying this?'

'I mean,' he felt her shifting on her elbows, 'it's, it's nothing much to you.'

'What are you talking about?'

'You know, with a servant.'

'That's how it is. But it won't be like that with you and me.'

The woman shouldn't be saying anything. She was paying too much attention to those wretched Bishops. The other girls, he remembered them.

Pulling back the cover, then stopping, she was somehow not there, absent, like a dead person. He lay still. He didn't want to hurt her. But she should be his, to do as he liked. He was stuck, half-way, like the rest of his life. She was so alive. Just to hold her, that was enough, for now.

Lifting his hand... then, gentle restling sounds, she was turning towards him. Light fingers on his face, stroking his forehead, his cheeks, his mouth, he could feel her leaning over him. Her lips brushing his, but then she slumped back.

Now, he could not stop, bringing his hand to cup her cheek, his mouth moving over her, searching for her lips, but she twisted her head to the side.

Dragging back the fur-skins, he kissed her neck, forcing down her tunic to free her breasts. Mouth came to nipple, hand straying down her belly, caressing.

'Please.' Another whisper. 'I can't.'

His hand froze.

'Why not?'

'If you have to, I won't cry out.'

He could ignore her, but the thought fled. The time of her menses?

Wet face, nuzzling cheeks, sinking into her sweet smell, lapping tears. The swelling of her breasts, a hand soft on his ear.

'I haven't done it.'

He stopped. Was she still crying?'

Waiting, he was startled when she spoke directly into his ear. 'It' not as if I don't think...but I want to be true ... I don't know what's going on.'

She was slight in his arms. His fingers grazed her cheeks; they were wet. Never mind. He was ready, a burning desire to get on top, to taste every part.

Loud soldier laughter came from the tent next door.

He lay back, shaking like a stranger in a harsh land. Her

hand touched his, delicate. Leaning over, kissing, grazing her lips with his. A surge of tenderness, caressing her forehead.

Her small voice. 'That's where they struck me.'

Something scuttled across his hand. Lice. He shuddered, and was annoyed with himself. 'Does it hurt?'

'It's sore, but I was lucky.'

'You don't seem fortunate to me, poor Nehtan.'

Thoughts invaded like barbarian armies. Was he Roman or Christian: couldn't he be both? Women like her were for the taking.

'It doesn't matter.' Her breath was on his chin, her arm across him, her voice low and urgent. 'Tell me ... tell me where you're going. How are you going to get out of here?'

Her small finger prodding his chest, his arm moved around her, pulling her close.

'Well, we're on our way to an audience with the Emperor. Goar will provide us with an escort to Treverorum. After that we'll head south and get to Italy.'

Silence. He squeezed her shoulder. There was no point in this talk.

'Why do you want to see the Emperor?'

He let out a slight groan. 'We're taking a message from the cities of Britannia.' The whole mission seemed tedious, long-winded, but she wanted to know – and, after all, it was important. 'We've thrown over the usurper Constantinus and we're ruling ourselves until we can get help from the Emperor. We have to convince him that we are loyal, so that we don't suffer reprisals when his troops come back. A letter by itself won't be enough. He probably would not even read it. We have to talk to him in person.'

He had her attention, but this was going nowhere.

Another nudge from her. 'Then what?'

'We want permission to arm ourselves. My father fears that Britannia will break up into little kingdoms, fighting each other. I have a secret letter from him to our cousin, Comes Gerontius.'

He should not have told her. It had come gushing out, and he didn't even know what the letter was about. 'You mustn't tell anyone about the letter. It's secret.'

Her mouth brushed his ear. 'The world's going mad. Why don't we leave the others when we get a chance, and find somewhere safe?'

Fromus shifted, staring into the darkness. 'What are you saying? My family; I'm a delegate; people depend on me. I have to deliver the letter.'

'Of course.' Her arm looped across his chest, her fingers circling. 'What about me?'

'You must come with us. Nowhere's safe. You know, Ursacius wanted to barter you for an extra horse.' Her breathing stopped. 'But they can't; I won't let them. You're a citizen, I'd sooner ...'

'What?'

'I don't know, I wouldn't let them do that. They couldn't. I wouldn't let them.'

He faced her in the dark, tracing her belly skin beneath the tunic. He leant in to kiss, but she turned her head.

'Would you do that?'

'I won't leave you here, they know that.'

Her arms clasped around his back, pulling him close. He stroked her hair. 'What about you? You must have people in Britannia?'

'Far away, in the north.'

'Tell me about them, and your life, before all this.'

'Not now, I'm tired. You wouldn't want to know.'

'But I do. I want to know everything.'

'Please, let's not talk about it.'

Her palm was pressing on his back. It felt as if a weight had been lifted off him. Seesawing back and forth, his hand caressing up to the edge of what he was permitted, then they were kissing, breaking away, dozing, whispering. She slept first, hugged lightly by him. The unbearable joy of feeling her trust in him, this wild thing he had found. The first rays of sunlight began to warm the tent as he fell asleep.

Men's voices rumbling, logs clanking. He jolted awake. She was there. Leaning over, slightly arched eyebrows, brushing back her hair, he kissed her high, round cheeks.

Her eyes opened, alert, her mouth tense. 'I'd better go and help.' She sat up, whispering. 'I have to go.' Putting his hand on her leg, her eyes softening, looking straight into his. 'They're starting a fire; I should be out there.'

'They don't need you.'

'It doesn't seem right.' She paused, eyes lowered, then slid out from under the heavy skins. 'Normally, I'm the first up. It's my favourite time of day, before Vitalis and Marcellinus get up.'

Outside, someone clanged a metal pot. The heavy voice of Bellator gave orders. A soldier guffawed. 'By Mithras, isn't he the lucky one? All night and still at it.'

Fromus froze. An angry bark: 'Shut up.' Bellator's unmistakable tone released him.

Fromus leapt up, putting his arm around Nehtan. She turned, lips parted, eyes anxious.

'I'll go first.' He nuzzled her neck. 'Wait a bit until you come out.'

Dressed, he opened the leather canvas and stepped into the sunlight. A blue, still morning. Sharp smoke hung about the tents. Red-cloaked Romans stood around a fire, and further off colourfully robed Alan women were beating clothes against a log. Fromus felt the soldiers' brazen eyes on him as he walked across the grubby patch of grass to join Novateli and Ursacius.

'Have they brought anything to eat?' He grinned. 'That stuff last night was disgusting.'

Novateli laughed.

A short while later Nehtan slipped out of the tent and joined them. Fromus watched her accept a pot of warm milk from Bellator, then stand back from the circle of men. She had nothing, no one, apart from him.

On the far side of the fire, a couple of legionaries half-turned towards a man behind them. It was the dark-cropped soldier. Fromus saw him flick his wrist and appear to make an obscene gesture with his thumb, half-hidden under his cloak. Surely, the man would not dare? Before Fromus could decide, the cavalryman mouthed something to the two men and walked away.

CHAPTER TEN

Nehtan's feet sunk into the mud amid the labyrinth of Alan tents and carts. Losing her balance, she rooted her hand in sludge so as not to fall over. Anything rather than reach out to a nearby soldier.

The huge Biarchus Bellator strode up. Pushing a stick into the fire, he stepped close to her and sniffed. Nehtan pulled the cloak about her neck, steeling herself to dart her eyes to his broad face.

'What do you think, will they let us go?'

The Biarchus kicked a log into the fire. 'There's some as swears Alans are cruel killers, but I reckon we'll be all right. If they say they will let us go, that is what they'll do - but who knows when? That's another road. Time doesn't mean the same to them as it does to you and me.'

She forced a smirk as Bellator lowered his voice.

'I was once in a cavalry troop led by a Decurion who was half-Vandal, half-Roman. You never knew if things would happen when they were supposed to.'

Shivering, she peeped at the legionaries huddled around the fire. They didn't mean anything to her, not like Marcellinus and Vitalis. In the fort at Vindolanda, the boy used to call her 'His Personal Pict, his Very Own'. No matter how many times she told him that she was not a Pict, that her tribe did not dye their skin blue, and that her father sold cattle to the Romans, Vitalis paid no attention. He would prod her, in his earnest little boy way, saying that she was not to worry, she was his Most Personal Pict and he would look after her.

He could sting like a spring nettle. She remembered

stopping Vitalis from taking a handful of raisins, his father's favourite luxury, and he had kicked her knee viciously.

But, most evenings, with his mother gone, he wanted to be cuddled, and they made up stories.

She had loved joining Vitalis's reading lessons. Sometimes, the three of them had taken it in turns to read from Marcellinus's most treasured possessions – fragmentary scrolls of St John's Gospel, Caesar's *Gallic Wars*, or, her favourite, part of Ovid's *Metamorphoses*. Marcellinus had been proud of how well she had progressed, though she had to be careful not to overshadow Vitalis. Usually, the centurion said little except at the end of the day when he wanted to know what his son had been doing. If the master was tired – and that was often – he shouted. A few times he had stroked her head and, once, his hand shaking, her shoulder and her bare neck. He said her name, then stopped. Soon after, he gave her the iron amulet with the Chi-Rho incised in the middle.

Now Marcellinus and Vitalis were on their way to the Lord. She was still in the power of Romans, but it was different with Fromus.

Through the smoke coming from the fire between the tents, a pair of dark soldier eyes glinted at her. It was the trooper whom she had pushed over. He was stocky and trim, even in the mud-filled camp. She looked at Bellator and gave a slight nod across the fire.

'Who's he?'

'Trooper Messor. You mind him, a hard man, good to have with you in a fight, but don't be crossing his path at night.' Bellator chuckled. 'No, if you want an army man who'll treat you right, go for a Brigantian, like myself.' A sudden tenderness in his tone. 'I'd know how to look after you. You'd know where you were with me. You need to be careful.'

She held his gaze for a moment, his eyes devoid of intent. Then it was over, and he walked off.

It had been about a year ago. Master Marcellinus's detachment was marching down to Gaul. They stopped for a few days in the army district of Londinium, staying in a murky hut that stank of leather-work. Few soldiers were left in Britannia, and the only cavalry troop had been summoned to Londinium. On the second evening, finding no beer for the evening meal, she rushed out to buy some before darkness. Minutes later, footsteps raced up behind and two men dragged her into an alley. She screamed as callused hands tore at her tunic. Then, one of them tumbled, his arm up to fend off knife slashes from a third man. The attackers fled.

Her defender slumped down, sobbing, pouring out confused and bitter words. She listened to the sound of the man, more than his words, for what seemed like a long time, their heads close. The sense of him was barbed and bristling with hurt, throbbing heart-bruises that went back to childhood and even before that, to the mother he never knew and the father whose few kind words had been buried beneath the mountain of his cruelty. He was showing her something always hidden. She told him that she understood what it was like to be alone; she was a slave. All the while, the man's hand was on her neck. At first it did not hurt, but he began clenching harder. She dared not challenge him, until she gasped for breath and grabbed his wrist. His arm snatched back, and the man ran off.

Nehtan stared at the fire embers. She had not seen the man in Londinium's face clearly, but she knew the tone of voice and his dark, bushing eyebrows. It was him, Messor. She hadn't been sure before, hoping that it wouldn't be so. There were barely any cavalrymen left in Britannia, so it was not surprising that he was one of the escorts for the delegates. He was another one who had power over her; he would tell them about her, when it suited him.

* * *

The day wore on until an Alan warrior, sitting bolt upright on his horse and wearing a shabby cloak, beckoned the Romans to follow him.

Philus inclined his head to Nehtan. 'You all right then? Ready for the feast?'

A soldier laughed. She shrugged her shoulders. There was always one who would twist the words.

A hubbub arose from somewhere beyond. Women and children started to stream past, families supporting old men. Warriors on horseback weaved through the motley crowd. Another man rode up and beckoned the Romans to join the Alan stream. They walked past a ring of wagons on the edge of the camp and reached a patch of bare land, studded with tree stumps, in the midst of which blazed a row of large fires.

A thumping noise grew, and a group of men approached on horseback, banging taut drums with padded sticks. The Romans stood planted to the earth, jerking their heads. Then came a shrill, rolling drone. Nehtan could not make sense of it until a line of women arrived, with plaited hair and painted oval eyes, playing bone pipes. They walked in a wide circle around the drum-riders, facing the men, who thudded short drumbeats in unison. The older women stopped piping and ululated as they swayed with glassy eyes.

The beat echoed in Nehtan, lifting, joyful. She tipped her head back, the sound like sharp rays of sunlight slicing through cloud. The ululating-drumming-piping world tipped forwards, cascaded down, gathered, pressing together before surging off again. On and on it pulsed, pouring across the sky. She searched for Fromus and saw him rocking with his eyes half closed. The women ceased ululating and the drumming became quieter until only a low beat and a plaintive pipe-melody floated in the air. The men jumped off their horses, took hold of the women pipers and hoisted them up.

The crowd erupted into a huge bellow of *ahay-yiy, ahay-yiy, ahay-yay*. Then, suddenly, it was over, and people were turning to each other and talking.

She saw Crispus raise his head to Novateli, who spread his palms wide and grimaced. Fromus strode towards her, his face beaming. He raised his eyebrows, and she wished she was back in the tent with him.

At length, Prince Goar arrived and dismounted to sit on a fur-lined chair. Beyond him, there was a flurry of activity and a Roman man and woman appeared. The man was perhaps in his early thirties, with short brown hair and a smooth, chiselled face and a dimpled chin. The woman was pretty enough. Whitener highlighted her fleshy face, and her neck was garlanded with a necklace of blue and green eye beads interspersed with wave stones. The lady laughed briefly to herself, curling her lower lip and keeping her grey eyes steady.

Goar spoke to the smooth-faced Roman in measured Latin. 'Thalassius Paulinus, allow me to introduce you to our new guests.'

'Flavius Thalassius Paulinus' - the prince let his right hand sweep down - 'I present Quintus Natalius Crispus. Friend Crispus, Paulinus has been most interested in our ways. Like you, he finds the rapid changes in the Empire not to his liking.'

Goar chuckled as the two Romans grasped each other's

forearms in the usual way. Nehtan detected a flicker of worry on Paulinus's face as his palm opened towards the lady. She was not the proper, matronly sort, but at least she was another woman.

'This is my wife, Sabellia Clara. We found our way to the noble prince's camp by accident and have been treated most graciously. It is time for us to leave, and I would be most grateful if you would allow us to accompany you.'

The Roman lady nodded and clasped her forearms. Another one of the Masters. 'We are gratified to know you, Quintus Natalius Crispus. Prince Goar has told us something about your mission.'

Crispus stooped. 'We are pleased to meet, in these, how shall I say, uncommon circumstances, and I am happy to accommodate your wish to journey with us.'

Nehtan watched the Roman couple flick their cloaks with a flourish and leave. These two might change the military dominance of the small Roman group.

Later, in the twilight of large fires, great chunks of smoldering meat were carved and drinks were passed round in horns and wooden goblets. Nehtan was amused to see warriors grapple half-seriously with each other to gain a drinking cup. Crispus waved away a metal goblet of frothing liquid.

'It looks revolting' Fromus said, 'and it smells like horse piss. In fact, it probably is.'

The Romans laughed, and Nehtan could not help smiling.

The sky disappeared as the dark came. A group of plainly clad men arrived, dragging huge branches, which they threw into the fires, lighting up the faces of the young warriors. A drumbeat started in a juddering rhythm. Long-haired men danced around the flames, erupting into bursts of loud singing. On the outer fringe of the yellow light, silhouettes of dishevelled figures huddled together. Nehtan remembered what it felt like.

She was squatting behind the Roman delegates, cut off from the heat. There was no sign of the old Alan woman. Two warriors wandered behind, peering at Novateli's decorated spatha sheath. The taller man laughed and put his hand to the pommel of his sword. In the shadows, a soldier jerked his head up. The Alans walked off into the night.

Several times a year, the clan had gathered in front of the elders in Colud. Once, her family had stayed in their hut, fearful, while the whole village crowded outside, yelling. Men dragged Grandmother out by her grey hairs, nymayr screeching while atir's arms were pinioned behind. Nehtan shuddered as she recalled clutching nymayr, shrinking from the hatred boiling on all sides, terrified that she would be next. The elders boomed: Grandmother was banished, and she would be killed if she came back. She had stopped them from dedicating Nehtan to the god Donn of the Underworld. Grandmother was cursed; it was she who had caused the cattle to die.

They had never seen Grandmother again.

It could happen anywhere, here... The half-obscured faces of the Alan warriors shimmered and dissolved in the firelight. They were restless, waiting for something.

Nehtan pulled her cloak tight. It felt as if fingers of flame were reaching out, pulling her back to her life in Colud. And then there was something else, the possibility of a different life, neither Colud nor Roman. Is that why she was here, to find a new way, perhaps in the south of Gaul?

She winced. Glowing embers floated up from the Alan fires, wafting towards the pinpricks of light in the far heavens.

Novateli was standing with his shoulders hunched, his back silhouetted against roaring flames. The ways of the Alans were strange, but the Romans were shut away behind walls, their burial places cut off from where they lived. In Colud, they kept the ancestors' bones inside the huts to keep out the bad spirits.

The old thoughts circled round. Why had God allowed the Picts to capture her? Had the High One led her to Marcellinus so that she could become a Christian? Or was she punished because atir had been selling forbidden things? Her fingers clenched as she sucked in the cold night air.

A hulking warrior emerged from a melee of Alans, pulling a slender girl by the hand. He hesitated as he was about to walk through the Roman soldiers. With renewed energy he strode on, letting go of the girl's hand. She followed, her head down. The two disappeared into the gloom.

The weight of her head on her neck was too much. She let her chin flop down to her chest. Lord, don't let Fromus desert me. Let me stay with him.

She could bind him closer if he lay with her. It would be a release, but it should not be like this, and it would lead to worse. She was trapped. He was a high master, an equestrian lord. They were on opposite sides of a wall that cut through the flowing land. Power had been bred into him from birth, even before that. Like all Romans, he was convinced that the world was his. Yet, he was young, and they were outside the might of the Empire. He liked talking to her, and there was a softening in him; he had prayed with her.

She remembered the leading Christians in the community at Bononia. They too had confidence in their place in the great scheme of things, though many were of low birth. They drew their strength from the end of time, when this world was gone. Was this what the Christ had written on the ground, a message of hope for those whom the world despised?

A streak of iron tightened in Nehtan's heart. She must hold to the Risen One, the eternal root of the world. Everything else would fall away.

Loud voices: Dorgolel was saying something to Crispus. Then they were trudging back to their tents. It started to drizzle. Fromus walked awkwardly in front of her. He left her standing inside the canvas-hide tent without saying a word. Soon he was back, hesitating at the tent flap.

'It seems – they insisted – we have to separate. Lady Clara has found a wooden tub, and tomorrow they are bringing hot water. She's taking our tent and wants you with her. I'll be with Paulinus and the others. By the Holy Martyrs, it is not right.'

'I must do as she wants.' She glanced down. By Saint Agnes, let him not make a scene.

'That wretched woman, why should she?' Fromus's eyes blazed. 'You're not her servant. It's completely unacceptable.'

'Please, I beg you.' Nehtan almost called him master. 'They don't like me being with you, no one does.' Her hand gripped his arm. 'We'll have time later.'

His long face broadened into a grin, then a scowl. Lady Clara had appeared.

'Where are you, Nehtan? I can't see anything. Go inside and make my bed. Bread of Heaven, how much longer must I put up with living amongst savages?' Her certainty was almost a relief. 'May the good Lord bless us for what we are enduring. It must count for something.'

* * *

111

Next morning four Alan girls brought a high-sided wooden tub. They giggled, but hushed when Clara stirred. Nehtan helped them to ferry hot water in leaky wooden buckets from a distant cauldron. Novateli walked past and shook his head.

Inside the tent, small trickles of water streaked from the sides of the tub. Grains of corn floated on the surface.

'Come, girl.' The lady dropped her undergarment. 'We've got to be quick or the water will get cold.'

Clara immersed herself in the tub. Flabby but powerful arms and a curvaceous body.

'My bathing essence, over there, in that box. You won't believe how long I've been waiting to use it.'

Nehtan found a lattice-carved sandalwood container under some clothing and lifted the lid. A luscious pungency spilled out. At the bottom of the smooth box was a mass of small, pale flakes.

'What should I do?'

'Bring it and sprinkle the flakes into the water.'

Clara was sitting with her knees up, leaning her arms over the side of the tub. Nehtan did what she most wanted, which was to dig her fingers into the delicate flakes, scooping them into her hand. The flakes melted into her pores, soaking her in the unimaginable world of the very rich. Was this how Fromus lived?

The lady raised her grey eyes. 'Go on girl, pour it out.'

She dropped the flakes onto the water where they dissolved above the folds on Clara's belly.

'Not like that, spread it round.'

'Shall I put more in?'

'Of course, all of it.'

She was about to plunge her hand into the sandalwood box

when Clara spoke. 'Tip what's left into the water, sprinkle it. Don't get it stuck on your hands.'

Nehtan tried to drop what was left into the small area of open water, but it would not come out.

'Give it to me, girl.'

Clara's hand brushed her fingers as she took the box and shook the remaining flakes out.

'Ah, that's good.' The lady beamed and Nehtan smiled back. 'I've been longing to bathe for weeks. There's lice everywhere, and the scabs on those old women ...' Clara shook her head.

Nehtan gazed at the steaming water. Clara's white flesh took on a rosy hue as she scrubbed herself with dollops of oily water.

'Give me a good rubbing with the towel, girl. You poor dear, you've never been in a proper household.'

Nehtan shook her head slowly.

'Well then,' said Clara, 'it's a good thing that you are with me. I know what it is like to be, well, someone like you. What's going to happen to you?'

'It's kind of you to think of me, my lady.'

'Yes, no doubt. Give me the green one first.' Nehtan pulled the long undergarment over Clara's head and waist. The lady's eyes narrowed, then she dropped her nose in the direction of the second tunic.

'I wasn't always a rich wife. There was a time when things were different. I know what it is like to be at the mercy of others. When you're used to wine and jewellery, with slaves running around, you wonder how you survived before.'

Nehtan heard Bellator shouting orders outside.

'They've told me something of your circumstances.' Clara pointed at her cloak. 'You're a sensible woman. You're young and you catch the eye. You need to take your opportunity when we reach a city.'

'I don't understand.'

The surface of the water in the tub was congealing round the edges.

'You're sweet on the young *Honestior.*' The lady shifted her shoulders, exuding warmth. 'They say he is partial to you, but do not be deceived, it will pass. Look, girl, I'm telling you for your own sake. I wouldn't normally say anything, but out here things are different.'

'As you say.'

'You should make the most of it while it lasts. Believe you me, I know. As for the future, well, he will be off to Italy and then, God willing, back to his estates in Britannia. Where will you fit in?'

'My lady?' Blinking, lips curled, Nehtan had to restrain herself for fear she might receive a clip across the ears. 'I ... can't think.'

'My,' Clara huffed and sat on a packing case, 'I hope you haven't got silly ideas. You will learn, one way or another, and so will he, but you've far to fall, whereas he ... Well, sweet is the apple when the orchard-keeper is away, and the world is a cruel teacher.'

Nehtan knelt to pull the lady's boots up her calves. She winced at the pressure on her head wound as her hair was stroked.

'Young woman, you've much to learn. I can still remember.' The lady sighed. 'You could join my household, but only if you promise to behave and do as you are told. I can't abide disorder amongst my servants.'

Paulinus was calling from outside. 'Clara, dear, we must be going.'

The lady's dark eyebrows held her. 'Well?'

'My lady, you are most kind.' Nehtan's head cried out that it would be better to live with this woman, away from soldiers, somewhere warm and dependable. But the Lord had given her hope.

'Young woman?' Clara's eyes puckered.

'I don't know. I'm not sure.'

'Don't make me regret my offer. I will not have you shilly-shallying. You must decide.'

Nehtan bowed. It was all she could do, but it was a gesture that meant more than she could say.

CHAPTER ELEVEN

The small column wound its way through a forest of alder, pine and birch, dotted with big chestnuts and oaks. The ground was springy and wet.

They were heading east, towards the city of Treverorum, guided by Alan escorts. Fromus let Papiteddo follow Dorgolel's horse.

Paths criss-crossed with bewildering frequency. It seemed that Dorgolel had no doubt about what was the main path, except every now and then, when he halted, and a couple of Alan riders shot off, without being asked, each speeding down an alternative route. Within minutes, they were back, usually at more or less the same time. One rider would nod his head slightly, while the other glanced swiftly up and back to where he had come from. No words were exchanged, and they never had to retrace their steps.

What would happen when these hunters settled down and forgot their forest instincts? The most treasured Roman virtue was discipline, but where was it now? Ursacius said that Emperor Honorius's opinions were those of whoever had last advised him, and that you could no more trust him than a flock of geese. Ursacius was a toad, but he knew his way round the swamp. The old world was doomed and Father was stuck in the past.

He felt Nehtan flick her hair to one side behind him. Together, they could create a future between them, at least for now, in their private moments while they were out here in east Gaul, away from the Empire and all those things you were meant to do.

Papiteddo jumped over a deep gash in the track, throwing Nehtan against his back. What did he want from this dark-haired, insistent young woman? Was it more than possessing her? As Catullus said, *better a sparrow, living or dead, than no birdsong at all*. And as for her, did she see him merely as a passage to a better life? Yet, if that was all she thought, she would have let him have her.

'What are you thinking?' Nehtan's lilting voice broke in.

'I was wondering,' he hesitated, 'about Rome, being Roman, and you.'

'So I'm last.' He felt her squeeze his waist, and a delicious warmth went through him. He wanted to hold her, to look after her, and let her shine.

She was pointing at a huge dog with drooping lips that was bounding past them, enormous compared with Father's hounds. 'Look, we've nothing like that in Britannia.'

'We do all right.' He smiled. 'I've a fine pack at home.'

'What's going to happen, with barbarians everywhere?'

Lemma Magna had no weight out here, but at least it was at peace. 'Things will return to normal,' he said. 'There are always raids, but the army gets back in control.'

'What did you mean about being Roman, and me?'

'I was thinking, you've no one to protect you.'

'What, not with all your cavalry escort?'

Her voice was low, but he sensed her smile. She was strong enough that she could tease him. Together, they were the young ones in this delegation of old men. What was she like, really like? and would there be time to find out?

They lapsed into an easy silence, lulled by Papiteddo's steady gait. There *was* something between them, despite everything. Or was he imagining it?

He kneed his horse to catch up with Dorgolel. 'I would ask

you something.'

'It is good to talk Roman.' The Alan's round eyes softened his jutting chin and weathered face.

'Your dogs,' Fromus asked, 'can you tell me about them?'

'Ah, you like! Best dogs, we say *Molossers*. I have two.' Dorgolel pointed to the massive brown hound with its pricked ears. 'This Motchkar, strong, he kill three.'

Fromus felt Nehtan's head flick up behind him. He coughed. 'You mean three animals?'

Dorgolel beamed and lifted the side of the cape strapped behind him. 'Head-skins.'

Under the cape were what looked like three crumpled and yellowing parchments.

'Who were they, I mean, what people were they?'

Dorgolel laughed. 'Vandals. Shanik Gochar, you say Prince Goar, he tell good head-skins, make them fear, we grow strong.'

'*Hei!*' Fromus could not help it.

'Why you say? Romans kill, make slaves, burn tents. You not like head-skins, but Shanik Gochar say Romans have games, people killed by animals, in circle of houses. Is it thus?'

'No, not any more, not now. The Emperor has banned it. That was gladiators – men trained to fight each other.'

Dorgolel glanced at Nehtan. 'Not animals? Shanik Gochar say animals kill people Emperor not like.'

They passed a massive old oak, its roots breaking up the track. Without missing a step, their horses picked their way through.

'Well, maybe they did that in the old days' - how could this barbarian judge him? - 'but that was many years ago; we don't allow it. We only had men killing men.'

Nehtan snorted behind him, and Fromus saw Dorgolel

wrinkle his nose as he spoke. 'This killing not for war or honour.'

Nehtan was squeezing his waist, but not like before.

'The Emperor stopped it, long ago. It was for the common people.'

He let Papiteddo fall behind the Alan's horse as the track narrowed through a tunnel of leaves and branches.

'Tell me, young Roman,' shouted Dorgolel over his shoulder, 'why you not like Alan?'

'But I do. I admire your skills, especially on horses.' Fromus leant forward to avoid a branch. Too late, he hadn't warned Nehtan, but she had already ducked. 'Decurion Novateli tells me that the Alans are the finest horsemen in the world.'

'We born on horses.' Dorgolel laughed and gestured towards the Alan warriors who were cantering past them through the woods. 'How many horses, that is a man. I am four horses. Old days, more than this, but many die when Huns come. You know Huns?'

'No, but I have heard of them. Have you fought them?'

'Many times. This why Alans leave land between great rivers and come to Romans. Huns together like mighty cloud of bees, stinging all in their way. My father killed, my woman killed. Huns have no *Tanri*, what you say, gods. Alans have *Tanri* of trees and rivers. Romans have Christ-God in the sky. Now Alans come to Emperor, fight enemies of Rome.'

'Do you want to settle here?

'Shanik Gochar, he watch ravens and eagles, discover which way they fly. He listen to *Tanri*.'

'And what about you, Dorgolel, do you like Romans?'

'Good you ask.' Fromus caught a glimpse of Dorgolel arching an eyebrow towards Nehtan. 'Romans speak, but they not hear our words. We see strength of Romans – high walls, houses of food, soldiers, always marching. These great things, but not for Alans. For us, warrior life, horses, riding with the wind.'

'And Roman gold?' Fromus caught Dorgolel's eye and grinned.

'As you say, young Roman, yes; Roman gold, and women also.' The warrior laughed. 'Fair women, fine clothes. Shanik Gochar ask small land, live in peace, serve Emperor.'

Dorgolel jumped his muscled beast over a log. 'Your horse strong. Your woman, her name?'

'She is called Nehtan.'

The Alan bowed his head and looked past Fromus. 'Nehtan, you Alan?'

'No.' Her voice was unafraid. 'I am a Briton, but one of my ancestors was a Sarmatian. People said that they were great horsemen.'

'Ha!' Dorgolel flicked his reins. 'Sarmatian is tribe near Alan, long times ago. You like Alan?'

'Yes, but my people live beyond the Great Wall in Britannia, and I am Christian.'

'This you say.'

Fromus lifted his head. She stood her ground. And she had rejected the old Alan woman. He pressured Papiteddo to keep up with the Alan. 'What of your family, Dorgolel?'

'I have son, brothers, new woman. Others are dead from Huns.'

The Alan clenched his knees on his horse and raised himself to peer ahead. 'I go, path clear.'

As soon as Dorgolel had sped off, Paulinus rode up on his black horse.

'Fromus – how fascinating, you have been talking with

our escort commander. When we were in their camp, Prince Goar put him at our disposal. He is a man I respect. Tell me, what did he have to say about our journey and the prospects ahead?'

'We were talking about Romans and barbarians.'

'Yes.' Nehtan's hand was on his shoulder. 'This man Dorgolel and his people have suffered much.'

It was surprising that she had spoken, uninvited. Paulinus smiled. 'Do please introduce us.'

'This is Nehtan' - Fromus quizzed Paulinus with his eyes – 'who is, that is, she's with us.'

Their horses bumped as the riders ducked beneath a hanging branch.

'Delighted.' Paulinus inclined his head in a slight bow. 'You know, if we were not in such a potentially ticklish situation, it would be a pleasure to be here, riding with this colourful company.'

'Paulinus,' asked Fromus, 'might I ask if you are from this Praefecture?'

'Indeed, in a manner of speaking. I was born in Pella in Macedonia, but I have spent most of my life in Gaul. This land has been ravaged, and I speak not only about barbarian attacks. Even before the Vandals took our city, we had problems. Roman justice is not what it was. That's why I had to leave Burdigala.'

'I am not sure what you mean.' Nothing was straightforward in Gaul. 'This was not due to the Vandals?'

'No, what can I say? When my father died, I was away, and by the time I got home things were not as they should be. Land that had been his was no longer ours; neighbours took advantage. Worse of all was my brother. Documents were lost, the promised patrimony was no longer mine, and my mother's portion was much reduced.'

Paulinus held his reins in one hand, his right hand resting on his hip. Well trained. 'Clara and I came north to sell land. We had no idea that things were so bad, and we were taken – how should I put it? – into protective custody by men of Prince Goar. We were outraged, but it could have been much worse. You know, sometimes I think I have to bear misfortunes piling up on me, like Christ.'

Fromus loosened the reins on Papiteddo. It was flattering that Paulinus, so much older, should share such things, but surely the man could not mean to compare himself like that?

'What have you lost?'

'By the Apostles, all I have left are the house in Narbo and Mother's lands in Vasatae and Epirus. I have been robbed, by my own flesh and blood. Worse, my brother does not feel as I do – the library, the vineyards, these were the mark of a true gentleman. They say that a well-bred horse doesn't care about a barking dog, but I will not rest until I have my rights.' Paulinus drew breath and smoothed his hair. 'Enough of me ... Fromus, what of you? What are you hoping to gain from this journey?'

'I don't know ... many things. We need to reach the Emperor, but we have far to go. Right now, I hope Papiteddo, my horse, keeps going.'

They were threading their way along a narrow, waterlogged track, with dense pine and alder on either side. The sky was cloudy and the light on the track, dim.

'And you, Nehtan, what are your hopes?'

'Me?' Fromus felt her hands loosen round his waist. 'I am here with them, with Fromus. I want it to be all right, for everything to go well.'

'My, you are as close together as this forest.' Paulinus

nodded. 'I remember when I was your age: it was simple. I wanted a swift horse with a fine harness, a fast hound and a splendid hawk. I wanted to be dressed in the best of styles, with sweet perfumes from Arabia, and I was not averse to a pretty woman.' Paulinus smiled. 'Now, here we are wading through the bogs of northern Gaul, with the threat of extreme violence hanging over our heads.'

* * *

They trekked on, pausing only to let the horses drink. Long before nightfall, they stopped and the soldiers put up basic shelters on the hillside. The Alans watched, laughing and chewing dried strips of meat while they scrubbed their horses with bunches of ferns. Fromus supposed that the warriors would sleep next to their horses and put up with whatever weather came.

Clara asked where she could bathe. Novateli suggested going downhill to find a stream, if it did not take too long. Two soldiers would accompany her.

'And the girl,' said Clara, 'can she tend to me? We have just the one servant, a man. My woman died after we reached the Alan camp.'

'I'm not sure.' Fromus looked at Nehtan, who shrugged her shoulders. The woman was insufferable; she would not take over Nehtan. 'I'll come too.'

'I'll come along,' Paulinus joined. 'I could do with a walk and a wash.'

They picked their way downhill, with a manservant carrying things for Clara. The soldiers shambled behind, muttering about being denied their rest.

Shards of autumn sunlight lanced through the forest

onto the grassy path. Not a breath of wind. Mounds of fungi glistened; fading heather and harebells added hints of purple to the small clearings between the trees. Pinecones nestled in lichen hollows. Midges and forest insects hovered in the sun's rays.

Fromus was heating up, his whole body burning with itches beneath his tunic. By the time they reached the bottom, everyone was swatting flies and bugs away from their reddened faces. Clara stopped when she came to a patch of open ground pitted with small pools of water.

'This is frightful. Paulinus, why didn't you find a better place?'

'My dear, I don't know what you mean; we've been following you.'

'You know perfectly well. Why are we here? I shouldn't be in the middle of this filthy wood, hundreds of miles from anywhere. It's ridiculous.' Clara stomped a few yards back uphill, then sat on a fallen tree trunk.

Fromus spied a small valley not much further on. 'I think if we follow this brook we may come to a good place. What do you say?'

Clara stood and brushed sticky leaves off. She beckoned to her manservant and started to struggle back uphill, followed by Paulinus. Either she didn't hear him, or she was damned rude.

The soldiers were racing uphill with new energy. Fromus shouted to the retreating Paulinus. 'Don't worry about us.' Nehtan's almond-eyes sparkled. 'We'll come later.'

He led her through a glade of birch trees to where the brook broadened, her hand tight in his. Fading brown leaves on the ground made a soft path. Everything glistened. Sunlight sparkled on the water as Nehtan let go of his hand to pull her boots and clothes off.

'I want to wash.'

'Should I look away.' Smiling, as he sat down to pull off his left boot.

'That's up to you.'

She was already naked: full breasts, curving form and a black pelt between her thighs. Wading into the stream, she squatted and splashed herself with water.

'Why don't you come in?'

He stripped and held his hands in front as he stepped into the stream, grunting as the cold penetrated. Nehtan swooshed a handful of freezing water onto his chest.

'*Heia.*'

Shivering in the icy stream, they laughed. The amulet around her neck glittered.

'Come here,' he beckoned, brushing dark hair out of her face. 'From the waist down I can't feel anything.'

'Just as well.' Nehtan giggled and scooped water over his head. He fingered her amulet, kissing her neck, breast, and down to her nipple.

'Enough.' She buried her head in the water and sat back on a stone, wringing out her hair.

Nehtan took his hand. 'Look.'

A wren flitted down to sip at the pebble-strewn brook edge. Everything flowed: breath brimming through sunlight, birch leaves fluttering, and the wren's quick movement.

Fromus reached for her, 'Nehtan.'

'Shhh.'

His hand dropped. Her eyes, the faint shimmer of her misty breath mingling with his. No need for anything, everything was right here, sitting in the tinkling stream, opposite each other on large stones, freezing but not feeling it.

One breath, able to look through her, and to be seen, without fear.

Then she was laughing, kicking water, pushing him sideways, skipping back to the grassy bank.

He could make it happen, but everything would be lost. Rolling on his stomach, he submerged his head in the stream. Slivers of liquid brown. He leapt up, racing towards her.

'No, Fromus, please.'

Grabbing her around the waist, he kissed her until, gently, she pushed him away. Then she pulled him close, her arm around his waist. 'We should stay here.'

'Me too, I don't want to leave, or be anywhere else.' He hesitated. 'I believe in you.'

Her eyes were close, in his. A great smile spread across her face. For a moment, everything was still except his beating heart.

'That's...' Her hand caressed his face. 'But I have to tell you... I mean,' she stopped, and took his hands in hers. 'The two of us. Would you come with me, away from everyone? Not go on with them.'

'I can't do that.' He stood up -, the coldness of the stream – his arm reaching for her.

'Not now. Later.'

'That's impossible.' His stomach tightened. 'We can go on like this. We don't need to tell them anything.'

The *tchit-tchit* of an evening robin-song rippled through the trees.

'They won't let me,' she was pleading. 'I can't go to Italy.'

'Why not? You'll be safe with me.'

'I can't.'

'But I'll protect you.' He reached for her hand. 'What's the matter? Is it too far?'

'Everyone, the soldiers, they look at me.' She shivered and he wanted to enfold her with his arms, but he didn't. She picked up her cloak. 'I can't go on, getting further away. I have to get back to Britannia.'

'You said you didn't have anyone there.'

'But I do. I have my people.' She collapsed onto a broken tree trunk, washed up on the side of the stream. 'Nymayr and atir.'

'Who are they?'

'You would call them mother and father.' Her hand was brushing a clump of grass. Why wouldn't she look at him?

'But I thought they were dead' - Fromus squatted in front of her - 'Marcellinus adopted you. That's what you said.'

'I can't ... it's confusing. I don't know. You've been so kind.' She turned away.

'Aren't they dead? Why were you with Marcellinus?'

'He did adopt me, in his way.' Her voice was small and quiet.

Fromus shook his head. 'I don't understand. Who are you?' He touched her shoulder, but she shrank back.

'You'll hate me.' She stood up. 'You'll throw me away.'

'What do you mean?'

'What's the use? I'm at your mercy.'

'Nehtan, you know I—'

'You're bound to find out. That man will tell everyone. Then it will all be over.' Her eyes were wide open, nostrils flared.

'What are you talking about?'

'I was taken... made into a slave. By Romans.'

His hand went to his head. The word was horrible. 'That's ridiculous.'

'What do you mean?' Her voice was soft again.

'It can't be.' Not her, not Nehtan.

'You think you can tell?'

Late afternoon sharp light filtered down through the tree-tops. His feet were cold. 'No, I mean, you don't seem ...' He straightened and looked her full in the face. 'It doesn't have to be like that.'

'But it is. That's how the world works.' Her head was bowed down. 'There's a mountain between us. It's different out here, but you'll change your mind when we get back. You'll have to.' Her voice lowered. 'They'll make you.'

'They'll do no such thing.' He paused. The slave-servants at home. Everyone had them. And in the brothels. 'I have to think. I have to work it out.'

'Leave me in Treverorum.' She was handing him his cloak and the crumpled money belt. 'You have your family and your duty.' A tremble, her palm resting on her waist. 'Please, if it's possible, if that man hasn't told everyone yet, don't say anything about me.'

'You won't survive, even if they don't know. You need to be in a safe place.'

'So be it, as you say.'

He and she were Christians, but also slave and master. *Render unto Caesar what is Caesar's.* And St Paul had sent the slave back to his owner. Is that what he was meant to do? Never! She would be put to work in the most profitable way.

A chill breeze and his shoulders shook. 'Is it true, what you said?'

Calm, almond eyes regarded him. 'It's getting dark; we'd better go.'

They walked back in silence, a long slow climb. He wanted to stop and talk with her, but she strode ahead. He called her name, but she went on up. The top of the hill brought the muffled sound of distant men's voices and the smell of wet-wood smoke, drawing them through the gloomy trees. There were two fires, one for the Roman soldiers and the other for the civilians and Novateli. The Alans were out of sight.

'We were giving up on you.' Dimple-chinned Paulinus greeted them from the fireside. 'Come and get some hot soup into you. Nehtan, you must be frozen.'

After wolfing down soup, lumpy with bits of tough meat, everyone turned in for the night. Fromus led Nehtan to a spot apart from the others. They criss-crossed small branches and filled a hollow with pine needles before spreading Fromus's fur-skins over the woody bedding. She lay with her back to him under a heavy cover, her hood up. Streaked clouds shrouded the moon. He hugged her from behind, but she was still.

'You all right?'

'Yes, I'm tired, that's all.'

'We don't need to say anything.' He wanted to sink into her. 'We'll keep going.'

A stick jutted into his shoulder as puffs of breath shimmered in the icy night air. He held himself round a motionless Nehtan and eventually fell asleep.

CHAPTER TWELVE

Days later, Nehtan watched an Alan horse and rider move down a hillside like water pouring over a bank. She was behind Fromus, holding on to the back of the saddle. The pommels felt smooth and reassuring, like knots of worn wood. To be with him was good, but she knew what would happen. She couldn't let herself go; her heart must get behind her.

She closed her eyes. If only she could be rid of her past, they could be free, like the Alans. The barbarians lived like the clouds, beholden to no one but their horses and their clan. One day, far in the future, even they would be gone. Everything would pass. All the world rests in the Holy One.

A shout. Dorgolel was wheeling his horse. 'River close. At city, we go back.'

A row of big trees along the riverbank came into sight. An enormous willow was leaning out of the river, its wispy branches being dragged at an angle by the water. It didn't look like it could last long, and yet it was there, swaying, hanging on.

'Do you remember the bird,' Fromus asked, 'when we were in the stream?'

'The wren. That was... I loved that. Those moments, but we can't... It was another time.'

'We're both Romans and Christians.'

'It's not enough. You know that, or I know that.' She must soften her tone. 'We have to live now, to pray. That was... not possible. Maybe...' She stopped, and shifted back in the saddle, opening up a gap between his back and her chest.

Fromus pulled his horse aside to let a trooper pass. She felt his chin graze her head as he turned half-back towards her. 'We're here, together on Papiteddo. I can't let this, this thing, I can't let it destroy everything. Later, later we will find a way. That is ...' He lapsed into silence.

She leant forward and squeezed his waist gently. Let the soldiers see, what did they know?

'Let's leave it for now. Tell me something... I wonder if we'll get good food in the city. You like salt. Marcellinus liked it too, though it is expensive.'

'There's not much left from what I brought, so we may as well use it up before the damp gets to it. Is that something' - his voice lowered - 'you would never have?'

'I didn't, no, except when the master wanted it added, like on Vitalis's name day.'

'I see.' He paused. 'A mountain between us, you said. But it's just as steep on my side.'

A patch of small purple flowers crinkled on one side of the path. Nehtan remembered that they used to crush their stalks and add the paste to offerings, lifetimes ago, in Colud. Then they would chant his name, Donn, crimson god of the hidden places, he of the dead earth and rotting corpses. It was he who would not let go of her. His short blade always curving into the guts of the living. Now was the time of Samhain, when the boundaries between the living and the dead are weakest.

She remembered the elders giving her something bitter to drink and taking her deep into the woods of elm and oak. They rolled her in cold ash, made her sip sour beech-water. Her head was bound, mud smeared over skin and hair. Old hands wrapped her in a cloak of laburnum leaves and lowered her into a pit, earth spilling up to her chin. The sound of footsteps receding. The long dark. Silence like a smothering. Then, creaking, rustling, the sharp tang of fox; warmth sprinkling onto clay-covered hair, and a soft padding away.

Slowly, like the rumble of a thunder which made no sound, a far-off quiet seeped into the forest, deeper than the stillness, soothing all animal tingles of pain and stink, washing everything away. A small bright hole grew and grew, glaring the shadows to death. There came a low howling, the earth turning to bone, dead hands pushing from all sides, shrieking and shrieking as skull mouths tore into belly, neck, chest. But she didn't care. Resistance melted, she dropped away. Nothing left, gone, she was not there, a great deep blast, being spat out to the stars ... past them, whirling into the blackness, a thousand thousand holes in one great ball of dark light. Melting, all essence evaporating, nothing bursting into no time, beyond tree, sun and moon. The ecstasy of no one knowing what cannot be known. Transcendent, before what a head can hold. No edges, an endless floating emptiness.

Then, slowly, slowly coming back. A stuttering, jagged screeching and wailing. It stopped at dawn when her lips closed. The old men returned and dragged her out of the hole. They made her slit the throat of a fawn, drink its blood. Pulling out its entrails, she said what it meant.

They carried her back to Colud. It was the time before the banishment. Grandmother screamed at the old men. They shouted back, but the old woman would not be quieted. Inside the hut, nymayr would not hug her, though she held Nehtan's head. Only Grandmother dared to hold her that night, mouthing smooth words, her hand stroking. In the daytime, outside, the world was raw, anxious, a new place where eyes darted away from her.

For years after that, on certain nights, a wild longing came back, a craving to let go, to plunge hands into blood and pull out a beating heart.

Nehtan looked at Fromus's fine cloak, his high shoulders. Why shouldn't they? The Christ was not kin of Donn - nor of Roman. He was all in all, and his people welcomed her. *By their fruits, you shall know them.*

They passed a decrepit hut with the roof fallen in; smashed pots speckled the ground. The track led uphill into forest. At the top they dismounted to rest the horses.

Nehtan walked into the wood. Three soldiers slouched near a big beech tree. One of them grabbed her cloak. 'Come here and I'll show you.'

Messor. A sharp pinch in her bottom.

'What do you think of that?'

Twisting, she raised an arm, but her hand was caught and forced up and down his trouser front.

A sickening laugh. 'Well lads, I'm ready for her.'

Shrinking from his hateful breath, black eyebrows, she wrenched her hand away. 'Get off me!'

'Stop that.' It was Philus, one of the other soldiers. 'Leave her alone.'

'You Christians.' Messor spat on a log. 'You make me sick, you're tighter than a goat's arse. Anyone would think you're all virgins.'

'I'm warning you, go on, get back.' Philus moved between her and Messor. He was tall, but kept his distance from Messor.

'Come on, Statarius,' Messor growled at the other soldier, a hairy man with a curving scar on his cheek. 'You were saying what you'd like to do with her.'

'Leave it out. Bellator's thick with Philus. I'm going back.'

The scarred soldier disappeared behind the trees.

'You cunting prick.' Messor snarled and stalked off.

Nehtan sagged to the ground.

'I'm sorry.' Philus bent down next to her. 'He's an animal when he gets like that.'

She trailed her fingers in a small heap of sticks and leaves, her whole body shaking.

Philus's hand brushed her elbow. 'Best not say anything. You know how it is.'

Nodding, taking a deep breath, she forced her chin up. 'What did he say...? Why were you here?'

'Look.' Philus pointed through a gap in the trees. 'It's Treverorum. It's enormous, a big bridge and gates. The houses go on and on, but I can't see any people.'

The red-roofed city was like a giant version of Clara's patchwork bedcover. Nehtan's shoulders dropped down, her eyes shut.

Bellator's heavy voice bellowed from below. Philus helped her up, and they made their way downhill.

Nehtan felt small and cold. It would only make things worse if she said anything; Fromus was barely aware of Messor. He seemed far away as he helped her up to sit in front of him, but he did ask, 'Are you all right?'

'It's nothing. I'm tired.'

They followed the Alan riders on a narrow path down a hillside of damp trees. Overhanging boughs scraped and scratched, and the riders stooped beneath low branches. The ground was matted with orange and yellow leaves. At the valley floor, they passed under an outcrop of rusty red rock and emerged in a narrow, overgrown meadow which ran along a riverbank. Beyond this surged a rain-fed river; Fromus said it was the Mosella. Nehtan could barely bring herself to look at it.

A dilapidated bridge, and on the other side, the castellated walls of Treverorum curved around the valley. Part of the walls and the nearest tower had collapsed. Red-tiled houses hunched beyond the wall.

The Alans wheeled and trotted back up the hill. No one spoke. The Romans started to cross the hump-backed bridge.

Dismembered branches bobbed in the grey river. On the other side of the bridge, the Romans traversed open ground before slowing their horses to pick their way over the rubble of a collapsed wall.

The place was desolate, the road littered with fragments of burnt and shattered buildings. Empty doorways gaped under red-tiled roofs, pockmarked with holes. The riders clattered down an avenue overgrown with grass and weeds. They passed a high stone wall in which were set two curved and ornate wooden window frames, looking onto the collapsed insides of a house. A statue of a laughing shepherd with horns on his brow teetered above a palace gateway.

Long streets stretched away from the avenue; rows of brick-built houses packed close on both sides. Debris everywhere – rubble, iron joints, shards of pottery, whitened bones. Through it all grew insidious green creepers and tough-tendrilled purple bushes.

It was good to feel Fromus's arms looped about her, holding the reins. The others, they couldn't know or it wouldn't be like this.

They rode on. An old woman scurried across a narrow lane with a load of cut grass. A man ran along the street ahead and disappeared over a broken wall. Two ragged children scuttled into a building. Small, filthy faces reappeared seconds later, frowning out of a broken shutter. Nehtan caught a bitter whiff from a dark-stained pile of dust.

Stray dogs stretched their forelegs and ambled out of the way. A thin man emerged from a side street, hauling a cart half-full of mud-encrusted vegetables. He stopped and hunched, staring with reddened eyes and an open mouth. A boy yelled something unintelligible.

They reached a large square bordered by stone columns, half of which lay shattered on the ground. It was hard to imagine there being enough people to fill such a vast space. On all sides were the ruins of once-ornate buildings. Three men lounged at the far end. As the Decurion rode towards them, they disappeared down an alley.

Nehtan shivered as the Roman group tethered their horses on a broken stone balustrade. Novateli told Bellator to find people to interrogate.

'I can't believe it.' Clara raised her hands. 'We are in the Forum and there is nothing. What a disaster. Decurion, where will we sleep, what about my lodgings?'

'We'll find out soon enough, Lady Clara. For the moment, we will rest and take our bearings.'

Nehtan flopped onto a broken step. She wanted to curl up in Fromus's arms.

Two men emerged on the far side of the forum. '*De quo vadis?*' one of them shouted.

Novateli cupped his hands. 'Bononia. *Venite et sic loquamur.*'

The men slunk back into a doorway.

'Shall I fetch them, sir?' It was Messor, his eyes lit up.

'No, wait for the Biarchus. Stay on guard.'

Nehtan scowled and looked away. A while later, Bellator and two soldiers returned, hauling a scrawny woman and a small boy. Nehtan shuddered to see that the soldier's grip was hurting the woman.

'I found her inside a big villa, hiding behind a cupboard.' The Biarchus plonked the woman on the ground. 'Everyone else ran away. I can't get much out of her. She says her name's

Vibia Pacata and that she's the wife of a legionary.'

The Decurion bent down, his face softening into a smile that Nehtan knew was for show.

'Would you like some bread?'

The woman's eyes lit over her spiky nose. 'Yes, we'll have that, won't we, Salsulus. Thank you, your honour, we're much obliged, only we was afeared ...'

She grabbed the crust and started gnawing it. The child tugged her sleeve and, after a moment's hesitation, the woman tore off part of the crust and gave it to the boy. Nehtan licked her lips.

'Now, Vibia Pacata,' Novateli resumed, 'you tell me what I want to know and there'll be more bread for you. We are Imperial cavalry and we have come a long way. There are soldiers here, is that right?'

'I don't know, your honour. I don't go there.'

'How many men?' Novateli's voice became louder. 'Who's in charge?'

Fool, thought Nehtan. The woman couldn't tell him anything. He should leave poor folks alone.

'Begging your pardon, your honour' – wailed the old woman, shuffling from side to side – 'they keep to their end. There was an old man. He was here when them long-hairs broke into the city. They took everything, what they didn't burn. It's been a long time.'

Novateli spoke slowly. 'Who is in the city?'

'Don't ask me, sir, your honour. I don't know nothing.' The woman shook her head and squeezed her eyes almost shut. 'I ain't got nothing. I told all I can, like you said.'

Bellator grabbed the woman and shook her. 'Answer the Decurion.'

The small boy, clinging to his mother's legs, started to cry.

Couldn't they see what they were doing? Novateli motioned Bellator to step back.

'Now, Vibia Pacata, the Biarchus tells me that your husband was a soldier, is that right?'

Her sobs subsided. 'I ain't seen him for years and years, not since long before.'

Bellator looked at the child and was about to speak when Novateli squinted at him.

'Then you are an army person, like us. Here, Bellator, give her another piece.'

'Thank you, your honour, thank you.' She hid the bread in the folds of her cape. Her child whimpered.

'Take your time.' Novateli hunched down. 'Tell me what has been going on since the barbarians left.'

'We've got to get back. Can't be late, getting dark soon. Please sir, let me go.'

Novateli straightened up and looked at Bellator. 'This is going nowhere. We've got to find someone else.'

The Decurion glanced back to the woman, who was pushing her child's hand away from her crust. He grunted. 'I'll give you one more chance.'

'Do you mean where we sleeps, and the fields?'

'This is hopeless. Who is in charge?'

The woman started to nod her head up and down, then she put her hands to her ears. Novateli grabbed her wrist. 'Who do you fear?'

'*Eia*,' she shrieked. 'Rusticus and his men up there.' She pointed towards where they had come into the city. 'Semicupa at the amphitheatre, he's the worst, and over at the Black Gate, I think his name is Arventus.'

'*Edepol.*' Novateli straightened up. 'She must mean Tribune Eventius.'

138

Novateli and the others moved away. Nehtan examined the filthy, freckled face of the small boy. She knelt down to smooth his forehead, but the boy hunched and raised his fists. She spoke to the woman.

'Vibia Pacata, that's your name, isn't it? And your son is Salsulus?'

'I had three, he's what's left. The girl got taken, though she were only six.'

'I'm sorry. I know what it's like.' Nehtan's voice dropped to a whisper. 'I was taken too.' The boy calmed as she stroked him.

'Where do you live?'

'Off Via Riochatus, past the water tanks, next to the old bakery, in one of them big places. Course, it's not our real home, but Rusticus lets us stay. I come down 'ere to get some old pots. I was right scared with them horses. Have you come from the Emperor?'

'No, we are on our way there.'

'By the seven stars, what wouldn't I give to get out of 'ere. I'm that sick of this life.'

'Can't you leave?'

'Nowhere to go. They say the south is better, once you get past the 'Gundians. Rusticus reckons they'll be back before winter sets in.'

Bellator's voice boomed. 'All right then, saddle up, moving out.'

The old woman glanced at the officer on his horse, then started poking in a pile of debris. The small boy sat in the dust, his mouth open, looking at Nehtan with large eyes.

When they were on their way, Nehtan told Fromus what the woman had said about the Burgundians. He spoke to Novateli, but, as Nehtan expected, the Decurion dismissed the intelligence with a peremptory nod.

Twilight came as the column rode through the decayed city. A trooper trotted ahead. They passed an enormous rectangular palace, clad at ground level with red and white marble, though much of it lay smashed on the ground. High up were two rows of arched windows.

Fromus whispered, 'That it must be the basilica where the emperors held court.'

Birds flapped through ruined windows and perched on outcrops of ivy. The clip-clop of horse hooves echoed off the pavements. They reached a street bordered on both sides by a colonnade of collapsed pillars and porticos. At the end a blackened and massive building hunched above the earth. It had round, protruding towers, connected by a long chamber with deep-set windows. Underneath the chamber were two archways. Helmeted men watched from the upper windows. An odour of burnt timbers.

'Is that it?' Her fingers were on his shoulder.

'It must be. The Black Gate.'

Men huddled around a fire in front of the stone fortress; regular soldiers, though their clothes were ragged. As they neared, Nehtan saw bows half-drawn in the high windows. The soldiers below stood up, with javelins and unsheathed swords. A solid-looking officer with a plumed helmet stepped forward.

'Who are you, what do you want?'

'We're from Britannia.' Novateli raised his hand. 'We were told that Tribune Eventius is here.'

'Your information is correct. Tell me, who is your Emperor?'

'Honorius. We are on our way to Ravenna, and we need shelter.'

'Isn't Britannia under the rule of Constantinus?'

'Not any more.'

The Black Gate officer paused. 'Your name?'

'Decurion Novateli, attached to the Decima Gemina. And yours?'

'Praepositus Tullius of the Twentieth, under the command of Tribune Eventius.' The officer glanced at the soldiers behind him. 'Stand easy. Decurion Novateli, you are welcome.'

The delegates and their escort dismounted. Nehtan followed Fromus inside the gaunt fortress, clambering up a spiral stairway. Not the sort of place she would like to live near.

They emerged into a cavernous hall with arched windows, most of which were closed with wooden shutters. On a small bed at the end of the chamber lay an old man with a crooked nose and a fringe of cropped white hair.

'You are welcome,' the old man panted. 'It's a long time since we've met loyal troops. We do the best we can, but it's not much.'

The old man rubbed his eyes. His wheeze sounded bad.

'I'm glad we found you,' Novateli said. 'You must be the last ones left.'

'The spring before last, soldiers from the usurper told us that we were under his command. Impudence. Calls himself Constantinus the Third. His men got the mint working, but it didn't last. We agreed not to bother each other, and I have not heard from him since his scruffy cohort pulled out last summer. His man Gerontius has turned against him.'

'We know about Gerontius.' Crispus broke in, smoothing his strands of hair. 'Tell me, what do you make of him?'

'*Eia*. An old soldier can spot rough ground.' The old man

141

sipped from a tumbler. 'I met the fellow when he came here, trying to patch up agreements to keep the peace. He struck me as an honest man, perhaps a little rigid, but you cannot tell; the wind changes too quickly. Praepositus Tullius tells me that you are bound for Italy, to the Emperor Honorius. Is that in connection with Gerontius?'

'No, no, nothing like that.' Crispus brushed dust off his cloak. 'We travel on behalf of the cities of Britannia. We're taking a message of allegiance to Honorius.'

'Got trouble?'

'Well, you could say that.'

'There is no loyalty; not the sort I recognise. *Mehercle*, it is best to endure what you cannot change. One day, the army will be back, and when they come, we will be here – won't we, Tullius?'

'Of course, sir. We may be dead, but we'll be here.'

Everyone laughed. Soldiers had a way of sizing each other up. Nehtan crossed to a stone window ledge and sat down, hoping the jagged pain in her hips would go away. Her head dropped and she drifted into a fitful half-sleep, nagged by cold and dull hip-ache.

Sounds of movement. She joined Fromus and the rest as they picked their way down the gloomy stairwell. Outside, they ate hot vegetable broth, into which they dipped lumps of hard bread. Soon, overcome with tiredness, she tugged at Fromus's sleeve.

Merciful God, she didn't need to say anything, as she couldn't. She felt herself being guided in the half-dark as they climbed to the top chamber of the fortress. Clothes and bedding lay strewn around the room, stinking of men-sweat and stale clothes.

'Where will the soldiers sleep?' she had to ask. 'I mean, our cavalrymen.'

'The Decurion said that the men are in the building outside, with the horses. Why do you want to know?'

'I just need to know where they are.' Her eyes were closing. For a moment, she couldn't remember what she was worried about. 'That's all.'

They settled down in the damp air of the stone chamber. She shuddered as the cold from the wide flagstones started to suck the warmth out of her bones. That soldier, Messor, he could tell them at any time. Then Fromus would be gone. But, for now, it was good to have his warmth nestling beside her.

* * *

She woke early with rumbles in her stomach. White light streamed into the room. Crispus, Ursacius and the others were asleep around the walls of the big chamber. She was bloated, constipated, though she had not eaten much for days.

Wondering if she dare, then poking Fromus. 'I have to go outside. Can you come with me?'

'Took me ages to get to sleep,' he muttered. 'You'll be fine.'

She shook him, but he was a dead lump. Across the room, a body stirred. She pulled on her boots and gave Fromus another shove, but he yanked the cover over his head.

Tiptoeing down the worn stairwell, she felt her bowels lurch. No time to be lost. At the bottom, light streamed through a gap beneath the heavy outer door. Two Black Gate soldiers were sprawled asleep. She nudged a man with her foot and asked him to let her out. He told her to open the door herself.

The heavy bolts shot back with loud cracks, and she let herself out onto the cobbled courtyard. The remains of a fire smouldered. On the right was the building where they kept the horses. She stole away to the left, picking her way round fallen columns and a collapsed building. She reached open ground, filled with stunted shrubs and prickly bushes. In the distance were the severed stumps of what would have been a row of trees. She passed round the edge of a wall and squatted. Finally. A relief.

Wind ruffled her hair as she walked back, balancing against a wall. Rounding a corner, she thudded into a man: Messor, with Statarius behind him.

Her back was shoved into the wall, his fleshy hand pressing hard on her mouth.

'Got you now, my precious. You've come to me, like I knew you would.' He turned to Statarius. 'Didn't I say?'

Fear pulsed through her as she stood, pinned and helpless. She kicked between his legs but the cape got in the way. An elbow smashed into her face, a massive jolt of pain.

'You bitch. Statarius, the rag.'

'Fromus,' ' she called, but her head was jerked sideways as a cloth was tied across her mouth. Statarius pinioned her arms as Messor leant close.

'I know all about you. You think you're high and mighty, up there with the maggot. You're mine, since Londinium.'

Everything drained to a bleached-white hatred. She twisted to find the other man, but Messor wrenched her back.

'You deserve a branding. I can do what I want with you. We're going to have a bit of fun.'

Statarius let go of her wrists and grabbed her under her armpits. She tried to shout, but it was no good. She kicked Messor in the face as he bent down. A mistake. A punch slammed into her chin, wrenching her jaw. They carried her past a ruined house, arms flailing, tiles crunching underfoot, bramble thorns scratching her face.

Not this! Save me, *Filius Dei*, mother of God!

Dumped onto the earth, her hip jarred. Around her, a blurred hollow, bunched round with purple-headed bushes and a crumbling wall. Messor stood above. Perhaps they had not decided. Straining her head back, she searched for the thick beard and curved scar of Statarius, but his blue eyes flicked away.

'We'd better get it over with.'

'What do you mean?' Messor growled. 'This is going to be good. Don't worry about her. She won't say anything, she wouldn't dare. That pile of shit wouldn't touch her with a galley-pole if he knew.' A boot rammed into her foot. 'Slave-slut.'

The man's eyes blazed as he undid his belt buckle and took off his sword. 'Right, hold her tight.'

Arms wrenched back, she tried to remember, find a prayer, anything.

We ask you, Lord, be our helper and protector...

Tunic and undergarment hauled up, thighs exposed. Monster weight squashing down, choking on her breath, a coarse thing pushing. Trying to shout but the cloth too tight. Hand mashing her shoulder, grinding numbness, grey-stone wall of nettles. Throat squeezed, no air, her arms beating against him.

Statarius's voice. 'Messor, let go or you'll kill her.'

'Fuck off.'

His hand was tearing her tunic, pawing, pinching. She dragged in a great gulp of air, smothering under the force of his chest, belly. Messor snapped back her head, her neck burning. Then, body squeezed, hair pulled, she lost all strength, head lolling to the side, the sound of grunting, her chest being squashed. Green leaves pushing onto her nose, pushing back and forth, a thorn waving, cutting her nostril. Head wrenched back, a flash of black eyebrows, his eyes crushed pits, something small in him. Grunting, emptiness, just the grunting and her eyes shut, coarse hair pressing down on her forehead.

Hip bones pounded, pounded. A shuddering, and the weight rolled off.

Gagging with vomit, she couldn't breathe. She dragged the cloth off her mouth, spitting sick.

His shadow loomed above. 'Go on, Statarius, you now. I'll hold her down.'

'No, I don't want any of this.'

'What do you mean? We're in this together; you can't stop now.'

Shaking, she tried to pull the tunic over her streaked thighs. Coughing, a broken throat.

Statarius was backing away. 'No, I've had enough.' He ran off.

Messor snarled back at her. 'You're lucky, you fucking rag.'

Another rib kick. She crouched in a ball, gasping, hands covering her eyes. She snatched a look: he was gripping his sword hilt, drawing the blade out.

'No, no, please.' Crying, drained to a brittle, marble white.

'You heard me. You say anything, anything to anyone, I'll kill you, and I'll kill that ring-fuck.' The weapon snapped back into its scabbard. 'I'm not done with you.'

She froze, eyes clenched shut, his steps crunching away, getting fainter. Then, no more sound - but inside, a wave of convulsive shuddering, splinters of ice, rocking back and forth, air juddering.

Bushes rustling. Him! She held her breath, shutting everything out. A hiss of spiked edges above her head. Then, breathing, her own breathing. Not his. No other sound.

She sat up, violence churning in her belly, her throat scraped raw.

From far off came the shouts of men.

Soiled, she felt his filth pulse in her blood. She was stained, every part of her ruined, taken over. His eyes burnt into her; it would never be enough for him. She was a twig wrenched from a tree, trampled to pieces.

She must wash him out. Get to the river beyond the Black Gate. Standing up, thighs grating, her skull a fragile eggshell. The wall fell towards her and bricks struck her head.

In the distance a soldier was leading a horse from the long building. He saw her. His head jerked away.

She collapsed back to the bricks. Lord, take me away, bury me.

She hobbled across the broken street and reached the arched gash of the Black Gate. Trudging through, reaching the river, tottering, she slipped down the muddy bank.

No thought – but her hands grabbed at brown tufts.

A gurgled yawp and she was ripped from her reed-hold, sucked into grey water, tumbling like a leaf in a mountain torrent. Her legs kicked against massive freezing. A flash of sky as water pushed in, a rope-cord twisting, impossible to hold. Tighter, choke-filled, tearing – gone.

CHAPTER THIRTEEN

Fromus padded down the winding staircase, his back creaking from a night on the stone floor. Where was she?

A loud clattering, and a soldier barged up, knocking him against the wall. It was Philus.

'Sorry sir, it's Nehtan; she's been in the river. It doesn't look good.'

A rush of terror sent him racing down the stairs and out the door. Three figures were on the riverbank, one on the ground, Bellator straightening up.

'Protadius found her. Her eyes were open but now she's out cold. We should pull her tongue, that's what they say.'

No! She had to live. Fromus remembered a river-drenched body in the countryside: an old man had known what to do. He knelt by Nehtan and turned her over. Heavy, water-logged. He lifted her from the waist, her head lolling down, and squeezed her stomach.

'Nehtan, wake up!'

Cradling her, momentarily nervous at showing how much he cared, then ashamed. He squinted at the dripping soldier.

'I was downriver,' said Protadius, shivering under a cloak. 'She sort of slipped in. The gods be thanked, there was a mudbank, or we'd both be done for.'

Fromus was pumping her waist, looking back at her sweet face. Suddenly, a retching; she spewed water, coughing.

'Can you hear me?' He lowered her gently. 'Nehtan, are you all right?'

Wrapping his cloak around her, he carried her to the upper chamber of the Black Gate, helped by Philus. She was awake, eyes anxious, not speaking. The soldier left.

Fromus hovered. 'You should take your things off. You're soaked through.'

'*Vae.*' She hunched down.

'What happened?' he whispered. 'Please tell me.'

She jerked away, and he tried again. 'What's wrong?'

No response, her eyes shut. He waited. From outside came the harsh clang of metal being hammered.

She lifted her head. 'I don't want …' Her head slumped. 'Can you leave me – please?'

Standing, the pain of her shrinking from his touch. He must do as she asked, and hope. A last look at the small figures huddled under a blanket. The creaking of the planks on the chamber floor as he walked to the stairway.

Outside, snowflakes clogged the air. A soldier was cooking leftovers in a large cauldron. Fromus forced his feet to keep going, a huge weight bearing down on him. An idea: she might eat. He watched as watery soup was ladled into a clay pot.

On the way back to the tower, he met Clara, her head swathed in a shawl. Her busybody voice demanded, 'How's the girl? They said she was in the Mosella. Is everything all right?'

'What do you mean? She's fine.' Stepping away, he clutched the pot, soup sloshing.

Crispus came over. 'What's up with the girl?'

'She fell in.' Fromus wanted to push the old man away. 'That's all.'

Ursacius appeared, speaking in a slow drawl. 'The Black Gate soldiers are looking at us in an odd way. Novateli shouldn't keep us in the dark.'

'I've spoken to him,' Crispus said. 'We need to stay calm

and wait for the Biarchus to come back.'

'I'll wager your woman is involved.' Ursacius flicked his head at Fromus. 'What's this story about her falling into the river?'

'It's not a story,' Fromus snapped. These people, why was he with them? 'This is an awful place. I'm going back.'

He strode to the tower doorway, slopping the soup onto his tunic. 'Damn, damn, and damnation on them all.'

At the top, he heard footsteps striding up the stairs; it was Clara. The woman swept past him and over to Nehtan.

'Now girl, we can't have you wasting away. Sit up.' Clara turned and took the pot from him. 'I think it would be better if you left me with her.'

'I should be here,' Fromus said, bending down. 'I'm looking after her. Nehtan, shall I stay?'

'The lady Clara, maybe ...'

Why? What had he done? 'I'll go. I'll be outside.'

Soldiers stood around the fire, watching as he walked across to Crispus and Ursacius.

'It appears,' Ursacius tugged his beard, 'that Bellator has gone off to find two of his men. They disappeared this morning.'

Something nudged inside Fromus. 'Who was it?'

'What did Tullius's man say, Crispus? I can't remember the names.'

'One was called Messor and the other has a scar on his cheek. Statarius, I believe.'

Ursacius smirked. 'Five crows were circling above the Black Gate this morning.'

Crispus frowned. 'What of it?'

'You remember what the old ones said – someone is going to die.'

150

'That's pagan superstition.' Crispus glared at Ursacius. 'There are laws about spreading such sayings.'

'I wouldn't worry about those edicts. We can say what we like now.'

'We must not forget who we are' – Crispus straightened up – 'and what we represent, especially now. Besides, we don't want to go back to the old ways.'

'Speak for yourself.' Ursacius raised his hand. 'I think we should return to Britannia. Gaul is in flames. We cannot risk our lives further. No one knew it was like this when we set out. They'll understand.'

'I hear you, Ursacius; you've made your position clear.' Crispus pressed his fists together. 'But Britannia depends on us. We gave our word. Unless the way south is barred, we will not change our plans.'

Fromus broke away. The bony old man only cared for his position. As for Ursacius, all he thought about was his money. What mattered was Nehtan. Fromus remembered those strange words of Catullus: *I hate and I love. And if you ask me how, I do not know: I only feel it, and I am torn in two.*

He strode past soldiers brushing down horses as he headed into the city. Kicking stones out of the way, he found a stick and beat back the weeds and brambles which choked the street. But they were too dense, and he had to go back.

Clara was at the doorway, adjusting the fabric around her neck. 'All is not well with your girl. There's no easy way to say this' – she paused, her voice low – 'she has been violated by a soldier.'

'No!' He turned to race up the tower stairs.

'Wait a minute.' Clara's sharp voice echoed in the stairwell. She grabbed his arm. 'She tells me that she was a virgin, though, frankly, it's hard to believe. You need to consider what you are up to. Do not mistake her for something she's not. You are an Equestrian, going to Ravenna. She's not for you,' the lady's voice hissed. She let go of his wrist.

Shooting up the stairs, he burst into the upper chamber. Nehtan's slight figure was slumped on the floor.

He crouched next to her. 'Nehtan, Clara told me.'

Dull eyes, her lips quivering. 'Don't ... you shouldn't.'

'What do you mean?' He reached for her. 'Who was it?'

'No.' She pulled away.

'The bastards. Both of them?'

'He, he was there, the other, he ran away.' She was sitting, crying, small, withered.

'I'll have them flogged to death.' Fromus felt dizzy. His legs shook.

She looked up. 'They won't do anything.'

'What do you mean?'

'You wouldn't know. Earlier, he grabbed me on the hillside. Philus stopped him.'

'When? Why didn't you tell me?'

'Please...'

'But if you'd told me.' He knelt beside her. 'You're coming with me; we're leaving tomorrow. That man, he's out there.'

Her eyes opened wide. 'Where?'

'That's what I'm saying, that's why.'

She was not listening. Eyes glazing over, she curled into a ball.

He hovered near her, but it was as if he wasn't there. A mess of filthy bedding was strewn across the floor. He stumbled down past the first floor and back into the courtyard. It hit him like a hailstorm: they all saw her as no better than an animal. This is what their soldiers did: 'our men deserved a bit of fun.' His family, Lemma Magna. They had slaves; most of the servants were slaves. They couldn't have children without permission, and their offspring were slaves. If someone killed one of them, Father would be paid compensation, less than the price of a horse.

What if she had a child? No: a woman cannot get pregnant from violation if she takes no pleasure in it.

Messor. Fromus had to find Novateli. A Black Gate soldier told him that the Decurion was in the tower.

* * *

He clambered up to the first-floor chamber. A blast of cold air swept through the open shutters. A map was spread out on a table.

Crispus noticed him as soon as he came in. 'The Tribune says that the road south is safe. The sooner we go, the better. We'll have to take our chances with any troops loyal to Constantinus.' The angular-headed old man spoke in a rush. 'We cannot cross the Alps as *Bacaudae* robbers have taken over the passes. We've got a long way to go, so we'll be leaving at first light.'

'Crispus, could I speak with you privately?'

'Later. We're planning the route.'

'I need to talk with you, right now.'

Novateli intervened. 'Natalius Crispus, I can continue with Tribune Eventius and Praepositus Tullius. Just a few details left.'

'Very well. Fromus, if you insist, I can give you a couple of minutes.'

Crispus joined him in the gloomy shadows at the top of the stairwell. 'What's this about? We've got a lot to do.'

Tribune Eventius was peering at them from the far end of

the chamber.

'It is about Messor, one of the soldiers.' Fromus tried to keep his voice low. 'Him and Statarius. They violated Nehtan – they attacked her. She is under my protection. They have dishonoured her and they're guilty of *stuprum*.'

It was wrong to call it anything else. Roman law might say that *stuprum* was the violation of an unmarried citizen, not a slave, but it was wrong. Moreover, she hadn't been born a slave.

Crispus glanced at the trio by the table. 'When did this happen?'

'First thing this morning, I think.'

'You think or you're certain?'

'I'm sure.'

'What do you want me to do about it?' Crispus's head came closer. 'You'll have to speak with the Decurion; it's his man, but not now, not here.' He paused, then added brusquely, 'I'm sorry, but this is the sort of thing that happens. I warned you.'

'But she's been violated – by one of our own soldiers.'

'Are you saying she was a virgin?'

Fromus was gripping his cloak so hard that his hands shook. 'We did not ... I mean, she kept her honour. Ask Lady Clara; it is not what it looked like. That man must be executed. That's what would happen if these were normal times.'

'But they're not, and we have to remember why we're here. We don't know who she is. She's not my concern. In any case, we have to get on.'

'But that's not ...'

Crispus was stalking back to the army officers. Fromus glowered at the group in the light of the flickering candles. He would have to tackle Novateli in private.

In the courtyard, he rubbed his knuckles and walked away from the Black Gate. He had to get away from this suffocating place. Near the river, soldiers were stuffing hay into a sack. One of the men was Statarius. Two soldiers moved to stand between him and Fromus, their heads down, pulling up stalks.

Wisps of grass blew out of the sack and floated away in the wind.

Scum. Who did they think they were? But Fromus was not going to dishonour himself by making a scene with common soldiers. Father would say that it was inevitable that this sort of thing happened if he consorted with a plebeian. Damn him! They were all wrong. They had to be. Nehtan was different.

Fromus went back through the archway and saw the Decurion ambling towards the stables.

'You know what happened?'

'Yes, I've been briefed.' Novateli quickened his pace. 'And we've lost Messor.'

'What about the other one? He's back here. You can deal with him.'

'What about him? I understand that he did not assault the young woman.'

'No, but he was part of it. He's almost as guilty.'

The plume-helmeted officer stopped. 'Aurelianus Fromus, you need to understand me. With all due respect, my job is to get your delegation to Ravenna and back. If you choose to take up with an unknown woman and she is attacked – I'm sorry that one of my men is responsible – but it's just bad luck.'

'Bad luck!'

'She's a stray girl, from God knows where, and I am not

about to cripple one of my soldiers for mucking about with her. I need the few men I've got. God alone, where do you think we are?'

Novateli moved as if to walk away, then turned back. 'You should not have taken up with her. It is dangerous having a pretty woman around, and the men had your example before them. I strongly advise you: it would be best to leave her here. They can look after her in the Black Gate.'

Fromus bellowed. 'What are you saying? Can't you control your men?'

Crispus had appeared. He hurried across. 'Fromus! She's in the way and we have far to go. Decurion Novateli and I are agreed.'

'What the hell are you talking about? What right have you? I'm not leaving her behind; it's out of the question.' Novateli was squinting at Crispus. These people meant nothing to Fromus. 'If she stays, so do I.'

Black Gate soldiers were watching.

'Fromus,' Crispus sighed. 'I promised your father that I would bring you back. I can see that you are attached to this young woman, despite her rank. I can remember – I was young once. Perhaps we can allow that you bring her with us, at least until we reach a safe city.' Novateli grunted while Crispus continued. 'But there must be no more scenes. We have to draw a line; remember where your loyalties lie.'

Fromus turned on his heel. God's curse should fall on the wretched mission and their *Romanitas*. As for himself, what an idiot! It was so undignified.

Yet, down at the stream, in the silence, her breath had been in him, her quiet smile encompassing everything.

CHAPTER FOURTEEN

Nehtan slumped in front of Fromus, sitting astride Papiteddo.

Another grey, used-up day. Sticky rain clung to everything. Riding and riding, that's all they did, for days and days, getting nowhere. What was the point? These Romans, desperate to keep their power – their empire of killing, violation and slaves. Barbarians were breaking in, on the run from even worse tribes. She had nowhere to go; even Colud had probably been smashed by Picts or Romans, or both. For a while there had been that place of peace in the oratory in Bononia, but it had been snuffed out. The Lord had deserted her.

Shutting her eyes, thighs burning, Messor's bulk upon her, relentlessly crushing... his filthy black eyes, his hand squeezing her throat. Her whole body ruptured, scrubbed with thorns.

What if she was with child? Too awful to imagine, shove it away.

The same thoughts kept circling round. That man had done what the others didn't dare. Fromus had held back in the tent, he had bathed with her, yet he had made her go out alone to the wasteland beyond the Black Gate. The soldiers – they thought only of drink, women, and cutting down anyone who stood in their way. Even dingy old Crispus; his eye was always on her legs. If this had happened to his daughter, he would have made that stuck-up Decurion jump through fire to punish the man who had held her down.

Dull brown fir trunks clustered beside the forest track.

She was not worthy; the Lord had judged her. This was her

punishment for leaving Vitalis unburied, with no prayers and no offerings. The Lord stood aside and Donn was taking his revenge.

Papiteddo leapt over a log, forcing her back into Fromus's chest. She recoiled. Statarius was at the front of their small column. Every man had to be watched: *a fox may change its fur but never its character.*

She must brush away the tears; they would see them as weakness. Where to go, to be alone, to find a silent place, to be still? Maybe the forest, or huddled at the back of some distant church. Jesus said, *blessed be the peacemakers ... thy Kingdom come.* What did these things mean? And yet, and yet ... he had been thrashed and trampled, stretched on a tree, speared. He knew what it was like to be powerless, to suffer.

The track widened as they came out of the woods into a patchwork of scrubby fields. Dishevelled figures were hacking at a meadow pitted with stones and weeds. Women were filling sacks with brown grass. An old one sat with her cheeks in her hands, fingers over eyes.

'Good boy, you can do it.' Fromus's voice was slight and striving, dropping into an empty space. 'Go on, jump.'

The rider behind them came up alongside. It was Clara.

'Hail and be well.' The lady's grey eyes levelled on Fromus. 'We'll never get out of this dreadful country. My clothes are filthy. Ah, me. How's the poor girl?'

Nehtan winced.

'It's not easy,' she heard Fromus reply, 'with one of those men at the front.' His head grazed her hood as he swung round to look at the lady. 'By the way, where are you from?'

'That's a few years back,' said Clara. 'I was brought up in Britannia, but I left.'

'Did your family have an estate there?'

Nehtan dropped her chin. That was all they thought about. She had to get away from all this. Even Colud.

Clara swept her hair back. 'To tell the truth, my father was the head of household for an important family of leather merchants. We lived on the Rhenus at Colonia, but we had to move because of barbarian attacks – they burnt down the workshops. The family had a cousin in the south of Britannia; you must know it – Durnovaria.' Nehtan shook as Clara continued. 'Your father's Lalbertus Aurelius Matugenus, isn't he?'

'How do you know?'

Nehtan couldn't help listening to their dit-datting voices, trying to make connections. Clara liked talking about herself; that sort always did. The saying was true: *they speak only to conceal their minds.*

The lady was pulling in her chin as she steadied herself on her horse. 'Your family have been Equestrians for generations.'

What was Nehtan thinking, imagining any sort of relationship with someone like him, except as his plaything?

'Do tell me' – Nehtan recognised his confiding tone – 'how did your marriage to Paulinus come about?'

'I made my own way. Durnovaria was nice enough; good shows in the amphitheatre, especially the bullfights. But, by the Lord Almighty above, it was quiet. In Colonia, things were always happening, and you knew what was going on, right across the Empire. My master used to entertain lavishly: that's how he got the army business. I used to help at the feasts – perhaps you did that too, Nehtan?'

'No.' She looked down as she spoke through pursed lips. 'Not me, my lady. We didn't have that sort of household.'

'Your father must have entertained his fellow centurions. What were his duties? Was he in charge of anything?'

'I don't know, I led a humble life.'

Nehtan stared at the wide puddle that they were splashing through. She could jump off the horse and pull that woman into the mud.

'Surely you would know?'

'I'm sorry, my lady.'

Fromus broke in. 'Clara, how *did* you get back to Gaul? You haven't told me.'

'My dear, you know, though I say it myself, I was the morning star of that family, although I was the daughter – well, as I've said, the daughter of the chief servant.'

Nehtan grit her teeth. The lady had all but said that she was the daughter of a freedman, an ex-slave. How did she dare?

Clara adjusted her embroidered cloak, taking time before fixing her large grey eyes on the young patrician, fluttering her eyelids. Hateful.

Clara went on. 'My mistress treated me like one of her own. Her daughters were older – two were married and one was at home, but she was plain and quiet. The mistress loved to chat with me. She let me use her kohl.'

Clara stiffened her back so that she was sitting bolt upright, ignoring the droplets of rain which spilled from the wet leaves above. Nehtan pursed her lips.

'My mother didn't like it.' Clara's eyes sparkled. 'She was jealous. Then, one of my master's army friends, Lucius Septimius, tried to persuade the master to send me to him, but the mistress wouldn't have it; she put her foot down, and I saw my chance.'

Nehtan stared at the lady. Forest damp made the woman's face shine as they came into a small clearing.

'She was tearful at first, then she saw the sense, as long as it was proper and respectable. I was to help bind the families together.'

The track narrowed and the horses jostled. A sharp pressure, as Nehtan's right leg was pushed forwards. Behind, Clara's leg pressed against Fromus's as they squeezed side by side. The lady laughed and leant forward to stroke her horse's head. With a flick of her whip, she pushed her beast to ride ahead. Clara's voice rang out.

'Septimius used to drink and have fun – not naughty games, but he had such a sense of humour. Ah, if only he had drunk more. When we were married, he sobered up and I had to be prim and proper. We lived in Burdigala. What a city – plenty of everything. Then, one evening, he ate a chunk of goose after downing a big dish of pike. He clutched his chest and fell over, right in front of our guests. By the hand of the Lord, would you believe it? He died there and then, and I was pregnant. What a disaster! The major domo tried to revive him by hitting him hard on the back, but that's what killed the poor man. He swallowed a bone and went puce. He grabbed me, like he was drowning ...'

Clara paused and looked back. Her eyes were watering. An actress's trick?

'I'm sorry; it brings it all back.' Clara wiped her eyes. 'Poor old Septimius, he went out like a lamp. It was terrible after that. I was with child, and I should have been well provided for, but his cousin took everything. It was a crime – the child was to inherit, and an uncle was to be the guardian. I knew where Septimius hid his coins, and not in a thousand years were they going to drag that from me. Thank Jupiter for Fastidius. He ran and fetched a friend of ours. This man came to the house to get rid of those vile snakes. You can guess who that was.' Her voice softened. 'My dear Paulinus.'

The lady shifted in the saddle and spurred her horse. 'You know, Paulinus is such a kind and clever man. He should have been born a hundred years ago, at the time of his grandfather, a great man of letters.' Clara giggled, then stopped. 'But here am I, babbling away while the world is turned upside down. Well, what do you think of all that?'

'You have an interesting story.' Fromus spoke slowly, and Nehtan felt the shape of his thoughts. He was so cautious. 'You said that you were pregnant: was there a child?'

'Yes, indeed – a girl, a lovely child, Artemia. I had to leave her in our house in Narbo. I miss her more than words can tell, but Paulinus has to face his brother, and he needed me. Isn't that so, my dear?'

The lady beckoned her husband, who had ridden up and was overtaking Papiteddo.

'My dear, you *have* been talking.' Paulinus's lips shrank into his dimpled face. 'I wonder if I might speak with you.'

'But of course. Fromus, you must tell me about your family when we next get the chance.'

'It will be my pleasure.'

At last, the woman was going and Nehtan would not have to listen to her loathsome prattling. But how did Clara stay so strong, despite everything?

Nehtan rocked with the movement of the horse. Her whole body ached. Hands clenched, she shut her eyes. Still there – the thorny wasteland and that grinding man.

'That's good,' Fromus whispered. 'Get some sleep.'

Everything had been lost on that day, years after Grandmother had gone. She and brother Eothar had been looking for nuts. As soon as Nehtan saw the blue-streaked Picts rushing at them, she knew it was bad. Squealing and kicking, she was wrenched from Eothar's flailing arms. Days of exhausting travel followed, then darkness and she was thrown into a pit. Soon after dawn, wiry arms wrenched her out, stripped her, and thrust her onto a platform surrounded by men. Squirming, her hands tied, greedy fingers prodding her thighs and breasts, her mouth forced open, people shouting. Terrified, she couldn't see Eothar, didn't hear atir's enraged voice. Nothing, no one to help her, all she could do was to bear it, eyes tight shut. Exhausting hours later, she heard a quietly spoken, older man with the voice of authority: 'That will do.' Coins clattered onto stone. She was pulled from the platform and taken under arm, limp. Eothar was shouting, 'Nehtan, Nehtan, don't forget me!' She could still hear his thin voice, but his face was a blur.

Hours later, stuck on horseback with Romans, birds were wittering, blackbirds. The mist had evaporated and the air was fresh. Clara was riding ahead, gabbing away, droning on to Paulinus. Nehtan snatched a glance at Fromus behind her. Even him, she would have to leave him.

He smiled. 'You're awake. We'll be stopping soon.'

'Fromus ... is this what you want?' An immense effort to speak, to think. 'I mean, why are you doing this? I can find my way. I'll stop at the next city.'

'Don't think about it; I'm not going to leave you.'

'Why? You can't take me to Ravenna, I'm in the way. No one wants me here. It will take months, and that man -'

'I know. I have been thinking. All I can say is, I am not leaving you, not like this.'

'Then what?'

'I don't know. We have to see. I need to talk to Crispus.'

Her feet and hands ached from the cold as she stared at Papiteddo's mane. The horse knew what life was: he obeyed and asked nothing.

163

A nudge from Fromus. 'What do you reckon, should I talk to him before we get to the next city?'

'I don't know, sir.'

'How can you still call me that?'

'I'm sorry, I don't ... I can't think.'

They rode on.

* * *

Long days on horseback and cold nights passed in a haze. Late one afternoon, they reached the city of Mediomatricum. The soldiers guarding the city gates let the party from Britannia in after a few questions. The city was far smaller than Treverorum, but it had not escaped the barbarians: broken doors and collapsed walls, and the huts outside had been burnt down. Nehtan gazed open-mouthed at a great vaulted bridge that strode across the city. Fromus said it was an aqueduct, bringing water into the city. The ruins of Gaul were grander than anything in Britannia, and the countryside was vaster, with distant hills and wide valleys. She could disappear anywhere.

They rode past a group of men grunting from the strain of heavy sacks on their backs. In the Forum, which appeared untouched by devastation, people were taking down market stalls or converting them into sleeping quarters. A gaggle of merchants in fine cloaks were talking in loud voices. Loose chickens clucked in a corner.

As they were unloading the mules outside the inn, a noise of cantering hooves echoed in the narrow street.

She fell back against the wall, almost dropping the pile of cloaks she was carrying. It could not be, but it was – him, Messor, his cloak spattered with mud, his horse limping and frothing at the nostrils.

The Biarchus bellowed. 'Messor, where have you been?'

'Sir, I've come to report. Unavoidably detained.'

Nehtan staggered into the inn and dropped the cloaks. Her legs trembled, pain pulsing in her belly.

She found the small room that had been assigned to Fromus and her. The latch did not work. Huddling in a corner, she tried to pray, but the words were blank.

Footsteps sounded outside. She clutched her hood. Throat dry, no shriek would come. The door opened. Relief washed over her at the long face and high shoulders. Fromus.

She could breathe. 'How did he get a horse?'

'I asked Novateli. It seems that he left Messor's horse at the Black Gate, a gift for Tribune Eventius. When Messor went back, they let him have it.'

'You mean that the Decurion left it for him?'

'That is not what he said.'

What was it that Bellator had said about Messor? A 'good man' to have on your side.

'You can stay here.' Fromus was hovering. 'The Decurion says that we will rest for a day.'

'I can't rest!'

'I'm going to speak to the Decurion. Nehtan, please.'

She turned to the wall. Escape, escape from all of them.

'Look, I'm doing what I can,' he said. 'You must come and eat with us. Crispus is paying for a feast, and he asked if you could join us. No soldiers – only the Decurion. It's an honour that he asked you.'

'Why!' Her fist hit the wall. 'I don't need anything.'

Fromus was still, his eyes searching hers. 'Very well, as you wish.'

'Lady Clara says that she can lend you some old clothes.

You'll feel better in them.'

Mudebroth! Fromus would not get anywhere; they would ignore him. She had to act for herself. The Lord must help her. But first, she would have to go to the feast.

* * *

The dining room had a low wooden ceiling against which the heat from the fire built up. Even before she got there, she longed for bed. As the men drank and talked, her head got heavier. She was sitting next to Lady Clara, who ignored her entirely. Their spirits lifted by wine, the group spoke louder and louder. Fromus got into an animated discussion with Paulinus.

'You are mistaken, my friend.' Paulinus put a bottle down. 'The white wines of the Mosella have been praised by poets for hundreds of years. They have a delicacy quite lacking in the Burdigalian red.'

Nehtan looked down and ground her nails into her wrist.

'That's as may be.' Fromus filled his glass. 'But there's nothing like a fruity red from Aquitania. Gluttony may kill more than the sword, so let the wine match the dish before we are all condemned.'

'I am sure it's good, but the Mosella—'

'That's where we were,' Fromus cut in, 'we came from Treverorum. The whole province is a mess, laid waste. It could be years before they make any more wine.'

What was she doing here? Nehtan reflected bitterly. Why hadn't she stayed with Vitalis, let nature take its course? Men were cruel, but she would not let them crush her. Nehtan toyed with her food. The only way was south; she must find new people. Nymayr and atir were fading. In Bononia, people said that true Christian communities were springing up on the southern coast.

'You know.' Paulinus sat up, his wife's eyes on him. 'I've drunk the best, and I can honestly say that the white wines of the Mosella are the most subtle. You hardly need to add water. As Ausonius says,

"These vines spread their grip over the long peaks
Of the naked rocks which wind in and out
To form new theatres on the hillsides."'

Crispus was booming, his cheeks shining. 'As Horace says, "drinkers of water cannot write poetry." Long live Rome!'

'Long live wine and fat hogs roasting for our pot!' shouted Fromus. Nehtan cringed as everyone else burst into laughter, even smirking Ursacius.

Nehtan regarded their beaming faces, leering in the firelight. There would be somewhere in the south. She would find it.

At last, the lady was standing up to leave. Nehtan slipped out behind her. Back in the small room, she lay awake.

Much later, Fromus came bumping along the passage, exclaiming as he hit the wall. She kept the cloak over her head. Fumblings at the latch, then Fromus fell into the dark room.

'*Vah!*'

'Are you all right?'

'Don't worry – a good dinner, that's all.' He belched.

Give him wine and he was a man with other men.

Moonlight shone through the window, silhouetting his form. She stayed in her corner as Fromus struggled with his outer tunic.

'I can't get this thing off.'

She got up and undid his belt. Heavy with the coins, the belt fell as she pulled his outer tunic over his head. Something dropped to the floor, and she picked up a small satchel attached to a leather cord.

Fromus remained standing in his under-tunic. 'That was a fine evening. Nehtan, how are you?'

'I've got to sleep.'

'I'll come next to you.'

'I've made your bed over there.'

'*Pol*. I want to be with you, like it was before.'

'I can't ... please.'

He sank down, squatting on the floor. 'I can wait. I'll have a rest, then ...'

She did not reply. He crawled to his bedding and soon was snoring. Nehtan opened her eyes. Lord, let him forgive me.

CHAPTER FIFTEEN

Fromus's neck was cricked and his tongue leathery. Bone needles pricked the back of his eyes. He swivelled his head, recoiling from the glaring whiteness of the low ceiling. Thank God, they were resting in Mediomatricum for a couple of days. Later, he would tackle Novateli about those two men.

He dragged himself out of bed to find water. A solitary tree with a few brown leaves stood in the centre of the courtyard. Bellator leant against it, wrapped in a cape and a fur-skin.

'Morning, sir.' The Biarchus looked huge. 'This is more like the old days. Lord bless us, we don't get much sight of them. Who knows where we'll end up, but I don't mind as long as there are evenings like last night. By the way, I heard your young woman let herself out, early.'

A jolt shot through Fromus. 'Where was she going?'

'We didn't speak. It wasn't me as seen her.'

Fromus steadied himself: he was overreacting. She had probably gone to the market, or the church.

A weight bore down on his head. 'As you say, that was a superb dinner.'

'We had a fair belting at the tavern.' Bellator shuffled down to sit against the tree in the watery sunlight. 'The local wine's got a mean head on it, right back-end stuff.'

Fromus made his way back to the room. She would return soon. But he couldn't sleep. He was staring at the ceiling when Clara's voice called from the top of the staircase. 'Nehtan?'

He stayed silent.

'Nehtan, are you there?'

The woman would go on and on. 'She's not here,' he shouted.

'When will she be back?'

'I don't know.'

'Hfff.'

Where was she? He got up and crossed the courtyard. The innkeeper's wife was stirring a pot in the kitchen. She looked up.

'You'd be Master Fromus?'

'Yes, where's the church?'

'I have a message, from your woman.'

'What?'

'She bade me speak only if we was alone.' The woman put down a wooden spoon. 'She said to say that she's gone to Narbo, she had to go that way – though it don't make sense- and she hopes you don't mind that she borrowed those coins you promised her. I think that's—'

'What do you mean, she's gone?'

'Like I says, she left at the crack of dawn. I was just starting when she comes in.'

'How can she travel?'

'I told her she'd best go to the Forum. If anyone's going, they starts there. They only goes south nowadays, though there's few as does.'

'My God, are you sure?'

The woman shook her head. 'That's all I can tell you, master. No, I forget, she said, as she wouldn't expect to see you again – though if you was to meet her, if you take my meaning, it would be in Narbo. She'll leave word in the main church. But you wasn't to bother, she would be all right.'

Fromus strode to the marketplace, holding back from running. Farmers and young men clustered around the sides of the stone square. A vegetable seller told him that a caravan, led by a Jewish trader, had left in the morning, bound for a southern port.

A wrenching pain in his belly. He was a drunken fool – but she should have told him. He raced back along the narrow streets, dodging dung and loose cobbles. She had pushed him away, and now she had left him. It was the sort of thing that happened with women like her. Why did he care?

No, that was what old Romans like Crispus would say. Her trusting eyes and flowing dark hair; she was more real than anything else. They could all go to Hell.

She was clever, resourceful ... the coins! Back in his room, he rummaged along his belt and found that a few were missing: it did not matter. It was better that way.

She had already been gone for half the day. He shot out into the corridor, colliding with Crispus.

'I'm sorry, Natalius Crispus, sorry.' He helped the old man to right himself. 'She's gone; Nehtan's gone to Narbo.'

'Steady on, what do you mean?'

'She left, early this morning, she joined some traders. I have to find her.'

'Let us not rush into anything.' Crispus pursed his lips. 'This could be for the best.'

'What do you mean? How can you say that?'

'Fromus, you have a duty to your family and to the citizens of Britannia. They depend upon us.'

'I can think for myself. I have to go.' Crispus had no blood left in him, a useless old toga.

Something else. Father's letter. Father had said it was safer not knowing what was in it, but that time had gone.

Fromus turned. 'Now see here.' Crispus was grabbing his arm. 'You agreed to be part of this delegation. We must stand together and get to Ravenna. By all that's holy, you barely know her.'

Fromus removed the grey-hair's hand. He should stay calm
– but the words tumbled out. 'By the Lord, do you think I
don't know how things stand? They killed my uncle in the last
clamp-down. Barbarians are everywhere and ... and I have a
duty to people we take under our protection.'

Crispus's jaw tightened. 'Now is not the time. You'd best
speak to Decurion Novateli.'

That did it. Fromus strode back to his room, closed the
door, took out the scroll and broke the red seal.

My Dear Cousin

*Greetings. May this letter find you and my son in
good health.*

*I wish I could write to you in better circumstances. I have
been a double fool. My wife and Rome have been my life,
and at one time, I thought you threatened both. I see now
that your closeness to the former was honourable, as was your
distance from the latter.*

Fromus could not concentrate. He read the opening again.

*Now that I am writing to you, I feel your absence even more
strongly. We are a pair of old asses.*

*Nevertheless, we were right – both of us, in our different
ways. Rome's authority fades and men of power in
Britannia have forgotten their Romanitas. Ancient tribal
divisions are opening up, Patrician no longer bonds with
patrician and neighbour eyes neighbour with suspicion.
Saxons and Scotti attack the coast, while the north is falling
prey to Pictish depredations.*

Total breakdown is not far off. If we were united, we could scatter the barbarians and restore peace, but we lack a leader, and military force.

Come back, with God's speed, and with whatever troops you can muster. Forget Gaul and its chaos, which is beyond even your capabilities. It is here in Britannia that your integrity and Generalship are respected and will make a critical difference. If you raise your standard here, you can save our island from the dreadful civil wars that I fear will soon engulf us.

It will not be easy; I make no bones about it. However, it is possible, and it is the right thing to do.

I have prayed, and consulted with a few. My son Fromus is already committed, though he is not yet as aware of this as he will soon be. Share this letter with him. My family in Britannia will survive or fall with me. Bring my son safely back and give him a taste of command.

Hasten, I beg you. As soon as you land, send word by the swiftest messenger to me in Corinium.

My affection to your most esteemed wife, Nonnichia, the absence of whose company in these long years I deeply regret, second only to yours.

All will ultimately be well.

Your friend and cousin

Lalbertus Aurelianus Matugenus

This changed everything. Or did it? He read the letter

again. It was as if he had known it all the time.

He took a deep breath and stared at the ground. His shoulders relaxed. Be calm. He remembered Nehtan staying quiet in the tent. The Lord would bring the answer.

Yet again, Father had not trusted him. In Father's eyes, the delegation's mission to the Emperor was merely an opportunity to get this desperate plea to Gerontius. He had let Fromus get all puffed up about being a delegate – and had told him nothing. It was too much. But if it was as bad as Father thought, Gerontius was Britannia's only hope.

Fromus thrust the letter into his inner cloak pocket. She had gone south. Gerontius was there. He would find them both and go back to Britannia. *More is lost by indecision than wrong decision.*

He raced to the stables and found the Decurion talking with Crispus. A trooper stopped rubbing down his horse.

Novateli looked Fromus full in the face. 'Does she have means?'

'Yes. I gave her coins.'

'If she paid them, the traders may have taken her with them, but we can't be sure.'

'What do you mean?'

'These are desperate times. If an unprotected woman gives a man money, there's no certainty that she'll get what she paid for.'

'Christ Jesus.'

'Let's not leap to conclusions.'

'We must leave immediately.'

'This woman,' Novateli nodded at Crispus, 'she can't continue with us ... too many problems.'

'Decurion,' Fromus said, 'I am not going to be put off this time. I am going after her, right now.'

Crispus sighed. 'If you are dead set, Fromus, perhaps Decurion Novateli can send a soldier with you, ahead of us. We should be able to catch you up. There are two hours of daylight left, and we need to finish provisioning. Is that not so, Decurion?'

'Yes sir, I suppose so – if you absolutely insist. I'll talk with Bellator. We might be able to spare one man, temporarily.'

Fromus rushed to his room. By the time he got back to the stables, Novateli was talking with Bellator.

'... that puts a different complexion on it,' the Decurion said. 'By all the stars, this time there'll be no mercy.'

'What do you mean?' Fromus interrupted.

'Ah, Fromus, something else. Trooper Messor took my horse, our best horse, and left by the southern gate.'

Chapter Sixteen

Dawn, ten hours earlier.

Nehtan reached the Forum at first light. An old man was barking orders to a crew of servants and armed men. She heard him saying Lugdunum, the big city on the way to the southern sea. The die was cast. Brushing down Clara's old cape, she walked up to the old man.

'Sir, may I travel with you?'

'Steady girl. You don't even know where we're going.'

'I heard your instructions, and I have to get away. My father and brother were killed by barbarians.'

The old man shifted under his patterned cloak. 'Where are you from?'

'I come from the north, sir. We'd been travelling for weeks and then we were attacked.'

'We don't take travellers with us. Not these days.' The old man swept aside a streak of grey hair. 'It's not my business. You must have other family.'

'I have silver, I can pay.'

The old man was still, fingering his beard. 'That's as may be. It is not the money.'

'I beg you, sir, I won't slow you down, I can look after myself. You won't regret taking me with you.'

The creases in the old man's face broadened. She must keep pushing. 'Sir, I have no one here, but I have family in Lugdunum. Please, Father is dead, our house is deserted, and it's not safe.'

'You have a wound on your head.' She raised a hand to cover the tender spot.

'Yes, sir, but it's healed now.'

'It's dangerous where we're travelling. No place for a woman.'

'I beg you, sir; my life depends upon my leaving. I tell you truly, I have to get away.'

She held his stare, her eyes pleading. The old man's lined face softened into a grin.

'Do you have the coin?'

'Yes sir. How much?' She reached for a coin in her cloak pocket.

'One silver, and it had better be good.'

She gave him the coin. He bit it and then peered down. 'By my forefathers, it's a long time since I've seen unclipped Theodosian Argentei. It takes me back. How do you come by this?'

'From my family, our savings.'

'To Lugdunum and no further, you understand? I am Yochanan ben Zakai, and we travel fast. My men do what I say and you must do the same. Is that understood?'

'Yes, sir.' She had done it! Hurrying after him: 'My name is Nehtan.'

'Hariulfus.' The old man spoke to a swarthy man with a broad sword, wearing a bearskin tunic. 'Give her the mule, the one we were talking about. Young woman, we ride hard, we stop only for the animals. If you lag behind, we will not come back for you. Mark my words.'

Nehtan nodded, beaming. She would ride her own beast to her own future.

* * *

Six hours later, she was at her limit. The wretched mule

had to be goaded all the time, even when the going was easy. The heaviness and her hurts submerged into one vast, aching exhaustion.

With every hill, the same story: the mule lagged further and further behind, and she only caught up with the others when they stopped to water or feed the animals. She would be lost if they came to a fork in the road and the others were out of sight.

The beast had to be mastered, with its hard back and bony rump. She had a good mind to call it Culus, the arse, but that would make her the laughing-stock. It was her and the mule against the men, but she would get there in the end, like the tortoise and the hare. That was it; she would call it Testudo, the tortoise.

'Testudo.' She poked the animal's neck. 'You are going to obey me.'

She whacked Testudo with the small whip they had given her, but to no effect. Then again, and again, harder still. A welt appeared on the beast's rump, but still it ambled. She struck Testudo with all her might; a loud hee-haw, and the mule hunched forwards. Then it kicked back with both its hind legs, but she held on. Another great thwack and Testudo jerked forward into a trot. Men cheered as she shot past the rear of the column.

Long days dragged by. Bracken and brambles clogged the land on both sides; thistles and nettles covered the occasional fields. The road was pot-holed; on hilly parts, the supporting stonework had been washed away. Only the packs on the back of the mules and the occasional clink of swords on chain mail beneath coarse cloaks distinguished them from common folk.

One evening, riding at the back of the column, halfway across a long clearing between two dark patches of forest,

Nehtan whacked Testudo, hard. He shot off, stumbled, and she wrenched herself up to stay in the saddle. A searing pain erupted in her shoulder.

When she reached the others, she was at the limit of her strength. They were re-mounting, but she could not go any further. She slid her leg over the mule and dropped into the mud.

'*Mudebroth*, Testudo.'

Yochanan rode his horse over to her.

'What was that about? Who's Testudo?'

'That's what I call my mule.'

Yochanan laughed. Nehtan's shoulder twitched and she winced.

'I'll get Josephus to look at that.' The old man scratched his neat beard. 'My cook and herbalist. Problems should be treated at once or they get worse.'

She felt the old man regarding her as she struggled to her feet.

'You are not used to being looked after.'

'No sir, my father worked hard; he was away a lot. I was busy.'

'I believe you – for the most part.' She was about to protest but Yochanan raised his arm. He spoke as if he were scanning a long scroll. 'I have been travelling the length and breadth of Gaul for twenty years, and I have listened to many stories. There is no end to what people will say to get what they want, and who am I to blame them? What are we but leaves blown hither and thither about the world? Who knows – one day you may be in a position to do a service to a Jew, and then you will recall the trust placed in you by this old purveyor of spices and fine clothes.'

She remained silent, hands sweating.

'We will see,' Yochanan continued. 'All sorts of people are fleeing the chaos, though never a woman by herself. You remind me of my daughter.'

'Has she been to these parts?'

'Nooo.' Yochanan blew out the word, making it sound like a chant. 'My family stays in Massilia – except my brother, who manages our store in Mediomatricum. I was hoping to bring him back with me.' The old man looked up to the grey sky, then levelled his gaze at her. 'Trust no one, and don't leave your family, when you find them.'

He turned and shouted. 'Josephus, you are needed here. The rest of you, dismount. We'll stay a while longer.'

A small man rode up, with darting eyes and a peaked cap. He sprang down and crooked his finger. Nehtan squatted with her head down while Josephus squeezed along her arm with his bony finger and thumb. It felt like burning oil was being poured into her shoulder. He rolled up her tunic to expose her arm.

Some guards edged closer. Josephus's eyes narrowed as he squinted at the men. 'Haven't you lot got anything better to do? Never seen a woman's arm before? You had better spend your coin in the right places when we get to Lugdunum.'

Guffaws, and a couple of the men walked off. Two guards lingered. One was Hariulfus. The other was dark-skinned.

'Go on, get on with it.' Josephus jabbed his finger at the big man. Nehtan's eyebrows rose. 'Unless you want me to take another look at that sore in your private parts?'

Hariulfus laughed in his bearskin and the pair of them walked away. Josephus stood up, unpacked a bundle from his side-saddle, and took out a small phial.

'Wait here.'

He darted off and came back clutching a wooden cup filled

with water. 'Hold this.'

After pouring a small amount of liquid from his phial, Josephus commanded, 'Drink.'

'What's in it?'

'Don't you worry, young woman; it is good for you. Henbane, knitbone and a few other things. It will help the mending in your arm, and it'll soothe the pain. Now, let me have a look at that thick skull of yours.'

'No!' Nehtan recoiled, but Josephus kept his hand out. 'I won't hurt you.'

His fingers were gentle as he probed her scalp. 'That'll do. The scabs are strong and there is no corruption of the flesh. It must have been a hard cut. You'll bear it your life long. But you've got youth in your favour; you've healed well.'

'It was the Alans. My father and brother were killed.'

'As you say.' Josephus lowered his eyes. 'I won't ask more'

'That's what happened.' She wished her voice did not waver.

'So be it. Now, I must work on your arm.'

Nehtan sat while Josephus made a poultice with mud and dried plants from his sack, then massaged his fingers up and down her arm. It stung and her eyes watered.

'Yochanan said about his brother,' she asked. 'Is he all right?'

Josephus's eyes flashed. 'All I know is that the master's brother wasn't there, though he should have been, and the store was ransacked. It looked bad, but you will not find Yochanan ben Zakai pitying himself or telling the world.' He shook his head. 'These are terrible times. Families are struck down and people lost. The ways of the One God are mysterious.'

A sudden vision flashed, of a sea of people clutching

bloodied arms and wounded heads, kneeling together on a salt-encrusted shore, with nothing but their shared pain.

'It's not much but it will help.' Josephus adjusted the sling around her neck. 'You should be resting that shoulder, but you'll survive.' He stepped back and peered at her. 'You're lucky the old man has taken a liking to you.'

She started to thank him but he brushed her off with a peremptory wave.

Alone, tears sprang to her eyes. This raw welling, this was new, something she used to be able to control. Another thing that man had done to her at the Black Gate. She must overcome it, overcome him.

She walked to a stream and knelt to scoop water. Instinctively, she turned to offer some to Fromus, then shook her head. That was gone. They had been close, almost as one, down at the stream, splashing water... He couldn't still want her, could he, not after she had taken the coins? A chance, a slip of a hope: Lord, let me see him once more; have mercy.

A man came, a servant sent by Yochanan, to give her bread and dried mutton. As they prepared to leave, she struggled at the side of Testudo.

'Hariulfus,' – it was Yochanan – 'get that young woman onto her saddle, and mind, I'm watching.' The big man grimaced, lifted her up carefully, and placed her on the saddle.

'Thank you.' Nehtan did not dare look into his eyes.

'I had a child once,' he whispered. 'She'd be younger than you. I don't know what happened to her.'

She hesitated, but the man strode back to his horse.

Pulling her hood about her neck, Nehtan steered Testudo to ride behind Yochanan. Winter was coming. The air was tight with cold as snowflakes fluttered down. She looked back and scanned the far trees. A dark patch in amongst the firs: it could be a man on a horse. She blinked the snow out of her eyes. Nothing there.

Night came and they camped around a small group of abandoned hovels. Yochanan did not invite her to come to his fireside – or into his tent – but he did send food. Nehtan curled up against the wall of a roofless hut. She was so tired that she had barely finished eating before she was asleep.

Next day, jerked awake, someone was touching her. She struck out.

'*Hei!*' Josephus stumbled back. 'What's wrong with you? It's time to get up. We're going.'

'Sorry. I – I thought it was someone else.'

Josephus raised an eyebrow. 'And the shoulder?'

'Much better.' She reached to where the swelling had been. 'How did you do it?'

'You've never been treated by a proper herbalist. You will be fine. The young heal quickly, or they die. Clearly, you are of the living sort.'

'I don't know how to thank you.' She smiled, but he was turning away, almost hiding. 'And who looks after you?'

'No time for chat, got to go. The master bade me give you this.'

He handed her a water gourd, a chunk of bread and a small cake. She bit the cake; it was sweet.

Yochanan was supervising the loading of saddlebags onto the mules, barking at his men. 'You there, Hariulfus, help Nehtan onto her Testudo.' The old man laughed. 'See, this young woman isn't complaining, though she's got a dislocated shoulder. Sharpen up. We need to get to Augustodunum and then push on to Lugdunum.'

After that, though she spoke few words with the guards and muleteers, they exchanged friendly smiles. Days passed, her shoulder toughened up, strength was returning. Her body, at least, had forgotten the Black Gate.

Snow fell, but it didn't pile up; it seeped into the ground, turning the track into a mushy brown paste. The column spread out as they went up a long hill.

A yell erupted from the rear: 'Let me pass!'

No, it couldn't be! Her whole body seized as she forced herself to look back. Messor! There, at the bottom of the hill. She crouched low on Testudo.

Yochanan rode downhill, past her, but he caught something in her face. 'What is it, do you know him?'

'He's evil.' Her voice choked. 'He attacked me.'

'That had better be the truth. I haven't got time for this.'

'It's true.' She shrank inside her cloak.

'The Lord God of Abraham preserve us. Hariulfus, come with me.' Yochanan continued downhill with the big guard.

'You dogs!' Messor's voice rang out. 'I'm an Imperial soldier, on orders to get that girl. She's an escaped slave. If you don't give her to me, it'll be the worse for you.'

Hariulfus moved in front of Messor, his huge sword across his chest.

'Get out of my way,' Messor shouted.

'Quiet!' Yochanan roared. 'Who are you? How do we know that you are telling the truth?'

'Why would I be here? You saw the girl in Mediomatricum with us.'

'I saw no such thing. Show me your orders.'

'There wasn't time. Listen, old man, it'll go badly for you if I don't bring her back. This is none of your business, hand her over.'

Messor caught her eye. 'Nehtan, you're mine.'

She kicked Testudo, trying to make him turn around, get

up the hill.

'Be off!' She heard the iron in Yochanan. 'A plague on you, I know your sort. I've a good mind to have you whipped. Be gone.'

'You haven't seen the last of me,' Messor bellowed. He would never let go. 'I'll get you, one by one. You're nothing but damned Jew merchants.'

Testudo wouldn't move. She looked back down the slope. Two guards and Hariulfus were following Messor at a distance, as he retreated. The cavalryman turned into a wood and disappeared.

Nehtan kicked Testudo hard with her heels. What were they waiting for? Her head ached with a deep throb from the base of her neck.

'Nehtan,' Yochanan reached her side. 'That's some piece of work you have after you. I thought there was something, but he's nothing to worry about. Hariulfus and his men are more than enough to deal with him.'

Holding onto Testudo's reins, she panted. Her belly churned, she leant to the side and spewed. Donn … Messor. Where could she go?

Light snow clung to swaying holly berries. Josephus handed her a gourd with a green stopper and a small sack of food.

'Take this. Drink some – just a sip or you'll be flying. The master will drive us hard for the rest of the day. We've a steep climb and then it's down to the river valley.'

His voice came from far off. She was back in the ancient place. She took a swig and tucked the gourd and sack inside her cape. A slow rush of warmth, and she was lightheaded as it reached the top of her skull. Snowflakes danced in the air. Terror was not the only power in the world. She was with

Josephus and Yochanan. That brute viper was slithering behind, but she had friends – and she was a branch of the Lord's sacred vine.

The hard grind of riding Testudo up and down the hills took over. It got colder. Flecks of white drifted out of a silent fir-lined expanse, covering everything. The ground was blank, except for the hoof prints left by the riders in front. At a ridgetop, they halted.

One of Yochanan's men appeared and grabbed her thigh. She howled and kicked him.

'No need for that. We've got to rest the animals.'

'You didn't tell me.'

The man hoisted her off Testudo and plonked her down on the narrow track. She should have stayed with Fromus.

The track was narrow where they were resting. Fir tree walls were closing in. She stamped her feet on the ground and rubbed her hands together. A guard was pulling on the reins of a mule as the beast dragged him across the track, jerking his head up. A muleteer was shouting, holding on to the animal's load.

Then the muleteer fell. The guard bellowed; the mule ran off.

'You there!' Yochanan shouted. 'Go and see what's happened.'

The man rushed down. Hariulfus followed.

'He got one of our men, shot him with an arrow. The whoreson! He won't stand and fight.'

Yochanan brushed snow off his head. 'Is he dead?'

'I reckon so. The arrow lanced his throat, blood everywhere.'

The guards peered into the dense pines down either side of the track. In the distance, an indistinct black movement.

186

'It's him,' someone shouted. Swords were drawn and a couple of guards remounted. Animals and men backed into each other.

'Steady now.' Yochanan strode through their midst. 'Stay where you are and be vigilant.'

The muleteers shrank to the side of the track. Snow descended in dense waves, sticking to the men's beards. Hariulfus returned.

'Nothing we could do.'

'We'll bury him.' Yochanan brushed snow off. 'Hariulfus, you stay in the rear. Take another man with you.' Narrow eyes in his big head; he swivelled on Nehtan.' 'This is not what I bargained for.'

A deep breath.

'You had best get back on your mule,' Yochanan said. 'Find Josephus and stick to him.'

The muleteers and guards scowled at Nehtan as they adjusted the loads on the mules and re-mounted. 'We never had a girl before.' One man jabbed his finger at her. 'And look what's happened.'

The line of animals and riders shuffled forward. The path was too narrow for Testudo to overtake the others and find Josephus. After an hour, the track broadened. Nehtan kicked and prodded Testudo and got him to pull out of the column and trot past a laden mule.

'A shriek came from the back: I'm hit!'

Shouting. Horses rearing in the pelting snow, mules crashing into each other, packs falling off. A rider on horseback rushed past Nehtan, roaring. Testudo brayed and twisted back down the track, following after the panicking horse.

'No, stop!' Nehtan clung on as Testudo crashed into the

side of a guard's horse.

'Damn you,' said the man. 'Control your beast.'

Snow stung her eyes. Testudo jerked his head and swerved. She started to fall, grabbed his mane, but she was not strong enough. Plunging onto the hard track, a wrenching pain in her shoulder, hooves thundering towards her head. She threw herself to the side, rolling into a snow-pile at the edge. Throbbing in her neck, no time, she scrabbled on all fours through sticks and pinecones, under a branch and into thick fir-brush.

A quick glance back. Yelling on the track, white flecks blanketing everything, a guard hacking at a mule, the flash of a raised blade. Something moving fast, a crimson cloak on a horse galloping towards her.

CHAPTER SEVENTEEN

'*Heia!*' Messor kneed his beast away from the puffball guards.

Fair lifted his spirits to plug an arrow into the idiot muleteer. Pick them off one by one, like crippled sparrows. He would snatch Nehtan from their midst and leave them spitting blood.

She was tormenting him. By Cautopates, let her be different, not just another one to crush. Fate had brought them together in the army district of Londinium. She had listened to him and he had felt a great weight beginning to lift. He remembered that moment of relief in the alley in Londinium. She belonged to him; only she could make him whole. The dog bite had been a sign: Mithras had made their paths cross again in this destroyed land, a place where he felt at home. Mithras was bringing her to him – she, who knew the black fireball at the centre of his being - and could heal it. It was in her eyes, though she denied it. With her, he could bear anything, and they could meet the sun god as one.

He pushed off to the side of the whited-out track. A small clearing ended in a wall of spiky fir. No animal tracks. He waited, sword drawn, for the first guard to brave his way into the narrow space. Flakes poured down. Hunched, tense on horseback, he stared at where the movement would come from. Soon, his horse's hoof prints disappeared beneath new snowfall.

Pissing Mithras, where in Hades were they? He fought to quiet himself as he listened beyond the muffling snow. No one was coming, they had gone on, too cowardly to face him.

Frozen droplets stuck to the hair on the back of his hands. He rubbed his knuckles on the horse's mane and patted the animal's flank. They would both feed the wolves if he did not find the way.

He dismounted and led his horse through the dense pine. There would be many woodcutter paths.

Damn this fucking wood. His arm smashed down on a brittle branch, making his animal rear up. He drove on, wrenching the horse behind him, ignoring pain from splinters. By all that's cursed, he would beat them. He had nothing, except that she must bend to his will.

Teeth clenched, thrusting through branch and twig, glancing back to keep a straight line.

Yes! He broke through onto a thin trail. It led at a long angle back towards the main track.

Mithras, let me get there first!

He mounted and forced his horse to canter almost blindly in the tumbling snow. Brushing sweat out of his eyes, slapping his beast's flank: he must make double speed to overtake the dog-head Jew.

A junction ahead, the trail intersected by a much broader path coming at a sharp angle from the left. Had to be it. No sign of hoof prints, nothing in sight.

Springing off his horse, he led it back between the trees and tethered it. Bow and quiver in hand, he rushed back and scuffed out his hoof and boot prints. Slipping behind firs, he skirted parallel to the track until he reached a triangle of bushing, low-branched pines at the edge of the ditch. Taking his time, he slotted an arrow to the string.

Long minutes, then a faint sound from down the track. It had to be them. Snatches of human voices.

Twilight on the luminous path. Snow cascading, denser

than before. A rider came into sight. She would be in the middle. He let the first two trot by, every nerve straining. Then, the joy of loosing an arrow into the belly of the third man, a muleteer, no chain mail. Shrieking, the man toppled. The next rider bawled, bent low, kicking his horse. Guards at the front yelled, fighting to turn their beasts.

He stepped into the track, amidst contorted riders, twisting flesh and pelting snow. A short profile rushing away on a flailing mule. Her!

Rushing back to his horse, he remounted, spatha blade out, spurring his horse in the direction she had fled. Back at the track, panicked riders sprawled on the ground, guards colliding. Horses braying, loose mules, packs on the ground, chaos.

A man on foot gawked. 'It's him!'

Messor held steady on his horse as he slashed, but missed. Three riders crashed in front of him, blocking the track. Too late, one of them saw the blade slamming down. A sinewy crunch: shoulder cut through to bone. Quick! A guard on foot tore at him, thrusting a spear.

Spurring his horse, Messor parried, jerking sword-point into face, time only to gouge the guard's nose. Others, flailing and yelling.

Where was the woman? Too many of them. Wheeling his animal, he flattened a man and sped through jumbled guards and packmen, his blade hacking recklessly. A sharp heat in his leg, and then he was racing down the empty track, no one following.

The bastards were scared shitless. By Saturn, it was good to fight.

He snarled at the blood seeping from the gash in his leg. Mithras was an ox-head for not helping him. Fuck, his leg stung.

He pushed into the forest and tethered his horse to a fir with a snapped top.

'Steady boy.'

The animal's eyes rolled, ears pricked, flank steaming, but he was still. That asshole Novateli had trained the beast well.

Messor worked his way back on foot through the trees. His leg burned but the cold would staunch the flow of blood. He had ridden right through that shambles. They would not last long if they were in the army.

He would skewer a couple more, find the woman.

Merda! His bow, he'd lost it. Dropping the quiver, he edged forwards, crawling under snow-laden branches. Two men were talking, one with authority. The name 'Nehtan'. Messor crept closer. The Jew bastard said she was missing. The other, a womanish sort, was trying to persuade the white-beard to find her, but the old man would not hear of it. A man with a huge belt and sword stepped forward: it was the cunt with the bearskin. The mules had been re-loaded.

Terse commands; they were leaving. No more to learn, he crawled back.

She was in the forest, on foot, alone.

Messor waited, then rode back, peering through blanketing snow in the dim light. A mussed-up patch of mud and snow led off the path and under branches, into the wood. It had to be her tracks. Dismounting, he pushed in, but it was no good. Within a few paces, it was inky black, snow pouring down. He went back to sit huddled in a hollow under a large fir, shivering under his cloak while his leg throbbed.

Next day he awoke with a drawn-out shudder and a rancorous hurt in his belly. It had snowed most of the night. Damn those cawing crows, her footprints would be covered, but she would not get far. She would be in the forest, away from the road.

'Come on, old boy,' he growled, patting the horse. 'You miserable bag of bones. You work all right for Novateli; you can do the same for me. What's a few days without food for the likes of us? We're soldiers. A shit life for a shit life; we can take it. Those bastards think they know, but they're worms, lower than the lowest raven, hiding from what it's really like.'

He glowered at the dull sky, the underside of a vast, scalding pan. 'A freezing day, an empty belly, and a smacking pain in the leg – that's what we've got, but I'll get her. Fuck 'em all.'

CHAPTER EIGHTEEN

Darkness, choking flith, encased in cold all round. A stem of light. She was buried, blanketed by earth, struggling to suck air, her body mired in mud. Hidden – she must stay hidden, deep in the ground, crouching in her burrow in a field ringed by dead trees and a collapsed dry-stone wall. Up above, a man with blood-red eyes, his foot about to clamp shut her breathing hole.

Messor! Nehtan sat up and a jagged wave sliced from toe to head. It was pitch black and she was shivering, deep in the woods, veiled by layers of snow.

Yochanan and Josephus had gone. She remembered falling off the mule and pushing into the bleached fir forest, scrabbling under branches and collapsing white mantles.

Eyes open in the night, blinking to flutter off the snow, she lay curled under a many-trunked tree, its branches heavy with snow, her cheeks rippled with dried blood, hands stinging. The thick cloak of the woods wrapped her tight. Twigs and lumps of snow matted her hair. A good disguise. No – more than that, it was a gift.

Trees were friends. She had been carefree amongst them, long ago, north of the Wall. The wilderness flowed, feeding the waters of the holy mountain. What did the Christ say? *Blessed are the poor in spirit; foxes have their holes.*

Men washed him, clothed him, fed him – and spiked him on a plank. Tree-killers did this, too busy to notice who they were.

Take strength from the pity of trees, cradled in silence, nothing to do but reach towards the sun.

She pulled her hood down, invisible, held in the palm of the woodlands, grey cracks of light stroking fir-tops. She would not go back to that black road. Yochanan had been kind, and Josephus, in his nervous, bird-like way, but they were better off without her. Fromus – him too. And her way was her own.

Fingers of sunlight crinkled down, softening the chill. Enough to sit and breathe, head nodding.

That leering, burning face.

Struggling to stand, she pushed downhill between waving branches. Had to move to get warm, and away. It was the right direction, judging by the sun. Firs stood with hands on hips, larches leaning, and the odd oak, thick arms open.

That stinking man, grinding her into the stony waste. He had tried to throttle her. Why? She was not born a slave, with no shame, no future. She was part of everything that was sacred in the heart of the Lamb of God, who was all in all. By the blood of the martyrs, she would not be stained to death by that man. A tree was no less a tree, even when cut down and set on a pyre of seething flames.

What if his vile seed was spawning in her, his hatred reaching into her guts, blackening everything? Sooner rip it out. Not dwell on it. She must not feel or feed his torment. Speak, pray out loud:

'We praise you, O God,
We acknowledge you as the Lord,
All the earth doth worship you.'

Memories of services in Bononia: singing in the sunlight, a woman holding her hand, men with kindly souls – or did they glow with secret lust?

Bending low to crawl beneath branches, she snatched glimpses of a soft sky. Hours passed; her legs ached, back sore, head hot. Wiping her brow, she aimed for the treetops at the bottom of the open slope. Her chest heaved; she forced words out between churning breaths.

'God of heaven and earth,
seas and rivers,
God of high mountain
and lowly valley ...'

Crumpling at the edge of whiteness, clutching a branch. Dry throat, gleaming sun, feet stuck fast. Get to the other side. Wooden thighs must work. What came next?

'He makes the light of the sun to shine,
He surrounds the moon
and the stars,
He made wells ...'

Knees sunk in snow, right shoulder jarring, aflame. Dark patches beneath the trees ahead, a jagged line, islands of white. A stream.

'... made wells, and, and placed dry lands
in the sea.'

Eyes closed, she snapped them open.

'He has a Son ...
a Son
co-eternal ...'

Three more steps.

'with himself and the Holy Spirit ...
who ...'

Leg. Lift. Up.

'... who breathes
in
them.'

She collapsed next to a spreading chestnut, a low-hanging branch scraping her cheek, chest heaving. Needles of damp chill. Sitting, she reached for Josephus's cake and liquid. Only drops left. Squeezing lumps of snow into the gourd. Drinking.

No clouds, no wind. Birds passing. Late swallows, heading for the warm south. That must be a good place for a new life.

Light bristled on the waxen snow. A flicker of movement: a roe deer splaying its forelegs as it drank from a stream, a buck with short horns alongside, its ears twitching. The doe ambled downstream, followed by the buck, nuzzling her behind.

Gold-beams warmed Nehtan's face. Snow crackled, melting. A crow flopped past, wheeling, looking for scraps. It cawed and was answered by another. The hillside basked in the midday sun.

Messor could not be near, or the roe would have been disturbed. Even if he was, what could she do? The Holy One must be with her.

The stream would lead south, towards Narbo. Hope, a new way was opening. The steep-sided, thickly ferned valley was like the dales around Colud. Walking on, the rivulet became a river, wavelets and mini rapids dotting the surface. Knobby shrubs of bog myrtle sprouted on damp mounds. Stems of aspen and rowan were bloated with moss. With sodden feet, she flew down the path: she was a fresh breeze flowing through the sun-dappled earth.

A fish rose in a pool. She stopped to scoop water. River-light flashed marble and deep blue night. She could keep going for days.

Hours later and there was a sudden whiff of badger. Then, she froze: footprints. Not his; he would be on horseback, contemptuous of foot-sloggers. But if there were other people, that meant explaining, watching. Was there a way to live without fear?

Only Fromus was unafraid, standing naked at the edge of the stream.

Sitting on a boulder, she stared into the swirling river. Iced lichen covered the tops of big stones. Water, water, pulsing down the valley, arriving and leaving, boisterous, peaceful in pure activity.

Starving, but she would hang on to the last of her food until nightfall. She sipped earth-specked water from the gourd and strode on. Birds darted, a kingfisher and a green woodpecker. A pair of mallards grumbled as she flitted past, sharp-eyed for soggy patches and the treacherous edge of the river. The path narrowed to an animal track that skirted under bushes and zigzagged around clumps of hazel.

Smoke, lingering in the air.

She crept from tree to bush. On the other side of the river was a round hut with a stone chimney. No one in sight. More huts beyond. She would wait until nightfall and sneak close to hear what sort of people they were.

She went back to where she had passed a place to ford the river. Taking off her boots and cape, she threw them across. Stepping into the freezing water, feeling for sharp stones, she reached a small island in the middle. As she prepared to leap to the other bank, a man's voice rang out.

'Tell me, young woman, where are you from?'

Him! No, not his voice. An old, creased face in the wood above. The man's accent was odd but she could understand.

'Nowhere. I'm passing by.'

'Well, let's have a look at you.'

The man advanced from the trees, wispy hair streaking across a balding forehead. Over his paunch, a dirty tunic and cape. His sandals were threadbare and he carried a heavy stick.

'What are you doing here?' he asked.

She crossed the fast-flowing river to reach her boots and cloak. Downstream, water oozed in a large pool. If he came too near, she would jump in.

'I'm on my way to Narbo.'

'To Narbo! My, that will amuse Brigomalla. It's a long time since we have had such a distinguished traveller.'

'You don't believe me?'

'Now, first things first. What are you called?'

She paused. 'Nehtan.'

They were within two spears' length of each other, her boots in her hands. Difficult to run.

'Put your things on,' the old man said, 'and come up to our hut.'

'Perhaps.' She peered at his lined face. 'What's your name?'

'Vigilantius is what my parents named me, a long time ago, in a fine Aquitanian city. I am sure my wife would like to meet you. Here, let me help.'

He started to walk towards her, and she darted back along the riverbank. He was old but he was a man, and she remembered Nymayr's warnings about forest people.

'I see the woods have not been kind to you.' The old man Vigilantius chuckled. 'Come up to Bonadeni when you are ready, or rest here if you will.'

She watched as he clambered up through the bracken. At the hut, he waved before disappearing inside. Smoke drifted from a stone chimney. Neat, purple flowers were trailing up the wall either side of the door.

The muffled sound of a woman's voice, followed by Vigilantius's too-loud reply. 'We have a guest for supper, a young lass.'

A pinch-nosed, big-boned woman emerged wearing a billowing smock. She had long blond hair, dancing green eyes, and prominent teeth.

'Girl,' she shouted, 'you've been through more than one snowdrift to get here. I'm Brigomalla. That useless man of mine hasn't told me your name.'

Nehtan smiled at the woman's wide face, then made her way up through the snowy layers of dead bracken, keeping an eye out for other men, but there were none. The roof of the hut looked ready to collapse.

CHAPTER NINETEEN

Messor heaved himself up a tall pine, cursing the throbbing pain in his leg. Snow dropped in clumps as he perched on thin branches. Strong winds wind shook the trunk. If he had been scouting for the army, he would not have climbed so high. He stopped when his head was a sword's length short of the open sky.

He peered at the wide horizon. It had been four days, and still no sign of her in the vastness of the frozen forest.

'You gods,' he breathed. 'Mithras, grant me the woman, and I will give her to you.'

Was this what that cunt Philus called prayer?

A bird scudded above jagged treetops, a raven, the emblem of the first degree of Mithras. A sign? An icy blast and his back shook as his body cried out for him to descend. His neck prickled and his fingers were frozen lumps.

Nothing but pine-tops stretching away in every direction, small peaks poking out of a huge patchwork of whiteness. Limbs aching, eyeballs raw, bitter air scorching his nostrils.

A distant bird cawed. By Mithras, he needed this emptiness. If he could stay like this, watching the world, like a rich man waiting for everything to come to him – that would be something. He relaxed and felt himself spiralling outwards, away from the black hole in his belly, its fire weakening. His head was swimming, reeling from javelins of piercing air. Not so fast; he gripped tight. Pinpricks of light penetrated as he squinted at the horizon.

What was that? Smoke. With a spurt of will, he shook himself and at once the pit of his stomach opened as the upper tree trunk rasped, cracking beneath him. Splinters lanced as he slithered groundward, leg searing with scalding heat. No strength left, he clung to the image of her dark hair, high cheeks and liquid-brown eyes ... slipping, branches crashing into his face. Thump!

He lifted his head from the mushy snow, his right side a pulsing jelly of rawness. Resurrecting on one leg, tugging on a tree branch, he hobbled towards his scabbard and sword. His belly torched and flared, but he would find that smoke-place; she would know him for who he was. His horse backed away, neighing and pulling against its tether. As soon as he touched its flank, the animal calmed.

The sky was clearing as chunks of white fell off widowy fir branches. A faint whiff of smoke. Hours later, he broke into a clearing of flimsy wooden shelters around a stone hut. A knot of people had their backs to him, singing in Latin. They stopped at the sound of his jangling harness.

A poor lot, threadbare, quivering, in thrall to a balding old man and a bulky woman in a smock. Next to them, an uneven table with bread on it.

'Where is she?' he bellowed. 'Tell me where the young woman is. You must have seen her.'

No one spoke. The old man flapped his arms.

Messor kneed his horse forward. The crowd tensed, shouts erupted. He lunged with his sword at a tall man who looked as if he might fight, flicking his blade, deliberately missing the man's neck. Uproar. Ragged men rushed at him. Wheeling his horse, he knocked a man over, slicing his sword at another, cutting him lightly.

Everyone scattered, except the blond woman, the old man, and a misshapen boy, hunched on the ground.

Wispy hairs fluttered across the old man's long face. 'What

do you want?'

Messor pointed his sword. 'Who are you?'

'I'm Vigilantius. We're celebrating the Lord's Day.'

'Fucking Hades, Christians. I can't get away from you.' There was something insolent about the way the old man spoke. 'She must have been here. A stranger.'

'We have not seen strangers.' The old man emphasised his words. 'Only neighbours and Christians.'

Messor's leg throbbed. The blond woman was too wasted to take his fancy.

'You, Vigilantius, help me off my horse.'

The woman backed into the stone hut. The boy stood up. He was older than he looked, with watery blue eyes and scabs on his neck and jaw. The lad advanced, smiling, one arm trailing.

'What's wrong with him?' Messor squinted at the old man. 'Tell him to get back. Any closer and I'll cut him.'

'No, he's innocent. He's Micchus, one of God's children.'

'What's going on here, what sort of place is this?'

'It's our community, Bonadeni.' The old man was half-smiling, half-wary. 'We welcome whoever comes.'

'See here,' Messor said, 'I haven't forgotten your woman. If she has a knife ... Tell her to come out.'

'Brigomalla, you'd better show yourself.'

The woman emerged from the hut, her jaw hard, elbows out. 'My man, Presbyter Vigilantius, welcomes you, as do I. Bid you enter our hearth and share what we have.'

Messor scowled. The bitch should shut the fuck up. She would soon shrivel if he slit her man's throat.

A wave of exhaustion washed his thoughts away. He bent through the doorway and sat on a rickety bench. It had been a long time since anyone had invited him into their home.

The woman brought congealed broth and two hunks of bark bread. Vigilantius was outside, talking to the lad, who was staring at the ground.

'The boy,' Messor asked, 'is he yours?'

'Micchus is not my child, but he's ours. We found him and brought him with us.'

'Old man, come here. Leave the boy outside.'

The greybeard hugged the crippled lad and settled him on a clean patch of snow.

'The woman, she's mine, my slave.'

The old man shuffled inside. 'What can I say? No slaves have been here.'

'Listen, Christian, you'd better tell me the truth or you'll regret it.'

It was taking too long. He leant on the wattled wall and began to draw his sword. A commotion outside, and the confused lad came hurtling in, tripping and sprawling onto the earth floor.

Messor whipped his blade out but hesitated as Vigilantius helped the boy up. Beneath the mud and grime, there were signs of scraggly facial hair. The lad stared at Messor with big round eyes, his mouth open. Brigomalla reached her arm around the boy's chest.

'Be quiet.'

'Why?' Micchus inclined his head. 'Why can't I talk to him?'

Brigomalla clenched her hand on lad's shoulder. He squawked, his jaw working back and forth, eyes wide open.

'Leave him,' Messor shouted, 'let him be.'

A smile crept over Micchus's face. 'They know where she went.'

'*Eia!*' Messor pounced, jabbing his sword towards

Vigilantius. 'You lied, I knew it. Where is she?'

He wanted to hug the lad, but the spatha twitched. The boy lifted his arm, slowly reaching up to the blade. The woman yelped; Vigilantius crouched over the small figure. All three were shouting, too much confusion. As if in a dream, Messor raised his sword, about to cut through the cloying feeling.

'She's gone.' Micchus's squeaky shout filled the room. 'Gone to the river.' The lad's shoulders dropped. 'She left us.'

Lowering the spatha, Messor wanted to put his hand out to the blue-eyed boy.

'It's true,' Vigilantius said, 'she left yesterday.'

'Why didn't you tell me?'

'She's going to the river barge.'

'Where, after that, what did she say?'

'She said she was going to Narbo, that's all we know.' The old man paused. 'We helped her.'

Messor bridled, but his bones were cold and his belly had been empty for too long. He sat down, the sword dangling from his hand. He shifted round to let the sun fall through the door-way onto his knees.

'I thought that Christians had big buildings and special things, rich clothes, and gold.'

'No, not all of us.' Vigilantius shifted to perch on a log. 'We minister where we're needed.'

'What about incense and saints, that's what you call them, isn't it? You worship dead people and bones.'

'We don't need them. Heaven and earth are one, even in this hut.'

'What's that mean? Why don't you have those things?'

'I don't know; it's not like that.' Vigilantius flapped his

hands. 'We don't need ranks of candles and people kissing bits of dust in a pot. We gather and bring ourselves to the altar.'

'Why, what happens?'

'My son, come and listen with us -'

'By Mithras, I am not your shitting son, who do you think you are?' He should flatten the old man, but Micchus was next to him. 'Your kind burns in Hades. You're a scabby fake, you lied about her.' He rose, just enough energy left to strike, but the boy broke in.

'No, please.'

Messor's arm hovered. He should hurt them, but it was not worth it. He was in a hovel in a pigs-arse dump, about to slash a pathetic old man, who wasn't even a proper Christian. It was grisly, pointless. He glanced into the lad's shining eyes and sheathed his sword. The old man put his arm around the cripple, and the woman smoothed her hand on Micchus's shoulder.

These people and their fucking forest; he had to get away.

CHAPTER TWENTY

Nehtan paused in the glooming wood, knees sogged in slush, legs like dead fish.

Dum-dum! The double-clunk of hooves.

Run, hands on knees. Get behind a tree, curl tight.

Another *dum-dum*, but it was a tree-sound: a tuft of snow crashing from a branch. Relief, then a wave of exhaustion as she steadied herself against the calloused trunk.

Two days of walking, lost in the forest, no food left. She had survived by foraging for chickweed, sorrel roots and safe fungi. Long, grinding days, thumping her chest and legs to stop the freezing, hoping that she was going in the right direction. She would not give in.

Squeezing out a corner of her soaked cloak, she sat on a fallen pine trunk: patches of a chant came to her:

> *Ruler of the sky,*
> *you make the tautened limbs unlock,*
> *you soothe the mind that is overwrought,*
> *and drive anxiety away.*
> *Now that the day has run its course,*
> *we sing the hymn you claim of us*
> *and pray for pardon of our wickedness.*

An image: Vitalis in the brambles. She would be forgiven. That man would fail. Forcing herself up, press on while there was daylight.

Hours later, she emerged onto an open patch of land. Below flowed a river, blurred, vast. It had to be the right one.

Huts were squashed at the edge of the grey torrent. And there, down by a smudge of land sticking out into the water, labourers were heaving crates onto a thick-sided barge.

She scrabbled downhill and reached a ginger-haired man wearing a thick sheepskin. He was giving orders.

She couldn't wait. 'Can I get passage downriver?'

'Girl' - the ginger-haired man glared - 'this is a Rhodanus barge, and we don't take just anyone.'

A farming couple sat on the barge, nervous and humble. Four bedraggled sheep stared blankly, tethered amidst casks and crates.

Looking back to the forest, then to the man's eyes. She was too tired. 'I can pay, I've got Argentei.'

The coins were small but the man's eyes lit up. 'Well, that's another matter.' He brushed his fringe, quick eyes darting back to the barge. 'I won't mind how you came by these. Where've you come from?'

'They're mine, I tell you.' Glancing back, still no rider. 'I'm God-fearing; my master gave them to me.'

'A likely story.' The man felt in his sheepskin pocket and snorted at a tall youth on the barge. 'No slacking, move those ewes up.' He turned back. 'Where were we? You want to journey on my barge? Maybe. Three Argentei to take you all the way to the coast at Arelate.'

'What! That's too much.'

'Take it or leave it. Stay here if you like. You'll get two meals a day while you're with me, and from what I see, that'll do you the power of good. I have no time to argue. Yes or no?'

Three silver pieces dropped into his open palm.

* * *

Thank God, the barge master was eager to get to a larger settlement downstream. The boat cast off in the late afternoon light. Raggedy foliage and drooping trees hung over the banks; the river surface twinkled. The oarsmen worked hard to keep the barge parallel to the land, avoiding mudbanks and the fast centre of the river. Nehtan tightened her heavy cape and moved to the middle of the barge, away from the oarsmen at either end. She sank into a blank state but was wrenched out of it by a convulsion in her stomach. She staggered to the broad deck-rail.

The ginger-haired barge master shouted, 'Not on the goods!'

He started towards her. She fled down the side of the boat, but the bargee plodded back to his tiller. Nehtan stumbled to the other side, her stomach churning, but nothing came up. She avoided contact with the oarsmen and the farmer's wife, who glared suspiciously. Later, the cold, watery evening meal calmed her stomach.

In the long days that followed, it was easiest if she stared at the passing land, examining irregular shapes for signs of human activity, alert to any movement on the barge. The insistent sloshing of water induced a dull reverie. The snow had melted, the air was warmer. Cascading hills and forest gave way to undulating fields and orchards, with the occasional small settlement crouched on the riverbank.

On the second day, an oarsman offered her a slice of cheese to go with the claggy gruel of rye and beans. She hesitated, but accepted when she looked into his kind eyes.

'Thanks, it looks good.' She bit into hard sheep cheese.

'You mustn't mind us,' the oarsman said. 'We're simple bargemen, cussing and poling – up and down, down and up.' The man's hands were thick with calluses.

'Where's your home?' she asked.

'I have one of sorts, but it's not for the likes of me. My Trulla is at Arelate, with the little ones. I'll be seeing her soon, but when I's at land, it's all as I can do to bear the stillness for a few days, a week at the most. Then my soul's itching to be back on the water, little uns or no. I was born at sea.'

'You don't belong anywhere?'

'But I do. I'm here, on this boat, or any other. My life has been at sea, the *Mare Nostrum*. No one gets rich if he is honest, but I can't complain; water's in my blood. I don't want no plough on my back.' The man stretched his arms wide, then dropped his elbows with a crick. 'My sailing days are gone. This riverboat is work enough, for little pay, but the big ships are laid up. The open sea is not safe like it was.'

The boatman needed little encouragement to talk about his life, the work on the barge and how much easier it was on the lower stretches of the river. She listened to his simple words.

Was this what her life would be like? Always moving, Messor in the shadows, herself cursed. And what of her family – nymayr and atir? And Fromus? The south. It had to be.

When she got to Narbo, pray God, Fromus would find her. But, he would – and should - do his duty and continue with the delegation to the Emperor. His people depended on him. The world could not be built on a short burst of comfort and pleasure, even if they had shown restraint. And he was a Master, a high-up. Impossible.

The only way was to trust the Lord. The vine of the tree, there before the foundation of the world. For each person there was a destination on this earth, and for her, at this time, it was Narbo.

* * *

More than a week later, the barge reached the inland town of Tarusco in the far south of Gaul, some miles short of the great Roman sea. The land was warm, even in this winter season, and spiked with red and yellow plants. The barge was continuing south to Arelate, but she had to leave: the road to Narbo led west from Tarusco. The friendly oarsman had offered a sleeping space in his home at Arelate, but she had said no. The Lord knew, the likelihood of seeing Fromus was small: it was a thin straw but it was the only one she had.

Walking through the streets, Tarusco was quiet. A family trudged by, in thin, dirty cloaks. The father carried a child in one arm while lugging a sack with the other. There were great puddles where the cobblestones were missing. A violent shout started from the far end of a side street, then ended abruptly.

On a corner, a woman picked at Nehtan's sleeve. 'Did you hear? The Via Domitia towards Massilia is plagued – everyone killed, churches burnt. They say it was Vandals, though Felix says it were Goths come over from Italy. Them useless soldiers have gone to Arelate, but I can't go until I find my old man. Have you seen him, with a red scarf, a big scarf?' The woman was peering frantically down the street and into smashed windows.

'I don't think so ... Is the other way safe, going west to Narbo?'

'I don't know. You'd best go to Arelate, girl; you'll need protection.' The woman tightened a ragged shawl under her chin. 'Mercy, spare me something. I haven't eaten for days.'

'I'm sorry, I haven't anything.'

'The likes of you won't last out here.' The woman muttered something, maybe a curse. She wandered back down the street, shouting, 'Faunus!'

Nehtan walked past red-tiled buildings, shuttered or

ransacked. Tarusco looked like it was slowly sinking back into the earth. She had to find people fleeing west to Narbo – as long as they included women.

After leaving the town, she hid on the edge of a wood above the road. She tagged along behind one band, but a woman with a sackcloth cloak snapped at her: she should find her own family and leave them alone. Nehtan fled back to the withered brambles in the bare wood. It looked like where they had been attacked outside Bononia. Had that been because of her – was evil being drawn to her? Yet, she was a believer. The deaths of Vitalis and the master were not her fault - though she had left their corpses for the animals. Is that why she had been punished at the Black Gate?

Vitalis, she prayed, forgive me. Have you already deserved to be in the presence of the Lord? Christ, king on the high tree, wash me with your flowing waters. Let me find Fromus.

How to find Paulinus and Lady Clara's house in Narbo? She would spin a tale of working for the lady and being sent to wait on her daughter while the master and mistress travelled to Italy.

Agnus Dei, what was Paulinus's family name? She must know it, but her mind was blank.

Small groups of rough-looking men passed below on the Via Domitia. Impossible to tell if they were travellers or robbers. In the late afternoon, she spied a string of carts pulled by oxen going west, led by two men on horseback. The front cart had a crude cross, tied to the side-rails. Women and children sat slumped inside the wagons; cows and men plodded behind.

She ran to the front wagon. 'Take me with you, I beg you. By Saint Agnes, I'm a good Christian. I have to get to Narbo.'

'Go home, girl,' growled the carter, grimacing as he

whipped the oxen. 'Where have you been? Dragged through the bushes? Go back to your village.'

'But it's on your way.' Limbs aching, she stumbled to keep up with the cart. 'Have mercy, take me.'

'Too bad, girl, we're full, we can't take every waif and stray. Even the great church of Saint Paulus Sergius has its limits.'

'I'm small; I won't take any space.' Her knees were giving out. 'My family worship at the church of Saint Paulus. You've got to let me on.'

'Look, girl, there's no room, try someone else.'

A woman called from the back of the cart. 'Apollinaris, be merciful. What does it matter if she's in a mess? She can fit in the cart behind. If she's from Saint Paulus, maybe he'll save us from attack, let her on.'

'Please, I beg you, in the name of blessed Saint Paulus.' Nehtan crossed herself. She took off the amulet around her neck and held it aloft. 'My Chi-Rho was blessed in his church. You can have it if you take me.'

She forced herself to smile at the hard man with the whip. The carter put out his hand and called to the driver behind.

Nehtan clambered up the back of the following wagon and huddled down with bleary women and children. A baby with sunken eyes curled on its mother's lap. The women were grim-faced, and one was wearing a blue mantle, dirty and threadbare. In snatched conversation, she learned that they had fled their village after a band of army deserters had raided them. The village men were armed only with farm tools and knives. They had been in a fight on the previous day when a crowd had tried to seize their cattle, and two husbands had been wounded. They were going to Narbo because their master lived on a large estate near the city and had promised to give refuge to anyone who worked on his lands. He had a troop of private guards.

Nehtan slouched against the wooden side, fighting the dizziness that sent her head reeling, but her fingers stayed clenched tight.

Days passed, maybe a week, in a haze of bone-jangling lurches and silent fights to stop the women on either side poaching her space. Once she had established her spot, they paid no attention to her. She sank into the stench of long unwashed clothes and bodies. Then, one late, grey afternoon, shouting at the front made her sit up with a jolt. The column had stopped. Her cart was at the back, out of sight of what was happening. The noise died down and a torpid sleep blanketed them all, even the babies.

For a long time, nothing happened. Then, straightening her stiff limbs, she climbed out and picked her way to the men at the front. They told her that armed guards at the bridge ahead wanted to charge a fortune to let anyone cross the river. The villagers did not know what to do.

The men at the bridge had spears and a few swords, holding them like soldiers. She dragged herself back to the wagon. Some of the women had roused themselves, staring listlessly up at the evening sky, reverting to an ancient mute patience – but she had to keep going.

The money, they would want it. Heavenly King, she prayed, be with me. Blessed martyrs, give me strength.

Clutching a silver coin, she walked to the bridge and approached a leathery man holding a long staff with a crude spear-point. The man regarded her, clenching his jaws.

'Sir, let me through.' She held the clipped Argenteus between thumb and fingertip. 'By Saint Agnes, it's all I have. Let me pass; my family are on the other side.'

The man's eyes narrowed. He bared his yellow teeth,

coughed, and held out his hand. She threw the silver piece, which he caught and pocketed. The men behind him stood giant-still, staring as she scurried by. Murmurs, then shouts erupted behind her, and the answering voice of the man with the spear-point. She ran and did not look back.

* * *

In the distance, a shimmering expanse. The sea. She hurried down the road, but it doubled back inland. She hadn't the energy to clamber across bleached fields to get to the seashore. Hobbling on, past shattered fences; the grapes on the vines were black and wizened: nothing had been harvested. As night fell, she slipped into a hillside vineyard, sleeping in snatches as the cold wracked her body.

Dawn and the first glimmers of warmth. It was tempting to stay put, but she had to get to Narbo. She reached for a moulding grape. It was bitter and her stomach churned when she tried to swallow. Later, the road slipped down to the sea edge, but, instead of lapping water, it was lined with grim-frosted saltpans – sluggish ripples and bone-white roundstones. The road wound up into shallow hills, hemmed by wizened trees with spindly branches.

That evening she found a village. Too tired even to thank, she gave a precious silver coin to pay for board and lodging for a few nights. In the daytime, she washed and sat outside restlessly, letting the sun bake into her, ready to flee at the sight of a horseman. At night, tucked down inside the hut, sleep came late, long after the second watch was called. She found herself being hurled around inside a huge barrel of water and blood. When the churning stopped, there was a pocket of air, but everything rolled and crimson-green slime sloshed into her mouth. She kicked and kicked, finally breaking through, and tumbled from the sky towards the battlements of the Black Gate, where raised spear-tips thrust up at her.

She awoke, breathing heavily. It was better to sit up, snatching shallow gasps of sleep. After two nights and four meals, she pushed herself up at dawn and set off, trekking west.

Four days later, in the late afternoon, a distant smudge greyed the horizon, a line of high walls: Narbo. When she could make out the stone of the ramparts, everything in her drained, but she pressed on. At the closed gateway, a small crowd was shouting, begging to be let in. A haggard woman, hunched in a black cloak, spoke to Nehtan as if she were not there. The Briton Gerontius was coming with Vandals.

The men outside the gates were becoming frantic. A fight broke out between two groups. Nehtan squeezed forwards through the hard bodies of women at the side. A loud rattle of iron on stone, and armed riders shot out of the city gate. The crowd surged towards the opening. Nehtan pushed with all her might behind a young woman with brown hair who was clutching a baby. With a huge heave, the two of them fought their way in, the last to break through before the tall gates slammed shut.

Nehtan and the young mother scurried away from the towering walls and angry guards. Walking side-by-side, they glanced at each other, not speaking.

The shadowy streets were lined with lanky, whitewashed houses. It felt as if invisible faces peering down from their square-stoned windows. Brass-studded doors glared, and sturdy pillars jutted into the narrow street.

They passed clumps of refugees sitting slumped on cobbled corners. Nehtan's companion stopped and wiped the brow of her baby. She opened her coarse cloak, and put the infant to her breast.

'She's so quiet.' The young mother shifted the babe in her arms. 'It's a miracle she doesn't bawl. I don't know where the others are.'

'Do you know this place?' Nehtan found herself whispering.

'I've been here on pig market days, but not often.' The woman relaxed her shoulders. 'Come on, Irena, be a good girl.' She fingered the baby's mouth. 'Our home is Enserune. My man Agrestis brought me here with the others. I don't know where they are.'

'Why isn't your man with you?'

'He had to go back to Enserune to be with Father and the pigs. We thought it would be safer here. Now, little one.' The woman pulled the cowl away from the baby's face. 'Be a good baby, Irena, come on.'

Nehtan leant over. 'What's the matter?'

'She won't feed.'

Nehtan saw a blue-tinged mouth. 'Is she breathing?'

The mother gasped. 'What do you mean? By all the martyrs!' She put her finger to the tiny nose. 'Nothing ... not a breath! *Edepol*, Lord help me!'

The woman looked skywards, her mouth open, almost dropping the child. Nehtan grabbed the infant, turned her over and squeezed its stomach with one hand, rubbing its back hard with the other.

Frantic movements, then a raspy wail from the baby: 'Waaieee.'

Crying, the mother hugged the child to her, showering her with kisses, wiping the small mouth. Nehtan staggered and sat down with her back to a house wall.

'There, there, yes now,' said the young mother. 'Don't you give me such a shock, no, never, what a thing. May the Blessed Ones be thanked.' She lifted her face to Nehtan. 'And you, where would we be if you hadn't – how did you know?'

'It was nothing, just something I remembered.'

'Thanks be to Saint Paulus, praise be his holy name! Now, Irena, you keep feeding and do what the nice lady says.' Large eyes looked up. 'Is your family here?'

'No.' Nehtan scratched her wrist. 'I need to find Artemia, the daughter of my mistress. She's with her grandmother, but I can't remember the family name.'

'The saints be with us. Do you know what quarter they're in, or what their trade is?'

'No, they're landowners. I don't know where they live. What can I do?'

'My man says, for a tough knot, take a blunt edge. We'll find the church, and if we pray, the Lord will grant that you be led to them.'

Nehtan took the young mother's hand. 'My name is Nehtan. I'm glad to have found you.'

'By the Great One above, it's I who am thanking you. It's a good omen. I'm Maria and this is Irena. My people are vinedressers. Where are you from?'

'Nowhere you would know. It's been a long journey.' Nehtan creased her hands over her face. 'Everything's gone wrong.' She paused. 'Can I hold your Irena?'

Clouds and high buildings smothered the light as Nehtan reached out for the baby. Maria hesitated, then handed her over. It was good to feel the gurgling young life. Maria beamed and took her baby back.

'If we can find the church of Saint Paulus,' Nehtan tickled Irena's chin, 'maybe we can get help?'

'Everyone knows Paulus Sergius.' Maria rocked Irena in her arms. 'Haven't you been there?'

'No, I'm not from here, I'm from Britannia.'

'I knew you weren't from these parts.' Maria laughed. 'That must be far away, but I won't ask more till we find rest.'

* * *

They found the church in the centre of the city. It was a plain stone rectangle, with an arched doorway approached through a wooden vestibule. In the paved square outside, Nehtan leant back on a wall, craving sleep even more than food. Maria made the sign of the cross three times as she knelt facing the church.

'Come, Nehtan, you should kneel.'

A crowd was gathering outside the church. Two tall cypresses, set back from a fountain, swayed in the chill evening breeze. Maria shrank from the noise, hiding her baby, but Nehtan pressed forward. A man's voice rose above the rest.

'I tell you, they're coming – devil-worshipping Vandals. Mighty Christ, help us. We should have a bishop like the one at Tolosa. Saint Paulus, we need you now.'

'Saint Paulus, Saint Paulus!' the crowd shouted.

'They sacked Elusa, burnt the basilica, killed everyone. Gerontius is leading the barbarians to ravage all Gaul.'

'May they burn in Hell!'

'Saint Paulus, save us, blessed be his bones.'

The noise grew as more people joined the throng. A man burst into the far end of the square, shouting, 'Flee! Vandals! The soldiers have abandoned us.'

'Mercy on us all!'

A huge man near Nehtan roared and threw his hands up

219

in the air. 'Damn the barbarian Vandals and Britons. Who betrayed us?'

'To the church, Saint Paulus, save us. His bones, blessed be his holy bones.'

The crowd surged towards the church doors, shoving aside an old deacon in a brown cassock. Nehtan found Maria backed against the external church wall, clutching Irena. They joined a confusion of bodies pressing into the wooden vestibule.

On the far side of the square, three soldiers on horseback appeared. Nehtan's heart raced with fear. One pushed nearer, a familiar shape. Messor! She ducked down and grabbed Maria's hand, pulling her along. She could not help glancing back.

'Nehtan!' His shout cut into her.

Her hand splayed against the cold stone wall. Maria clutched the baby, her eyes wide. Nehtan hauled herself up, still gripping Maria's hand. Messor was screaming her name and trying to force his horse through the mass of people, waving his sword.

Nehtan yanked an old man out of the way and ground her elbow into a woman's shoulder, forcing her aside. She gave a huge shove, dragging Maria behind. The vestibule heaved and swayed. Hooves crushed on feet, shrieks of pain and the yelling of the soldier. The block of people was wedged in the narrow entrance.

'She's mine,' bellowed Messor. 'Get out of my way.'

Stuck tight in the pressing mass of bodies, Nehtan felt shielded from him. Someone's hand shoved her head down, a child was trampled underfoot. Then, she was propelled through the doorway into the church, falling with the others in a heaving pack onto the stone floor. She rushed with Maria behind a pillar.

'Can he get in?' Nehtan panted, her hand on her bruised chest. 'Where can we go?'

Maria peered round the pillar. 'I can't see; he's outside.'

Frantic roars inside. Then, a massive rattle, the fierce ring of wood slamming down as a cross-bar locked the wooden door shut.

Maria put her hand to her mouth. 'Thank God.'

The young mother sat down and started rocking her baby, singing a lullaby. Nehtan sagged, heart thudding, alert to the doorway.

Three hefty farmers thumped their fists on the inside of the door. 'Be gone, you scum, you won't get in here.'

A presbyter was at the altar, leading prayers. Candles cast a weak yellow glow; pale light slanted from windows high up the narrow nave. Gradually, people quietened or joined the chanting.

'Let the world be silent,

let the luminous stars

not shine,

let the winds and the clashing rivers

die down ...'

Nehtan's breathing slowed. She made herself focus on the chanting. A calming sense of things being pieced together, a cloak spreading over all, fine incense threading its way.

Then, a bitter-sharp reek, not incense.

'Fire!'

'They're burning the door.'

'Almighty God, help us!'

'Vandals!'

Frantic men and women rushed to the altar. Maria grasped Nehtan's shoulder.

'Who is this man? Are you a spy?'

'No!' The shout burst from Nehtan. 'Maria, by Saint Agnes, you know me.'

'I don't. Who are you?'

Two women turned towards her, their faces contorted.

'I swear by my faith in the Holy Lamb, I am innocent.' Her voice quavered. Two men rushed by. 'Help! That man is after me; he's possessed.'

Maria's lips curled. 'Why?'

A huge crash came from the wooden portal. The farmers leapt aside, scrambling back towards the altar. Another jarring thump and the doors fell inwards.

Light and smoke flooded in. The silhouette of a man, kicking at a burning timber.

CHAPTER TWENTY-ONE

Somewhere in the south of wretched Gaul. Fromus groaned as he led his horse on foot, aching from weeks of hard riding and little sleep. He raised his hand to shield his eyes from the relentless downpour, half-hoping to see Philus in front turn off to find shelter. They had not spoken for hours, marooned on separate, moving islands of squelching mud.

The track was edged by limp, fruitless vines. In the distance, black dots bent low, scratching the earth's hide. Once, the sun had been high in the sky and it had been glorious. Now, the Roman lines were smeared and almost washed away, succumbing to the ancient force they had sought to control.

Philus's horse stopped and Papiteddo's nostrils brushed against Fromus's back, swathing him in warm horse air.

'You want to stop?' said Philus.

'No.'

'The horses must eat.'

'We go on.'

The heavy saddle creaked as Fromus heaved himself up. He shut his eyes; Papiteddo would follow Philus's horse. His whole body sagged. It was a bitter, rain-soaked twilight and the road was sinking into a frothing sea of mud. A biting wind rasped and cut into the back of his neck. At once, a giant bird seized him from behind, its claws squeezing his skull, burrowing deep into his brain. Arms flailing, he tried to scream but no noise came and his lungs filled with thick drops of foul liquid. Thorny black wings beat against the side of his head, scratching through skin, dragging him back...

'Sir, sir, wake up.'

Fromus grabbed the saddle pommel to stop himself falling. He quivered, shaking off the talons raking the inside of his mind. The hood-cloth over his head was threadbare, and his shoulders ached with strain. Virgil said that *bad fortune is conquered by endurance*; pray the Lord Christ that the poet was right. His chest heaved. He clung to the memory of her sparky, almond eyes peering calmly up at him as she brushed hair away from her face, down at the stream. What did this shattering journey matter, when that man's foul violation had turned Nehtan from budding delight into solitary anguish? If he found her, she would not be taken from him.

* * *

Days passed. A shout from Philus.

'Look sir!'

In the distance, a line cut across the landscape. The taut walls of Narbo, clearer now that the rain had stopped. Its citizens were streaming out.

The first person whom Fromus and Philus reached was a lone man lugging a small cart. Philus moved his cloak aside, letting the light catch the metal studs on his scabbard.

'What's happening in the city?'

'Masters, let me go. I've nothing you'll want.' The man looked up sideways as he flipped back a cover to reveal chipped pots, a metal disc, and a jumble of wooden timbers.

'That's not what we're about.' Philus pulled on the reins as his horse pawed the ground. 'How goes it in the city?'

The man's jaw tightened as he looked behind him. 'They say the soldiers are leaving quicker than an ebb tide.'

'What do you mean?'

'Vandals, they're coming with Gerontius. The city will fall. Have mercy on us all.'

'How did you get out?'

'Through the east gate, but it's shut now. Them as is left has to take their chances.'

The man trundled off, his back twisting as he wrenched the cart down the road.

'Now what?' Fromus shook his cloak. 'Where do we go?'

Philus peered at the city walls.

'Well, sir, if that man knows what's coming, everyone will.' The trooper lifted himself off his saddle. 'If they've any sense, all the gates will be closed.'

'I could try to get in on foot.'

'It is possible, sir, but if I may say, I doubt you can, and they'll suspect anyone who sounds like a stranger. You said she was going to the main church. Good people will be there. I'm thinking, our best chance will be to find your cousin, the Comes Gerontius, then we can enter the city with the first of his troops.'

Fromus was silent. He should storm into Narbo, but it wasn't possible. His head must rule his heart. Where was his Roman soul?

They rode on and rounded north above Narbo, high up on a hillside. The port looked like it was squatting on the edge of the shining Roman sea. Glancing inland, they spied a dark line snaking towards the city from the west. A troop of cavalry was in front – it had to be Gerontius's advance guard. Philus and Fromus rode down to the valley road. At the bottom, Philus reined in his horse.

'This will be ticklish, sir. They don't know us, and their blood will be up.'

'*Mecastor!* Have you done this sort of thing before? What

should we do?'

'One time, when I was in Armorica; we crossed our arms on our chests. I remember the officer said that it showed that we meant no harm. Leastways, it worked then.'

'You'd better be right.'

Horsemen were already racing towards them.

'Sir. ' Philus thumped his hands on his chest.

Fromus's hands shook as he clutched the upper part of his cloak. The riders were outlandish warriors with long blond hair and spears with streamers held high.

'Vandals,' murmured Philus.

The leading barbarian and his horse crashed down the side of Papiteddo, waving his sword around Fromus's head. Another rider yelled in a strange language, his lance stabbing the air above Philus. The warrior shouted again and pointed at Philus's sword.

Fromus urged, 'Let him have it!'

The Vandal draw Philus's sword and trotted away, wielding his trophy high in the air. A wild-eyed rider gestured at them both to dismount. Fromus turned, pretending not to understand. Instantly, the edge of the rider's sword was at his neck.

More hooves thundered towards them. Then, a familiar tongue, a command in Latin. 'You men, stand aside. Obey me.'

A Roman officer in a plumed helmet barged on horseback through the Vandals. The warriors' eyes flashed, but they lowered their weapons.

Fromus let his hands unclench. 'The Lord be thanked.'

'Who are you?' the Roman officer asked. 'What are you doing here?'

Fromus searched for signs of friendliness but saw none.

'I'm looking for Gerontius.'

'You mean the Comes.'

'Yes, I'm sorry, I meant no disrespect. The general is my cousin.'

'*Di Omnes!* Is he expecting you?'

'No, but I have something for him, an important letter.'

'Show me. We haven't much time.'

Fromus rummaged inside his cloak. 'Here.' The crumpled parchment looked dirty and worn. He moved his thumb to hide the broken seal.

'Give it to me.'

'I cannot do that; it is only for the eyes of the Comes. I am bound by oath.'

The officer glanced at the restive Vandals and snorted. 'You'll go back under escort.'

'I understand, but can you send us with Romans?'

'I can spare one man, but I warn you, any nonsense, no mercy. You understand?'

'Yes, I do.'

A short while later they reached the head of the foot-soldier column and pulled their horses off the road. A bustling melee of rough-cloaked and trousered Vandal warriors hurried past, chins pushed out. They carried axes or heavy wooden spears with metal tips. Several groups carried long ladders.

A yell erupted from the midst of the Vandals. A boy, a local peasant judging by his clothes, was shoved out, crumpling to the ground next to Fromus. The youth clutched a black gash in his shoulder, stiffened and his eyes became cold stones.

A detachment of Roman soldiers passed, carrying multi-coloured banners emblazoned with shining dragons, Imperial laurels and signs of the zodiac. Behind them came red-cloaked Roman cavalry.

The cavalryman guard called to a passing officer, 'This man says that he has a message for the Comes. What shall I do?'

'Take him to the back.'

'I must talk right now with the Comes,' Fromus bellowed. 'It's imperative; I'm his cousin.'

'Wait.' The shout came from the midst of passing cavalry. 'What's your name?'

The speaker was hidden behind a wedge of horses and plumed helmets.

'My name is Fromus, son of Lalbertus Aurelius Matugenus. I bring a message from the Comes's family.'

'Bring him,' ordered the weathered voice.

A trooper brought Fromus to ride alongside a bulky man, wrapped in a dusty-red cloak. He looked like an old bear which still had sharp claws. The officers around him frowned at Fromus, as the big man broke out of the line.

The voice was hectoring, but the green eyes were kindly. 'Who do you say you are?'

'I am Manius Aurelius Fromus,' Fromus leant forwards in his saddle, 'of the house of Lalbertus Aurelius Matugenus.'

'Tell me, where were you born and how are your siblings named?'

'I was born in Corinium in Britannia and I have two sisters, Barita and Sida.'

'Is there no other?'

'No,' Fromus paused, 'there was Titus, but he died.'

'My God, you *are* Fromus. It's been so long, I didn't recognise you, and I'm sorry to hear about Titus.'

The old man dismounted and gave him a sweaty hug. Fromus remembered nothing of the Comes except a vague unease when he was in their villa.

'By all that is sacred,' Gerontius's eyes danced, 'what are

you doing here? I last saw you when you were a child.'

Fromus produced the letter. It was all taking so long. The Comes fingered the broken seal but said nothing. An officer on horseback arrived, out of breath.

'Sir, I beg leave to ask for final instructions.'

'Wait, Dubitatus, this needs my attention.'

Gerontius plumped down on a hummock at the side of the road. Vandal warriors and Roman soldiers trudged past while the old man sat as still as stone, holding the scroll close. A soft light shimmered on the blackberries rotting on spindly bushes behind him. Fromus studied his own filthy, torn cloak and scratched his ear.

The big head rose. 'You have read this?'

'Yes ... sir. I opened it because, well, things were going wrong.'

'We'll stop here,' the Comes barked at an officer. 'Give the men what food we have.' He nodded at an orderly. 'Bring us something.'

Gerontius beckoned to Fromus, who followed him as they walked down into an olive grove. The Comes strode ahead, trampling through the undergrowth. He found a broken wall and sat on a large stone, indicating Fromus to perch on a shattered olive trunk.

'So, you are Fromus.' A long sigh escaped the balding head. 'It has been many years. Tell me, how is Lady Aula?'

'She is in good health. All is well at home, except, of course, the letter, my father—'

'So I gather.' The old man's large head moved closer. 'Fromus, this break between your father and myself was a matter of misunderstandings, no real cause. But enough of this; you must know what is happening here. Afterwards, we can talk. I have to collect my thoughts for what lies ahead. Tell me, did you come from the city?'

'No, we came from the far side. People were fleeing towards Arelate. We met a man who claimed that Constantinus's men were deserting. He said the east gate was shut.'

Gerontius massaged his forehead in small circles with his fingers. An orderly brought food, which they ate in silence. The old man looked tired and made no effort at the usual pleasantries.

At one point, Gerontius picked up a chunk of hard cheese and offered it, looking Fromus full in the face as their hands touched. Behind the gruffness, there was a suppressed eagerness. Fromus remembered the peasant boy killed by the Vandals, and hardened his jaw. Then he looked back at the old man whose help he needed.

The Comes was gazing up at the sky, perhaps calculating if it would rain; a disadvantage for the attackers. The officer who had been waiting by the roadside joined them. The two conferred in brisk tones. Minutes later, the officer was beaming and running back to the road.

'Well, Fromus, you are welcome; you'll join my staff.' Gerontius began walking back to the road. 'We are about to find out if Constantinus's troops will stand and fight.'

'Sir,' Fromus said, 'I have something to ask.'

'Well, what is it?'

'I beg you to allow me to join the leading men. I must get into the city as soon as possible.'

'*Hei!* Even more of a firebrand than your father.' The Comes remounted. 'I'm sure we can use a man like you, but I want you by my side.'

'I need to explain. I'm sorry, it's not what you think. It is because of a person, a woman in whom I am particularly interested. I hope she's in Narbo.'

'*Mehercle.*' The Comes squeezed his horse to rejoin the column. 'Young man, glad though I am to see you, your private affairs will have to wait.'

Fromus scrabbled onto Papiteddo and pressed his horse to ride alongside the Comes, who was answering queries from one of his officers.

'Sir' - Fromus ignored an officer's raised hand - 'I request most urgently to be allowed to ride with the advance cavalry. I swear I will not disappoint you. I have ridden for weeks to find her. I have to get into Narbo before it is too late.'

'Good Lord,' Gerontius chuckled, 'you are persistent. We have hardly met and you want to rush off to find a woman in the city I am about to attack.'

Fromus held the gaze of the green-eyed old man. 'It's what I'm here for, after giving you the letter.'

'*Di Immortales*. You are stubborn.' He paused. 'Perhaps this meeting is a sign from Heaven. This woman must be quite a lady. What is her name?'

'Nehtan.'

'Not Roman, I see.' Gerontius spoke to a young officer. 'Sabinus, take my cousin Aurelius Fromus to join Dubitatus. Mind you look after him with your life. You are to stay at the rear, and bring him back to me.'

'Thank you, thank you,' Fromus wanted to shake the old man's hand, but it didn't seem right.'

'Young man, you are to steer clear of any engagement, is that clear? No foolishness. Do I have your word on that?'

'Yes sir.'

* * *

Fromus and Philus followed the young officer, Sabinus.

They hurried down the road and found Dubitatus and his troop approaching the western walls of Narbo. Sabinus tried to explain who Fromus was, but Dubitatus was pushing his horse forwards, listening to a scout. The north gate was open.

At once, Dubitatus shouted orders. They joined a headlong rush of about forty cavalrymen. Fromus scanned the red-brick walls. The ramparts appeared deserted.

The troop careered around the city walls and came to a gateway with people pouring out, shrieking at the sight of the riders. Dubitatus led his cavalry straight into the thick of them, crushing people in his way. The troop stormed in behind him, swords raised, with Fromus and Philus at the back. Civilians scattered as Dubitatus's men cantered up a cobbled street.

Fromus slowed Papiteddo and shouted ahead. 'Philus, stop, stop!'

The trooper looked back, his face flushed with a kind of leer.

Fromus put up his hand. 'We are not going with them.'

'But, sir, we can't get separated from Sabinus.'

'I don't care about that. We're here for Nehtan.'

A man lay groaning on the street-side. 'You there,' Philus shouted. The man tried to crawl away. Philus pointed his sword at the bloodied head. 'Where's the big church?'

'I beg you.' The man held his face, his ear hanging by a thin red stem. 'The other side of the river.'

They raced through narrow streets, following a riverbank until they reached an imposing bridge. A stone basilica loomed. Fromus urged Papiteddo forward, overtaking Philus as they shot into a square.

On the other side of the square was the high wall of the church. The entrance was on fire, collapsed wood strewn on the ground, bodies lying nearby, people rushing away. A man was mounting a horse.

'Messor!' Philus shouted. 'You bastard!'

At that moment, exultant yelling erupted behind Fromus as four Roman cavalrymen roared into the square. On the far side, Messor squinted, wheeled his horse and rode away. The Roman riders had black raven insignia on their capes, marking them as from Dubitatus's troop. Their eyes lit as they drew their swords.

'Stop, you men!' Fromus struggled to hold his horse still. 'We're on the same side; we're with Dubitatus.'

The troopers swirled around them, bristling with intent. 'How do we know you're with us?'

'I am on the staff of Comes Gerontius. I'm his cousin. You will answer to him if you do not obey me. I am riding with your officer, Dubitatus.'

It was awkward to be in a civilian cape. Thank God for Philus in his cherry cloak.

One of the cavalrymen, a redhead, spoke. 'Decurion Dubitatus isn't here.'

'I am aware of that.' Fromus narrowed his eyes. 'What's your name, soldier?'

'Sorry sir, Charietto, sir. Can we go?'

'No. I want you to get rid of that fire and open the church door. Dismount, and use the bench over there.'

Puffing and grunting, the four cavalrymen, led by Philus, heaved up a long wooden bench. They ran at the burning wooden vestibule and smashed their improvised battering ram into the twin doors. Flaming timbers fell as the vestibule collapsed. Fromus peered through the smoke.

'Once again, lads,' Philus urged. A massive crunch and a gap opened up between the doors. Ragged cries came from inside.

'One more go.' The bench rammed into the buckled frame and the doors burst open. Dropping the bench, the soldiers unsheathed their swords.

'No, put your weapons away.' Fromus urged Papiteddo forwards. 'We're peaceful. I want to get the people out.'

Inside the smoking doorway, men were coughing, clutching heavy candleholders and wooden staves. Fromus cupped his hands: 'We're Romans. You can come out.'

'Soldiers!' yelled a throaty voice from inside. 'You expect us to trust you! You'll rob us, you're with the Vandals.'

Shouts came from behind the heavyset man who had spoken.

'We won't harm you, we're Christian.' Fromus dismounted and lifted his cloak. 'I'm not armed; I'm coming in.'

Shielding his eyes from the smoke, he leapt over the burning timbers, falling onto the hard stone floor inside the church. Rough hands dragged him to his feet.

'Where are you from? Who are you?"

Jostling men, snarling faces, and a heavy candlestick raised above his head.

'I'm from neither side.' He spoke loudly. 'I'm looking for my woman. Why would I come in unarmed if I wanted to harm you?'

They were shouting, prodding him. 'He wants our plate, the sacred vessels, don't trust him.'

Another voice rose above the rest. It was the big man who had first spoken. 'I'll check outside.'

A hooded man thrust his chin forwards and held a knife to Fromus's throat. The big man's voice came from the square. 'There's only a few soldiers, and four of them are getting back on their horses. They're going. It's all right.'

The man with the knife released his grip. The bench was pushed aside, and a torrent of tattered people poured out of the blackened church entrance. Wide-eyed children clung to their parents as they surged towards the sunlight.

'Nehtan?' Fromus stood back. 'Where are you?'

Wails shouting for Saint Paulus Sergius rose louder and louder. Fromus pushed against the stream of people. 'Nehtan, Nehtan?'

The crowd was thinning. An old couple hobbled forwards. Behind them, a pair of frail women with stooped shoulders.

Fromus squinted as wafts of smoke billowed around him. Was there no one else?

CHAPTER TWENTY-TWO

Long face and high shoulders. It was Fromus! Nehtan rushed to the doorway.

'Thank God!' Falling into him, burying her face in his cloak.

His arms wrapped around her. 'You're safe, that's all that matters.'

She looked up, her body tensing. 'Did you see him?'

'He's gone.' Fromus's eyes beamed. 'I have been such a fool. I didn't ... Are you all right?'

He had a sprouting beard. Reaching to feel it, she shrank back, coughing. 'Let's go outside.'

Outside, a small cloud of smoke blew from what was left of the burning vestibule.

Philus beamed, his arms out. 'Nehtan, the saints be praised. They've gone, but we've got to go before the Vandals get here.'

Knots of people, loud voices ringing in the paved square outside the basilica. Two pale-faced children clung to each other. A woman was howling above a bloodied figure.

A young mother was walking in a daze, holding a baby: Maria and Irena.

'Maria, Maria.' Nehtan's voice dropped. 'It's Fromus. See, he came.'

The woman's eyes darted from Nehtan to Fromus. Clutching her baby, she looked like a field mouse which was about to bolt back into its hole.

'Please, Maria,' Nehtan insisted. 'I want you to meet him.'

Tugging Fromus's cloak, she reached out to Maria. The

mother backed away, her baby crying, swathed in a dirty, grey shawl. An ill-kempt family pushed past, dark lines under the man's eyes.

Then, arms were encircling her from behind. It was Fromus. She froze. He whispered, but she did not hear, breaking free.

'Maria,' she called.

The mother clasped Fromus's hand, her baby's head lolling inside her cloak. 'Sir, forgive me, I shouldn't have doubted ... I didn't know.'

'What?' He turned to Nehtan. 'What's she talking about?'

'Don't worry about it.' She stroked the young mother's shoulder. 'We were all afraid. Look, Irena – she needs you.'

Maria shifted her shawl and gave her breast to Irena. Fromus's hand reached out to Nehtan, but she busied herself with shielding the baby from loose embers in the air.

It was settled quickly: they would leave the city, Maria riding with Philus. Fromus wanted to take them to safety with Gerontius, but first they must get away from the Vandals. People were rushing away, others pushing back into the church.

Minutes later, their horses picked their way down a street, around twisted bodies. Nearby, flames roared from a collapsing roof. Down a side-street, Nehtan glimpsed two Vandals plunging their swords into a man lying on the cobbles. A third Vandal straddled a woman, one hand pinning her down, the other tugging at her smock.

'No!' Nehtan's arms beat on flailed. 'Stop, no!'

The woman stared blankly, a limp arm pointing to a bundle of rags in the gutter, tiny legs sticking out.

They raced on. Philus's horse careered into a knot of people, nearly dislodging Maria. A hoof landed on someone who screamed as if his soul were leaving his body. Nehtan lost her grip, but Fromus whipped his arm back around her.

A pit of narrow streets erupted on all sides. Things smashed to the left and right, flickers of orange hatred. Men ran pell-mell, women dragging children, bodies mangled against red-blazing houses. Everywhere, rage-vomiting Vandals with flashing steel and the eyes of frenzied dogs; an overwhelming screech, winnowing belly and throat, splitting heads. This sound, this blue-metal sound, ripped nerves from bodies of jelly. A howl was an echoing in a vast space, grating and grinding the dust of the earth into pure fear.

A voice.

'Nehtan, you've got to hold on.'

She opened her eyes as they shot through a gateway, thumping into a cluster of shrieking city-folk and sword-slashing barbarians with green and black cloaks. A tall Vandal raised his axe. Philus pressed his horse forwards, slashing his sword down as the warrior fell backwards over a fallen body. Vandal spearmen raced towards them. Philus's horse smashed one down. A spear flew past Nehtan as she clung to Fromus. She reached for her amulet, but it was not there. '*Agnus Dei*, protect us.'

They cantered down a small road. Papiteddo's flank was steaming. The horse stumbled; Nehtan held Fromus tight. Then she recoiled as he shifted beneath his cloak.

'Don't worry', said Fromus.

He spoke again. 'Philus, where are we?'

'I don't know, sir. We might need to go back to get our bearings. I don't think as we're in the right way.'

'Please sir,' Maria spoke up. 'I know where we are; we're on my village road. Do you see that hilltop?' A low crag was dimly visible. 'Beyond it is our home, Enserune. I told you about it. Saint Paulus has guided us. Praise be to him.'

They agreed to go to Enserune, which had Maria laughing and telling her baby that they would soon see Dadda.

The horses plodded past smashed frames in grey-shrouded vineyards, overgrown fields and knots of pine trees. Clouds threatened to obscure the moonlight by the time they reached the hilltop.

'Agrestis,' Maria called, as they rode up a steep track. No one appeared. Near the top, the bushes rustled: men jumped out with spades and spears, grabbing the horses' bridles.

'Whoa! Who are you?'

'What are you doing here?'

'It's me!' Maria shouted. 'Agrestis, Agrestis, these are my friends. Let go, let me go... Agrestis!'

A tall man reached for Maria, exclaiming loudly. He took the baby and helped Maria off the horse. They were led into a lightly fortified village on the hilltop.

Maria's husband clasped Fromus and quickly let go. 'I don't know what we were doing. I'm that grateful to you, sirs. I was at my wit's end. The city's burning. I would have gone back at dawn.'

They sat around a small fire and ate crusty bread. Maria and Philus did most of the talking. Nehtan could not bring herself to speak, but Agrestis kept thanking until she burst out.

'It was horrible, the women, those soldiers. I can't stop thinking about it.'

No one spoke for a minute, and most of the villagers drifted away. Freezing night air seeped into their backs as they faced the flickering fire.

'We see you're tired, sir,' said Agrestis.

'And you've found your woman, you must be happy,' an

old woman added. 'I remember what it's like.' She called to a grizzled man, 'Duccius, they can have the Javolenus hut, can't they?'

Philus was taken to another hut while the old woman, carrying straw-filled sacks, led Nehtan and Fromus to a circular hut with a low entrance.

'They've gone. If this is your ember night, let it be blessed. You will have burdens, I'll warrant. Let them fly with the night.'

The old woman shuffled off. Nehtan's chest heaved. By Saint Agnes, she could not be stuck in that small space with a man, even Fromus.

'Let's get in,' said Fromus, and all the old weight came back on her.

They crawled inside. The entrance was littered with wood-rot and animal droppings. A stick snapped: Nehtan jerked up, her head dislodging twigs and earth. She was being crushed under a mass of earth; her stomach churned.

Behind her, Fromus was carrying straw-sacks and a spare cloak. 'The sleeping area's in the centre.'

Scurrying, walls pressing in. She stopped in the dark.

'What is it?' Fromus asked.

'Nothing.'

Jutting sticks flapped against the outside wattle. She heard Fromus fall, smashing clay pots. 'It's like the Alan camp.'

'No, it's not. I hate it, I hate it. I've got to get out of here.'

'Nehtan, I'll protect you. It's just us.'

'I can't be stuck in here, with... with someone.' She pushed past him in the dark, going back to the lattice door.

'No, wait.' He was too close, but his voice was calm. 'Let me go, not you. I'll be outside, I won't come in.'

'Holy Lord, I can't breathe.' Holding her hand to her mouth, she sank down. 'If you don't go ...'

Vomit burned in her throat.

'I'm going,' he whispered, squeezing past her.

The door fell back with a broken-stick smash. Alone, leaning forwards, the vomit subsiding, she gulped blasts of cold air that put bone back in her head, her flesh tingling.

Rustling wind, a wide-awake quiver, her toes ice solid. The old woman said hides and rags were in the middle. Nehtan slipped under them, hovering on the edge of sleep, kept awake by the serrated warmth of thawing toes and fingers.

Mice scratched at the edge of the shelter. Another sound, a faint flapping outside. Then again.

'Fromus, is that you?'

'Yes.' A long pause. 'I'm here.'

'Are you cold?'

'Don't worry, I'm fine.' Slurred voice.

'You're freezing. Come into the hut.'

'Are you sure?'

'Yes, I'm ... I'm all right.'

The hut shook as a weight fell against the outside. The flimsy door opened and Fromus collapsed onto the hard earth.

With an immense effort to throw off the sacking and crawl into the cold, she reached him in the blackness. 'May the saints forgive me.'

'I'll be ... soon.'

He slumped against her. She found his face; his cheeks were matted with frozen droplets.

'Can you hear me?'

No answer; she dragged him to the bedding, pushing him beneath the sacking. His forehead felt cold; no, it was hot ... she could not tell. Was he breathing?

'Fromus?' No response. 'Help!' she shouted, but it was a croak.

'*Eia.*' His voice was fluttering.

Curling round him, kneading his hands. He was shaking and his fingers felt like graveyard earth; they could go black by morning and have to be cut off. She had seen it in the army camps.

She tried to pull his hands to her armpits, but the angle was awkward. She grabbed his hands and pulled them down, under the bedding. Pressing his fingers to her warmest part, between her legs, she shuddered as his cold penetrated like an ice flow. She scissored her thighs back and forth, like a blacksmith's twisted bellows, pumping heat back into him, while her hands massaged the raw flesh of his back.

'Come on, come on, stay awake. You've got to make it.'

His feet? Pray God his fancy boots were enough.

'*Heu.*' His breath on her face.

'What is it?'

Rubbing his back, pressing his hands between her thighs.

'I didn't, I didn't think' - he wheezed – 'that we'd ever do this.'

Starting to laugh, then her body convulsed into sobs. A sudden release, everything let go. Harsh years poured out in spasms, sloughing off layers of bitterness and the exhaustion of always holding herself together.

Stubble grazed her cheeks. Fromus wrenched his hands from her thighs and brought them up towards her face. She cupped his fingers in her hands and held the rigid tips in her mouth. He shook as they thawed together, awkward still frozen, no words, no names, a spring breeze wafting through a hillside copse, and there was all the time in the new-made world.

CHAPTER TWENTY-THREE

Twilight. Messor dropped back into the half-collapsed hut at the foot of the hill, huddling next to his horse. The days were warm, but nights were bitter when the wind blew. Nothing solid in this sickly southern land. Feeble trees and the soil little better than sand. The horse was wasted, the whites of its eyes too big. It would have to make do with whatever stubby grass it could find beneath the cypresses.

Nicking the officer's horse was like taking a knife to your leg. He had to do it because his own wretched horse was lame, but Novateli would never forgive him. Messor wanted to shout to the sky: he was a fool of a deserter, skulking here until she came down from that goat's arse village. Frigging Cautopates, they had better not stay long or he would have to haul up and wade into a stench of cowing families.

What was he doing? Easy cavalry life thrown away for a slut of a girl, following her like a dog on heat. They had barely spoken, though he had had her in that city dump. It should have been a sweeping annihilation of pain and the past, out-blasting head and belly. Instead, the clamping taste of ash, her whimpering, and a lingering sense of failure. He couldn't face the soldiers after that; he had to leave before they saw that he had lost his certainty. Besides, there wasn't any point in going on with them: they were doomed. It was his life, and something was shifting.

That fucking coward, Statarius; he should have killed him – and perhaps her too. Could have been the best part, watching as she throttled purple, even kissing her, sucking out the last breath as she went over the edge.

His body shook.

It hit him like a cudgel. He could not kill her, did not want to. Needed her soft, open eyes, her gentle hand. His life was useless. He was not the things he had made himself do. How to find a way beyond the humiliation burnt into every memory? Nehtan! She - she knew without words how to help him. Too late, maybe, after what he had done. Even so, he must make her heal him.

He looked up through the smashed hut-roof. Clouds were scampering across the night sky, branches moaning in the wind. Midnight lit up with no light.

What else was there? What did they want, those snivelling families, those whimperers on street corners? Why did they like squashing together?

The army used to make sense: riding high above everyone else, squeezing drops of mastery into the cups of real men. Now it was falling apart: no soldiers and no coin. The rich would not pay; nothing touched them, not even this barbarian mess. Their guts should be hooked out.

Euhoe! Boil them all.

Nehtan! Mithras was nothing, another fake. Only her.

If he didn't find her, what then? Run off to the woods, find a patch of sod-scrapers, lord it over their little lives? But civilians were useless, good only to cut or crush. He would have to join some rotting band of *Bacaudae* in Armorica.

Slash and move on, slash and move on. No end to it – unless she was with him, like in Londinium.

Why hadn't Da shared? They could have been together, like after the temple of Mithras had been torn down by fucking Christians. Da had yelled in the street, cursing their priests and the cock-sucking Emperor Honorius. Those crawling shopkeepers had run, fearing Da's plague words.

Da hadn't pretended, at least not then. *Merda*, what a prick-head, after his big words, for Da to run away to the other side of the city. As if anyone would take Da seriously; as if they would know him more than a spiked rat, spewing its life out in the mud.

Da should have brought him into the temple, shared the feasts, and taught him the special curses. But Da had not let Messor in, said he was too young – didn't want to pay the fees.

The world was one big cunt, with her legs clamped shut.

* * *

Dawn, a burning knot above the eyes, time to move nearer. Messor took cover in a clump of holly oaks, spying up the track, shivering as sunlight stabbed through pinched green leaves. It was all or nothing. That bony whore, Vibia Pacata. Couldn't do it with her, even when she squealed and fought back. Left her and the brat alive. Messor's body would not obey him. Nehtan, her cool-hard eyes, her warmth around him.

That strange man in the forest and the crippled lad who told about the girl. Could have worked with the lad. Could have looked out for each other, taught him things. Something of the pale blue sky in the boy's eyes.

Noise from the track. Two men passed with creased faces, carrying a hoe and a wooden plough. Sod-scrapers, what a life! He could follow; clobber one and make the other say what was going on - but the energy was gone.

Must hobble his horse. Shadows shortened, not a breath of wind.

Voices and laughter. *Merda*. More peasants. Couldn't they be quiet? Must be clodhopper market day.

A silvery laugh. Her! Walking down the track with the pisspot holding her hand. The fool didn't need any bells. Slice his prick, he had no right – and that motherfucker Philus, beaming beside them, looking like he had been double paid.

They were saying good bye at the junction, a village idiot leaping up and down, hugging that prancing Fromus. Made you want to puke.

Messor drew his blade, felt the edge. He would get rid of them and have her to himself. But not like last time.

What was that? Horses neighing, loud voices in dog-Latin: Roman cavalry with their crimson cloaks. Saturn! They must have come from Narbo. Within a minute, half a troop were milling around the maggot. A loud voice took over: they were taking him back to the Comes.

Messor's leg throbbed, his shoulders ached. The bastards were mucking everything up. Nothing for it; he would have to follow.

CHAPTER TWENTY-FOUR

'No.' Fromus glared at the men round the table. 'It's not like before. I'm not going with you.'

'What do you mean?' Crispus pursed his eyebrows and looked across to Gerontius. 'Someone has to talk sense into this young man.'

They were in a frayed military tent outside Narbo. It had been too dangerous for the delegation from Britannia to travel east to Italy once they reached the coast, so they had gone west to Narbo, hoping to find a ship. Instead the delegation had found Gerontius, a pillaged city and Fromus.

The Comes sat in the only chair, his arms folded, his green eyes settling on Fromus. 'Are you certain?'

'I am going back to Britannia, with Nehtan. I've done as Father asked.'

'How can you say that?' Crispus slapped the table. 'We have our duty to the cities of Britannia. You've forgotten your place and who you are – and who she is.' He turned to the heavy figure in the chair. 'Most honourable Gerontius, I know that the world is not what it was, but we must stick together. You come from Britannia, and this young man's behaviour ... Each of us has a responsibility to the Emperor.'

'As you say.' Gerontius lifted his large head. 'But Honorius has his own problems. You and Ursacius can still go to Ravenna. You don't need Fromus to take your petition.'

Ursacius shifted towards Gerontius. 'And what counsel, Comes, do you have for Fromus, if I may ask?'

Fromus was bursting to speak, but Gerontius's composure was catching.

'Fromus has briefed me on the situation in Britannia.'
Gerontius smiled and put his hands on his knees. 'You
know that I wrote to his father, Matugenus. Of course, I
am concerned about Britannia, but I have much to do here.
Winter is coming, and I need to tell my cousin what I intend.'

'Are you able to let *us* know?' Ursacius clasped his hands.

'You will hear in due course.' An orderly raised the greasy
tent flap. Gerontius nodded. 'Crispus, I must go. The Vandal
host has crossed to Hispania, and I must return to Tarraco
for the winter. I can put a ship at your disposal to take you
to Italy. As for Fromus, he will take a letter from me back to
Britannia.'

'That is most interesting,' Ursacius pushed forward. 'I also
intend to return. The two of us can travel together.'

'That is not possible ... it's ridiculous!' Crispus was
panting. 'What are you saying, Ursacius, is everyone going
mad?'

'It seems that this young man has better ideas.' Ursacius
tried to stand taller, but a piece of his cloak was stuck under
his boot and he had to step back. 'It's too dangerous. For
heaven's sake, barbarians are everywhere.'

'That's not why I am going back.' Fromus held Ursacius's
eyes as he spoke. 'In any case, I will not travel with you.'

'Why do you say that?' Ursacius's hand smoothed his
short beard. 'I applaud your good sense in having done with
this mission, but I don't understand your reluctance to
journey, well, together. My views are evidently not important.'

'*Honestiores,*' Gerontius's throaty voice broke in. 'I must
ask you to continue your discussions elsewhere. I am sorry,
but my men are waiting for their orders. Fromus, I can give
you an escort for half a day, no more than that. I leave it to you
to decide who travels with you.'

Old man Gerontius had said nothing of taking a letter back to Father when they met on the previous day. It did not matter; Fromus would do this service for him, and it fitted with his plans.

Speeding out of the tent, ignoring calls from Crispus and Ursacius, he was bursting to tell Nehtan. They had been at Gerontius's camp for a week, but he had barely noticed the military preparations. Only she mattered, though she had remained listless.

A stench of smoke lingered in the air. Soldiers were standing around in small groups, restless and less formidable, now that their Vandal allies had gone south to Hispania.

Philus was sitting on a log, not far from Fromus's tent. His fingers were playing along the edge of the sword that Fromus had given him.

'It's all as I could do, sir' - the trooper stood up - 'she won't eat or come out of the tent.'

'Very well.' At least Philus was dependable. 'I have news for you both. Nehtan and I are leaving for Britannia. I must say, I am very grateful for your help. I could not have done it without you, but, I'm sorry to say it, you should return to the delegation.'

'If it pleases you, sir, I too am grateful, but I'm not sure about the delegation. I'd like to stay with you; I'll be useful.'

'I cannot think of a better man, but it's not up to me. You'll have to square it with Decurion Novateli.'

'I know what he'll say. I beg you, sir, you'll need me.'

Fromus glanced over the top of the tent behind the cavalryman. No one in sight. 'What about your friend, Bellator?'

'I can't live by him. He'll understand: these things happen.'

Crispus and Novateli would damn him forever if he took

one of their men. 'Look, Philus, I am not going to encourage you, but if you happen to join me when I leave, then that is your choice.'

'That's all I need, sir.'

Fromus went to pack his things. It hadn't taken much, but he was now part of the reason why order was breaking down.

Familiar faces were coming towards him.

'*Ave*, friend Fromus.' Paulinus spoke with a broad smile. 'I'm glad we've found you. Our beloved Artemia is with us, and we're going to Tolosa. It's not too far and it's been kept safe by its splendid bishop.'

Clara grasped her husband's arm. 'Praise the Christ, we found our daughter in good health, and the Comes said that Tolosa's walls are strong and their baths are still running.'

'I'm glad for you.' Fromus scratched his chin. 'I also am about to leave, but not with the embassy. I am going back to Britannia, with a message from the Comes.'

'My, that is unexpected.' Paulinus glanced at his wife. 'But one has to be flexible in these troubled times. Your journey will be difficult, but, as the poet says, *fortune goes with he who dares*.'

'Paulinus dear' - Clara squeezed her husband's arm – 'there is something we can do. Fromus, I don't know if she mentioned it, but I made an offer to Nehtan. Events overtook us: that unfortunate business at the Black Gate. Nevertheless, I'm prepared to take her with me, if she understands her place.'

'That's not necessary.' He could not help a high-cheeked, glassy smile. 'She's coming with me.'

'Young man' - grey eyes flashed – 'no doubt you have the right, but it would be better for her if she's placed in a respectable household.'

'You misunderstand. She's not my concubine. We're travelling together; it's her choice.'

'Her choice! Whatever can you mean? She's plebeian, probably a slave -'

'That's not ... We'll find another way, a Christian community that doesn't care about such things. She could stay there.' Thank the Lord that he did not have to travel with Clara.

'You can't mean to live in such a place - with her!'

'My dear,' Paulinus intervened. 'There's no point in getting angry; it's his life.'

'You don't understand,' Clara shouted. 'Neither of you do. It's impossible, the difference... you've no idea. Community, you say? Scratch a Christian and you'll find they are just like everyone else.'

'We'll see. I didn't say I was going to live there. I have my own plans.' He frowned; he hadn't thought ahead beyond leaving for Britannia with Nehtan.

Clara shrugged Paulinus off and advanced a step. 'You couldn't live without your family's wealth and power. When push comes to shove, you'll get no mercy. You'll see: each day is a battle, scrabbling to find food, stealing from neighbours, no thick walls between you and them.'

'My dear, we can't part like this,' Paulinus started, but Clara was walking away. 'I must apologise on behalf of my wife. It is inexcusable, but she's worked up; she was thinking of you.'

'Don't worry, I understand. Besides, she's saying the truth - the bad part of it.' Deep lines shadowed Paulinus's eyes. Fromus stepped closer: he must tell someone. 'You know, Nehtan means a lot to me.'

'So I see.'

'You're the first person I've said that to.'

'What have you told her?' Paulinus shuffled his feet. 'What have you promised?'

'Nothing, I'm not sure - maybe, in a way, everything.' But he couldn't live in a hovel, and she couldn't come to Corinium, not even as his concubine. 'What about you, Paulinus? After all, you married far below your rank.'

'True enough, though the family came round to it, or at least Mother did. Funny: Clara lives like I used to, and I, well, sometimes I think that I'm more like her, using my wits, doing what I can, to get by.' Paulinus brushed back wisps of thinning hair. 'But I do miss the old days, reading letters quietly on our terrace, sipping fresh wine, our men toiling peacefully amongst the vines, the world waiting at our fingertips. I'd do anything to go back.' Paulinus shrugged his shoulders. 'Too late, it's gone. Best be off. Farewell.'

They grasped each other's arm. It was difficult, this final leave-taking: so much that could be said or asked.

Then it was over, and Paulinus was walking away, carefully skirting a large puddle. Now Fromus was truly on his own, with her. It was what he wanted, and yet – and yet, something in him held back.

Back at his tent, he pulled back the tent-flap. She was crouching on the fur-skins.

'Did you hear us?' he asked.

'I was lying down.' Nehtan pulled her cape tight.

'What is it?'

'Nothing. I can't talk here.'

'Why, what do you mean?'

She stood up. 'Can we get away from the camp, down to the trees?'

She shot out past him, without waiting for an answer.

It was not like her, but he followed. They went downhill through a morass of felled trees and around a trampled field, its dry-stone walling collapsed to the ground. The bitter stench of latrines hung in the air.

He caught up with her, sitting on a pine, fallen amongst a jumble of boulders. 'I've good news.' He was about to put his hand on her knee, but stopped. 'I have decided: we are going back to Britannia. And I'm taking a letter from the Comes to my father.'

Silence.

'It's agreed, it's official' - Fromus continued, though her eyes were shut - 'I'm not part of the embassy, we can go back.'

Her head was bowed, her nails scratching the pine trunk.

'It's what we wanted, isn't it?'

'I've been sick.' Her voice was tiny.

'We'll soon set that right. You're exhausted. We both are.'

'No, it won't ... it's not that. It's something else.' Her eyes flashed. 'Something inside.'

'What?' Fromus started, his voice high. 'Not...'

'You can go back without me. You've got your letter.'

'Are you sure? Couldn't it be something else?'

'You don't understand; there's no escape.' She gripped her knees. 'I'll kill it!' This fury, her hard cheeks. 'I want to die.'

'You can't ...'

Her hands clenched like claws. 'It's all for nothing. You couldn't know.' She was beating the back of her hand on the pine trunk.

Snatching her hand. 'You're bleeding.'

'Lamb of God, what can I do?' She slumped to the ground. 'I'm cursed, at the mercy of Donn. He's everywhere, even here.'

'What do you mean? Who's Donn?' He cradled her head,

but she pulled away with a retching groan. 'Look at me,' he said, reaching for her arm. 'Don't give up, not you ... Are you certain?'

Her lips pursed into a weak smile. 'You should go back to the delegation. That's where you belong, and it's right. It has to be. You have your duty. I can't go with you; it's ridiculous, I can't bear it, let me be.'

'No, I'm going back to Britannia, like I said. I've got a message to take. But that's not the main thing. You are, I mean, you're the only thing I'm certain about. How can you be sure?' He hadn't meant to say that. Could he really take her with him to Britannia, and her with that man's child?

A low evening light draped the tree-tops. A pigeon flapped, a blackbird flitted over a bush.

Nehtan looked up. 'I'm two months late. It's never been like that.'

'It could be something else, maybe just one of those things, what with all the awful times you've had.' His hand hovered above her knee. 'There's nothing constant in the universe. We can pray to the Lord.'

'Don't you see? Your family, who you are. You can't possibly ... I could never be - and you won't want...'

'I'm not leaving you, not here.'

'You're first duty is to your family. My future lies elsewhere...'

She buried her face in the folds of his cloak. Streaks of mist were gathering above the trees. Fromus stroked her black hair, his stomach clenching. Everything was falling apart. The only way was one thing at a time. Let tomorrow take care of itself.

* * *

Later, he was summoned to the tent of Comes. He insisted that Nehtan went with him.

Gerontius handed over a parchment. 'Here, it's not sealed. Read it and commit it to memory, then burn it.'

'Shall I wait outside?' Nehtan said.

'No,' Fromus said. 'Comes, cousin Gerontius, by your leave, may she listen? Two will remember better than one.'

'It's not how things used to be, but so be it.'

Fromus unrolled the thin sheaf and read aloud.

My Dear Cousin

I was overjoyed to receive your letter – and to meet your worthy son, Fromus, well able, and with his own mind.

Nothing gives me greater comfort than this opportunity to renew our friendship. We are indeed a pair of well-matched old asses.

Fromus will tell you how it is with me, and the situation in Gaul.

At present, I cannot leave my soldiers and those who are loyal to me. I have hopes of a reconciliation with Emperor Honorius. If I succeed, then I will come back to Britannia, with whatever troops I can muster.

We are in the hands of the Almighty Father. May he look down and bless us, as my sweet Nonnichia would say.

My most cordial greetings to Aula.

All, I trust, will indeed be well.

Your friend and cousin

Jovius Aurelianus Gerontius

'Well?' asked Gerontius. 'Can you memorise it?'

'Of course, sir.'

'Good, good, the die is cast. We must be bold, Fromus, if we are to triumph. Your family awaits you in Corinium. Do not fail them.'

'Of course, sir.' Fromus bowed his head, brightening when he saw the old man's sparkling green eyes.

Gerontius nodded, stepping towards Nehtan. 'And as for you – don't worry, I won't bite.' A wide beam engulfed his shaggy face. 'Look after him, young woman, and may the Lord God be with us all.'

CHAPTER TWENTY-FIVE

Messor strode past a soldier trying to scrape mud off his sword. It had been too easy to get into Gerontius's camp.

Call themselves Romans, just because they had pricks with plumed helmets. Bellator would have a fit if he saw how they turned out in the morning. This lot would crumble like wattle if they came up against proper legionaries.

Security was a joke. Everyone knew that they were calling for six riders to escort the maggot and his whore for half a day's ride north. Messor had almost volunteered - that would have set the cat amongst the pigeons.

If this was what the new world was like, it was made to order. Everything was sliding towards him, all the rules breaking down.

Messor swaggered up to a group of soldiers standing around a campfire pot. Four bearded faces. He picked a thin lad with his sword hanging loose.

'Here, you, I've been told to fetch your rations.'

'What? But this is ours.'

'Look, sonny.' Messor scanned the other faces, before settling back on the boy. 'You do what you're told. See here,' he put his hand on the pommel of his spatha. 'I've come for provisions for the cousin of the Comes, special instructions, and you'd better give them to me. It's orders.'

'Fucking typical,' one of the others exclaimed, jerking his head up. 'What about the pot?'

'Get it back from the quartermaster's tent.'

'Pissing officers. They'll give us a pot with a hole in it.

What about our grub?'

'Not my problem.'

Messor walked away with their pot of warm mush. He wolfed some of it down behind a horse enclosure. The rest he crammed into his leather pouch.

He was ready, keen to be away. The camp was fit for nothing but a shit. He was stealthy as a pike, getting whatever he wanted while half-baked soldiers sat around and gossiped.

A familiar voice. It was Philus, on horseback, telling someone to get out of the way. Messor ducked low, chucked the pot aside, and raced back to his horse.

His belly was tightening, burning in a long line of hurt. She was his, because he willed it. Those fools said it was written in the stars. More lies: the world wanted to be deceived, and so it was. Da held to baubles of sun-feasting Mithras and the distant blood of his bull, the ramblings of old men. Da knew nothing, none of them did. What had Mithras and his service in the temple done for Da? His whore had been smashed by his own son and there had been no punishment. The only unconquered sun was the fire in a man's belly.

Nehtan would soothe him, put her hands into the flames and unwind the barbs, her eyes burnt wide-open in the world as it was. Her guts were like his, twisting while they danced round the earth's cauldron, the heat only lowering when new flesh was thrown in. He longed for a woman to stand alongside him, to share the livid scream, to feel it thicken beyond words and memory, sinking into pure animal throb. It was her, though she pretended not, she who knew and listened to the depth of him – she would bring him out of the pit and show him another way.

* * *

258

Two days later, Messor watched from a hill as Nehtan and Fromus walked in a deserted valley, as if they had not a care in the world. Lackey Philus was leading the two horses behind, on foot, a bad position.

Time to end it. She was his - bees sting if you take their honey. Best to catch them in the shade, after the road slunk into a wood.

Damn his horse, hardly moving. It needed whacking with the flat of his blade.

The track straightened inside the wood. The three of them were walking down a slope towards a ford at the edge of the trees, beyond which were huts.

Sword out, gasping into a trot, Messor raced past the rear horse. Hay-top Philus spun round too late, the blade already slamming down.

Fuck, nearly missed. Philus's back slashed, the bastard was down. Now to skewer the maggot, stuck-still in the ford, no weapon, the woman behind, shouting.

Merda! His horse stopped, frothing at the mouth, buckling at the knees. Too late, Messor thudded sideways into thin river-water, smashing onto stone.

Shoving up, sword tip in the waterbed, hip shattered. Checking behind: Philus writhed on the ground. In front, the maggot was his! The woman clung to him; he was alone, pushing her away, no one protecting him.

'You ring-fuck, you don't know her! Nehtan, you belong to me.'

Messor stumbled forwards, one leg dragging, Fromus backing away. Nehtan grabbed maggot's hand and they ran to the huts.

Hip loose and raging, Messor fell forward, smashing onto his out-swept arm. Again thrusting up. Papiteddo! The idiots.

He turned back to the grey horse, heaved up onto the saddle, forcing himself, exultation exploding inside pain.

'Nehtan!' He shouted. 'You're mine!'

One blade-whack and the big horse charged over the ford towards the huts.

'Come out, Fromus.' The name spat out. 'Let her go.'

He backed the beast against a hut wall, pulling its head sideways, smashing the mud-packed sticks. Shouts from the other side as Fromus and Nehtan burst out, racing to the wood. Too far for them to make it, running against the horse.

'I'll kill you, gonna rip your head off!'

Maggot turned, mouth open, face white. This was it. Sword-arm up, Messor kicked the horse, pounding towards the hated head.

At last. Blade plunging into soft neck, beautiful red spilling – that look in the eyes. They were always surprised, the clay men on the end of his blade, not pretending any more, nothing but shit.

Something else - a heat scorching his belly, a fireball bursting, javelins of pain lancing up his crumbling spine.

CHAPTER TWENTY-SIX

Fromus dashed to the ford, driving Nehtan in front.
Had to reach the trees, the low branches and tripping
roots.

Hooves thundering. A rupturing shriek: that man, his
chasm-ravenous mouth. Not enough time; they could not
make it, not both of them.

Turn, stand between her and the mad soldier.

Fury pulsing from the rider's lips, high up on horseback.

One chance, grab his leg, pull him off. My God, so massive!
The beast's eyes were flecks of fire. Bend, grab the man's boot ...

Too late, the falling blade-edge, nerves shredding – nothing
but this arc of flesh and metal.

Twisting, turning to see her face ... distant almond eyes,
her voice a tinkling green. Everything leading to this moment:
Nehtan, family, *Romanitas*, and a place of emptying heat and
cold.

Chung! Chill sweetness crashing through neck, vastness
opening out, an abyss of blinding white radiance.

There, at the edge, a frenzied figure on the salted track, the
dream-dreaded face – himself, mirrored, the soul of all beings
sinking into ocean waves. This was why he had been born: to
know that he had always been part of one inexpressible love.
No more striving, simply let the myriad drops rise and merge
in intimate peace.

Silent, I. Silence.

Roaring seas raging across the sky, trees flowing, water still
as stone.

Light singing in a thousand beats - laughter - wind
clapping - white flowers raining on snow.

CHAPTER TWENTY-SEVEN

Nehtan screamed, throwing sound in the way of the sword chopping down on Fromus.

Run, stop it! But edge was screeching into neck. A grinding flicker and his head cracked sideways. No difference between blood and blade: the taste of burnt iron as it bit through flesh and bone.

His neck spurting, a caress of his soaked hair as she threw herself down.

Catch him, hold him together.

Body-drops, one eye crimsoned, the other urgent, pulling her in ... glazing into a blob of jelly.

For an instant, an old sound blotted everything out – *swish-crack* – Nymayr beating wet wool on round stones.

Movement; her mind snapped. The horse neighing, Messor sliding off, his eyes darting to the bright red spilling from his belly. On the other side, Philus falling backwards, his sword clattering, his face contorted.

Messor plunged to earth, his legs tumbling over Fromus, his arm reaching out, his face drowning in a black frown.

'No! She shouted, thrusting herself away. 'You can't ...'

The angry body crumpled.

Hunching to her knees, Nehtan cradled Fromus's head, his mouth twitching, the neck-stem a mess of throbbing pink.

A groan, Messor, his face rising from earth, dark eyebrow-lips reaching towards her.

'I ... I ... *you*.'

'No!' Her foot kicked out with the force of a river, catching his chin, snapping his head hard back. A low wheeze, stuttered gargling.

Quiet.

A patch of earth held by tufts of grass, Fromus on her lap. Her arm coming up, she watched as wet fingers closed the brown eyes.

* * *

Leaves drifting by, drops of rain. Distant crackling, light wind and the yielding soil.

Red, soft red, and drumming.

Nymayr, holding her up to the sky and laughing; a wren calling, water pure, twinkling at the brook.

* * *

A croak. Philus, his fair hair muddied. 'Nehtan.'

'I can't ... I'm not leaving him.'

Through hazy greyness, she lifted her head; a stone in a hollow plain.

'We have to bury him.' Philus dropped to his knee. 'Maybe later.'

The soldier winced as he reached towards the bloody gash across his shoulder. Fromus lay flopped on the mud, the other man further off. She did not remember moving away.

A black beetle wound its way through a forest of tough grass and passed out of sight. For a while, nothing.

* * *

Two farmers came by, stopped and gaped.

Wrenching herself up, coming back to the cold earth and the next things to be done, she mumbled, 'Help.'

'What's happened?'

She forced the words out, and found that the men came from a hamlet close by. They would bury Fromus, taking Messor's horse in exchange. The animal lay on its side, an upper leg twitching.

The older man shrugged. 'If it can't pull a plough, it'll fill our pots.'

With an immense effort, Nehtan raised her head. 'The digging has to be done now, we'll wait. When you lift him, be careful. Your village' - she nodded in the direction of Philus - 'can they heal him?'

'Can't say as they can, not with him in that way, but if you keep going' - the villager pointed away from the wood – 'it'll take you an hour, less on your horse. You'll find the veterans' settlement. Can't miss it. They'll know what to do.'

Walking to the clearing behind the huts, she saw two mounds in a fenced patch, a makeshift cross between them. She pointed, and the villagers heaved long spades onto their shoulders.

Philus needed help to get to the stream. At the water, he nodded towards the stain on her hands and cloak.

Part of him, part of her.

The cavalryman's cheeks and eyes were worn. He was waiting. She looked at the dark red on her arms. Why not wash, if Philus wanted her to? Squatting, she let her fingers dangle in the brook, like colliding sticks. Philus sagged down. Cupping her hands, she brought water to his lips and he drank. He dipped his good hand in the stream and poured drops onto her cheek.

'Hey up, you should clean off. You've to start somewhere.'

'I can't. Not now.' Stream water lapped and sloshed past. 'What about your back?'

'It'll wait till they've finished.'

Heaving herself up, she let her mind slide. A torrent of tiredness washed over, heavy bones dragging on flesh. The words of the old shaman woman in the Alan camp came to her: 'you will bear a great warrior.' No! She was revolted. She didn't want any such thing. She had to be out of the world, away from warriors and soldiers. No more killing. No more struggling to get what she wanted, scrabbling around like an ant on fire. She shook her shoulders, and sat down heavily. Fromus... nymayr, atir. Far, far away, she'd never be with them, didn't deserve to. Fromus had died because of her, and she had pushed him away, hadn't dared to trust him.

A great wave of pity and sadness. A thundering, blinding sea, memories dropping away. Standing empty, wind on the face, she saw legions of people clinging to the teeming earth, seedlings pushing up through snow. Something beyond the emptiness: the place that was no-place and where suffering and laughter were perfect like the vast night sky, nothing lacking and nothing in excess. Let everything go, if she could, and there would only be one thing, where everything was.

An ash tree waved on the other side of the hut, each twig fluttering, its rutted bark creaking with immense slowness. Across the world, ceaseless change, blood dissolving into light, anguish shattering into rock - and the rain would wash and wash until there were no edges.

Everything was simply itself, a time for all things, even this. She had been taken to where she would rather not go - and yet, she was alive and there was the late afternoon leaf-light. And Fromus, his hand gently on her...

Nehtan and Philus sat as the sun dipped and the two villagers hacked to make a hole next to the fence. Low mumbles. 'This here land is stone-ridden; that's why they left.

It's no good for my back.' The men straightened and wiped their brows.

'Come on, lads,' Philus spoke. 'No flagging, we need to be done. You've far more than a fair wage in the horse.'

Her hand scooped yellowing dust and rubbed it between fingers. Eyes shut, a gasp filled her nostrils. She was drowning at the brink, a tiny bubble popping in the void.

The sun cast long shadows as the villagers carried Fromus's slumped form to the shallow grave.

'I think he would want you to have something.' The cavalryman swallowed. 'You should take his belt. The money, we'll need it, and they'll mind me better if I can pay.'

Fromus would never laugh, never ask her thoughts, could not be warmed. Curly hair, soft brown eyes. Kneeling, she put her hand to his side, staring at mottled leaves netted into the mud.

A quickening in her belly. A rush of fear, then tenderness for what would be, what would soon become. Her heart knew the way: let one foot follow the other.

The noise of shifting feet: Philus, clutching his shoulder. Poor man, he needed tending. She parted Fromus's cloak and tunic and took the inner belt with coins. A presbyter should ease his passage, and he should be remembered in the Sacramentum, but that would have to wait. His skin was hard - had it always been like that?

His family, they would want something. They should know that he had not abandoned them and that he had died honourably - though they would be shocked if they knew about her. She could take them his gold ring, perhaps - and stop the villagers stealing it.

Philus spoke. 'We should say something.'

It was true. It was the next thing: she was in the way. Look up, look around, be of service. She sniffed water in the air, mist coming later. And the farmers had to get the horse to their village. She nodded at Philus, and they stumbled through the ploughed field of prayer.

'Be with us, merciful God, and protect us through the silent hours of the night,

That we who are wearied by the shifts and chances of this fleeting world,

May rest upon your eternal constancy ...'

Noiseless, her head in her hands, she sensed Philus's arm above, holding back. The blank-faced farmers waited, puffing. Final words, she could not say them. A long pause.

Philus grunted. 'We mourn him, his life was cut off, but we seen who he was. Lord, we commend his soul to your mercy.'

'Amen,' said the farmers.

The men lowered Fromus into the shallow hole. They looked up, but she was still. Loose mud fell in. Bending down, she picked up a clod and threw it. When the earth had been spaded onto him, she gestured at them to drag an old roof beam on top.

A deep breath, and with it came a tang of rotten wood and turned soil. What was it they sang? *Many are the light-beams from the one light; many are the branches of the one tree.*

The men started to dig another hole.

'No!' The word came from her belly.

'Why?'

'Because ... because he shouldn't.'

Their long spades rested. 'I know as he were wicked, that's what the soldier said, but it don't seem right, to leave him like a dead crow.'

'He's a beast.' Her fists clenched, the farmers' mouths dropped. 'Throw him in the wood, not here.'

Swaying, she sat down, her heart beating as they dragged Messor away. She remembered her kick, snatching his life away, and was glad. She had won.

But Fromus? Everything was dashed down, all bone-blood shattered, nothing whole any more. Nowhere to look or feel good about.

Listening to her own breath, a great gulp of air. So simple. Everyone breathed like that. Why must she be always filled with fear or hate? She knew what the world said, and what she felt. It was right. But how did that help? It was all gone, those things and those people. Could it all be part of one thing? Even Messor. Had he been seeking, in his warped way?

The memory of another death - Vitalis, bowed amongst the brambles, crumbling in the leaves, the last faint straws between them dissolving. Her chest heaved. Christ was fallen from the tree, and all creation with him. Courage. The true Master had conquered the world, though the world knew him not.

They had stopped. One of the villagers was bending low over Messor's corpse. 'Begging your pardon, but you won't mind us, will you?'

They pulled off Messor's boots, removed his cape and belt, and put them with his saddle and sword. It was good to see him stripped. Now they grasped his arms and legs. For an instant, she was amazed that he did not struggle, but the body had only its own weight. The two men heaved it towards the wood beyond the ford.

Her head was heavy, body drained. She had to shoulder all these things, those pointless and necessary things, but she would let it happen. Look at the birds and the lilies; see the flowers of the fields, each ringing in glory. She would keep going, back past the Black Gate, back to splashing in the stream, back to Fromus blushing next to the Alan warrior, back to long before, to the warm hut and tender voices. Then, back beyond all of it, to the new place that she already knew – a thread of light, full of joy and sorrow, gazing on from an impossible distance.

It could not be explained, but it held together - the trees above, the fearful blood gashes, her monotonous life as a slave, the grasping cold. Fromus. Bad and good could be looked in the eye because that was how it was, an essence before knowing. *Shoulder my yoke and learn from me.* Everything was a gift, like rich wine pouring out all the time, sloshing to the ground, no one noticing. Her head had never been so clear, though it felt like a black wall was waiting to collapse on her.

'Best be going.' She tapped Philus's arm. 'We'll get help.'

'I'll pull through. I've seen the like before.'

'We'll go to the veterans' village. Then we'll find the people I told you about, the ones in the forest. We'll rest up and work out what to do.'

She helped Philus shuffle over to Papiteddo, kneeling to let him use her shoulder while he lugged himself up onto the saddle. Taking the reins in hand, she led the horse up the road and away from the darkening wood.

Chapter Twenty-Eight

Nehtan felt more relaxed in the spring sun than she had done for a long time. The birch trees near the settlement were bare but further off the firs were bushy-green. She and Micchus were in a clearing. The lad was on his back in a patch of brown grass, near Papiteddo, who had been rolling. They were alone, and the boy-man was imitating the horse, blowing air through puckered lips.

Nehtan laughed and nearly slipped. 'Don't!' Her hand went to her belly.

'Papiteddo.' Micchus was kicking his legs up. 'Happy.'

Nehtan smiled. Everything should be simple like this. She loved old Vigilantius and Brigomalla, but they were tense, perhaps because of the marauding barbarians, or perhaps because of her. She brought demands for change, even if she didn't mean to, not least because she gave time to Micchus to be himself, rather than to try to make him be the son they would never have. Micchus had no ideas about himself or others. Of course, it was easier for her, she knew, because she didn't depend on Micchus, unlike Vigilantius and Brigomalla, whose own relationship seemed to centre on Micchus, especially as far as Brigomalla was concerned. The lad's insistence on things being done the same way and in the right order made their hut into a home, and he loved them as if they were his real parents. In a way, the old couple had already grown to need her to keep the sweetness between them; Vigilantius had his place in the village as the priest, but the wife kept herself at a distance from the others. She was lonely, and liked having Nehtan to talk to. Brigomalla must have been attractive when she was young.

Nehtan felt her belly: too bad that soon she would have to leave. She went up to Papiteddo and stroked him.

Micchus picked himself up. 'Can I do that?'

'Yes, but you be careful, and move slowly. Remember about his nose.'

She stopped to listen to the evening twitter of blackbirds. The warm day had thawed the ground, making it pockmarked wherever Papiteddo walked. The flanks of the horse were caked in mud: Fromus wouldn't have liked that. He would have wanted a clean, presentable animal at all times. Her heart tightened, and she looked back towards the hut.

Brigomalla was walking towards them with a disapproving frown, but her face brightened when their eyes met. 'My dear, I haven't heard you hoot like that for weeks.' She turned to Micchus. 'You're soaking. You'll get a chill.'

'Sorry, my fault.' Nehtan helped Micchus up, holding his hand as they walked back to the hut.

It was near the end of the day and Vigilantius was putting sticks on the fire.

Nehtan stopped outside. 'We need wood, Micchus. Can you bring a big log, the one we found near the river? Then we'll dry out your cloak.'

The lad scurried down the slope. She took a deep breath and went inside, nodding to Vigilantius and Brigomalla.

'I need to ask something.' She paused. 'One more thing.'

'I thought it might come to this.' Vigilantius brushed ash off his beard. 'But not so soon.'

'Young woman,' Brigomalla said, 'I've seen your look and I've a mind that you're turning to your wild ways.'

Nehtan made herself take Brigomalla's hand. 'I have to go. I like it here, with you and everyone, but I need to travel before the worst of the spring raids. I can do it in stages, first getting somewhere up near Bononia and the sea.'

'Stubborn as a mule.' Vigilantius brushed a streak of hair over his balding head. He spoke in a way that made her think he was chuckling, but he wasn't. It was just that his eyes shone with kindness.

'You know,' Nehtan said, 'I have to deliver a message to Fromus's father, it's important. And I have to tell them what happened. Then, there's nymayr and atir. If I don't go now, I'll never leave and I'll never see them again.'

The old man sat down. 'Oh, for the bravery of youth! I've been watching this brew for weeks. That frozen island will swallow you.' He patted the space on the bench next to him. 'Reflect on it, stay here, and give yourself time. Have your child with us. Brigomalla will love it to high heaven. You'll not want for anything we can give.'

'Nehtan,' - Brigomalla put her hand on Vigilantius's shoulder – 'all is in the hands of the Lord, but it helps if you're sensible. You're five months pregnant and the land bristles with murderers. You think you can do anything you please, and never mind what the world is really like - and you in your state, bringing a new life into the world. It's not bravery but the craziness of youth, sheer pride... His family won't be better off for what you bring them, and your people can wait a while longer.'

'Perhaps, but I have to try, while I can.'

'If he was the man like you told us,' Brigomalla said, 'Fromus would not want you to take this risk. And with his child in you.'

Nehtan dropped her head, her hand on her belly, wishing

272

again that there was nothing there. 'I'm not going just for him, but for me, for what I owe.' A trickle of water wound its way across the earthen floor. 'I can't let them down; they need to know what Gerontius said. And I have to see my family, let them know I'm alive... Anyway, I'm over the sickness. I've a good three months walking in me, and I have coins enough. I can pay for passage across the sea, and get there, but not all in one go. First, I'd have to get up to the coast. '

Vigilantius put his hand on Brigomalla's. 'Let her be, give her time to find her heart's true course.'

'What do you mean?' Brigomalla's eyes flashed. 'You're not thinking right, like her. We can't let her go. And you've forgotten the child she's carrying.'

Nehtan fled out of the hut. They were old and didn't see her energy and determination, despite the life inside her. She could do it, bit by bit; she could cope. But, if Brigomalla was like that, it was better she go immediately, unless... maybe Micchus could help her find the right way? It was better to talk with him because ideas did not get in his way.

Micchus was dragging a long branch up the hillside.

'Come and help,' he panted, beaming from his round eyes.

Nehtan looked out across the small valley. 'Micchus, you know I'm going to have a child?'

'A baby brother.'

'Or sister.'

'Or sister. 'Micchus's big mouth broadened.

'The thing is, I have to tell his family.'

'We're here, and Philus.'

'Yes, but he is not the father.'

'I know, they told me.' Micchus's mouth dropped. 'You mean, the one who died, the patrician. Brigomalla said you loved him.'

'Oh, I don't know... maybe, but I wasn't ready.'

Nehtan was surprised at her own words. She paused while Micchus looked eagerly at her. Love, she thought, what is love? It is more than a quickening of the heart, more than lying in his arms. She stopped thinking and let the words come.

'It seems like a long time ago. I was much younger then, I didn't know what I was doing, what I was feeling. I was too... buried... though it couldn't have worked: we would have been wrenched apart. The world, they wouldn't have allowed it.'

'But he's the father.'

'No.' Nehtan felt a traitor for saying the word, but it was also a relief.

'Then who?'

'Not him, someone else.'

'A friend for Micchus?'

'No.' She would have to tell it all. 'You'll never see him.'

'Why not?'

'A bad man. He's dead, he's gone. He did terrible things.'

'Why?'

'I don't know. He was... he was torturing himself, and he did it to others. ' Again, she was surprised at herself. That man, he too wanted time to slow down, to have space to breathe without needing to crush those around him, to allow himself, his boy-self, to surface and be cherished.

What! How could she think about him like this? A beast who had done those things to her – and to Fromus! ... Never, never again would she feel Fromus curl around her. Never could she learn what it was like to be him; never share feelings, delighting in touch without fear.

Her hand went to the old wound on her head. Micchus was still standing next to her, his mouth half-open, his eyes shining. 'Do they know him?' The lad pointed up the slope. 'Could they help?'

'No,' she shrieked. 'Sorry, I didn't mean that. He was a monster.'

'Why did you let him?'

'I didn't. Look, Micchus, let's not talk about it. Can you keep it a secret?'

'Will the baby be a monster?'

'No, of course not. How can you say that?' Again, she was shouting, and Micchus was scrabbling away to the hut. She was knotted up inside, all those feelings breaking through. The only way to cope was not to think of Fromus; she had to block him out - until she was ready. Better if she was on her own, praying without words.

As for the old people, how could she steel herself to tell them about the father of the child in her? She must find somewhere in the forest, a place to let be and see what came to her, what the Lord might say. She needed strength, for things to be clear. For now, she had to shut away that time, to move on, to keep that part of herself alive but hidden.

She started towards the woods to find a quiet place where she could sit without thinking, but she fell twice, face down in the soggy snow. Her clothes were wet, her legs and chest chilling, so she turned back to the hut. Donn, she thought, this was his power, and Messor, him in her belly. She must forget also about them, but she couldn't. Wherever she was, they were with her.

* * *

Back in the hut, she sat on the bench and forced herself to smile at Vigilantius, who looked the same. It seemed that

Micchus hadn't said anything to them. She could sit between the fire and this old man and say nothing, bathing in a blessed silence.

Vigilantius didn't move, his hand stretched out and resting on the bench, staring into the fire. Looking at his callused fingers, she knew that she couldn't speak about the father of the child: it was too much to tell them - and too hard not to tell them. She had to leave, to not have other people interfering, to find her own way in her own time.

Brigomalla came in, a jostle of energy. Nehtan's jaw hardened as she glared at the mud-floor while Brigomalla went through her plan, blasting holes in it. When she had finished, Nehtan looked up. 'I'm sorry, it's how it is.'

The wife left in a huff and the old man heaved a great sigh.

Nehtan fingered a hole in her smock. 'I'll be careful. Anyway, last week you said it's not safe here either.'

'True enough.' Vigilantius hunched his broad shoulders, and edged closer. 'Tell me, why did you come here with Philus?'

'We were looking for a place to rest, a refuge.'

'Nothing more?'

'I trusted you both. It's good here.'

The old man placed his hand on her head. 'Perhaps it is more than that. Let the Christ lead you. Find who you truly are.'

'What do you mean?'

'Give yourself time. Search deep inside, not in words nor even in prayer. Let go of all striving. Find a place to be still, and let be whatever is. You'll know, because you'll no longer feel that you are rushing.'

He stood, his eyes twinkling. Her shoulders dropped and a light gust of wind blew drops of water from the door-lintel into the hut. Vigilantius closed his eyes and she copied him. She heaved in a great breath of air and let her jaw relax.

The only sound was the distant clunk of wood being chopped.

Somehow, with her eyes shut, she knew that the big, dishevelled man was smiling. She could not resist opening her eyes to check, and he was. 'Try doing it,' he said, 'on your own.'

'I will, later.' Energy welled. 'I've prayed silently like that before.'

Vigilantius stepped away to tend the fire. Her head felt cold. She hesitated, then spoke. 'I know you don't believe in praying for the dead, but can you remember Fromus in your services?'

'We'll include him, as all others. And we won't forget you, of that you may be sure.'

'Could you give me food for the first few days?'

'What, already?' Vigilantius moved aside as Brigomalla returned. 'Of course, we'll give you what we can - and, if you've time, you'll sup with us tonight?'

Nehtan's silvery laugh rang out.

Brigomalla raised her eyebrows, but her face softened into quick, half-smile. 'For you, we'll dine on the finest roots. Foolish though you are, a young thing with no sense, not in this world anyway. But you'll see, who knows, I don't suppose you'll get far.' Brigomalla's eyes stopped flickering. 'And on your own head be it.'

Soon after, Nehtan went to find Philus. She met him striding out of the dripping forest, an oak staff in one hand and three snared rabbits in the other.

'We'll have to make more holes in our belts before spring pickings come, though you needn't, seeing as you're feeding the two of you.' His eyes narrowed. 'Hold fast, I seen that look before.'

'It's time.' She was staring at the ground. 'I said I'd wait until you were healed and the snow was melting. Well, I've done that.' Words tumbled out faster than she intended. 'I'm leaving, in a few days. If you come, if you want to ... We'd be companions, but nowt else, as you say.'

Philus dropped the rabbits and rested his chin on the top of his staff. Taking a long breath, he straightened up.

'Any way I think of it, you're mad, like those men raving all over the Empire. If I was to go with you, you'd only be encouraged.'

'That's as may be, but it's not as if it's too much for me - we women work through to birthing.'

'You can't walk to Bononia. It's still winter.' Philus thumped his staff into the ground. 'There's snow, robbers, and the sea to cross.'

'I have coins. I'll rest up before trying to buy passage across. It's best to go while the barbarians are still warming themselves in folks' homes. I'll stay in the woods and buy food from homesteads.'

'You mustn't go.' His face was pinched, his eyes glinting. 'You won't make it.'

'There is always a way, but it may not be what we will.'

'I won't come. It's not right, you'll see. I tell you, I am staying here. I can't be the one as leads you on. What did Brigomalla and the old man say?'

'Never mind them. I'm a cussed girl, so don't belt yourself. I'll be fine.'

* * *

Two long days later, Nehtan relaxed on an ash branch sprawled on the ground. It had been much harder going than she expected. She had crossed a wide valley where the river had flooded. Her boots and trouser legs were soaking.

A tightening, her hand went to her belly. A faint kick. Five months, and the poor thing did not know what was coming. A bigger kick! Life, defenceless, hers alone. It had no choice but to trust.

Heu! Was she any different?

She rested, blank, letting go. Took a deep breath, and another. No future, no past; not neglectful, not indulgent. No fretting, thinking gets in the way, let it come from wholeness, from silence. The Christ will lead, from that place of blood and darkness, even as he was nailed to the tree: *Woman, behold your son.* That could be hers; it was not the child's fault.

Wind ruffling, the ash-bark no longer digging into her as she sat on the branch. She yielded, letting the aches speak, her wet feet stretching out. The air was fresh-sweet.

Her head spun. Too early for food, but she would stay awhile. A pigeon swooped low as the sun moved across the sky.

Her shoulders shook, and a lethargy spread from her belly, which, at first, she resisted, then she let it take hold. Her eyes shut, though she knew she must stay awake - but it was good breathing deep and slow, alert to the smallest wriggle inside.

For a long moment, there was just the two of them, until a spit of wind tugged her eyes open. Blinking, squinting, she spied something moving on the track far behind. A man, judging by the leaps with staff in hand across boggy patches. Where to hide? But he had seen her, and she was too tired. She clasped the knife in the pocket of her cloak, and waited.

At length, she saw fair hair, a familiar, tight face. Philus fast-walked the last stretch, making her laugh.

'You took your time.'

'Look lass.' His eyes narrowed as he rested on his chin on the tall staff. 'I left the horse as they'll need it, and it'll only mark us out as fair game. I'm here on your terms, but you mind my advice about the best way and when to lie low.'

'I've been thinking...'

'I feared as much, you mad woman.' He held out a chunk of bark-bread. 'Bite on that, if you can. As for the rest, if you mind where we're going, I'll mind you.'

'That's what I'm saying. I can see now. It's best.' She looked into his eyes.

'You're not saying...'

'I am: back to Bonadeni.'

'Ha!' He hoisted her up above his head.

'*Hei*, Philus, careful.'

'I know, I know.' He put her down, chuckling.

From far away came the screech of a buzzard, sending a robin darting over their heads.

She sniffed the air. 'Let's be going. Shall we sing?'

'There are those as prefer I keep my peace, but they're long gone. When they see us, Brigomalla will be mighty pleased, and him too.'

'Then let's sing her song.'

> '*The Wren! The Wren! The king of all birds,*
> *In mid-winter frost was killed in the furze.*
> *Though he be little, his joy is so great,*
> *He makes a new home near anyone's gate.*
> *So up jump, good people, and free him to fly,*
> *The small king of Christ-light is not hallowed to die.*
> *The Wren! The Wren! The king of all birds,*
> *Bless his seer-call and hail him with words.*'

A high wind blew. It would bring rain, but they could take cover under the tall trees ahead. They stepped up their pace as the first drops fell.

Historical Afterword

Late antiquity and the year 409

Though the main focus of *Beyond the Black Gate* is the emotional and spiritual journeys of the principal characters, the historical context is interesting and little known.

The summary which follows has major caveats. First, nearly every aspect of this period is disputed within academia, beginning with the broad categorisation of the 5th century as part of 'late antiquity,' a time of great change but also continuity. Alternatively, it is described as the definitive onset of the 'dark ages', a period of ossification and cataclysmic decline.

Second, the sequence of major events north of the Alps in the early 5th century is unclear, especially regarding the migrations (or invasions) of non-Roman peoples (or barbarians) into the Empire. Third, the spread and penetration of Christianity, and the extent to which the new religion led to a 'closing of the European mind', is a matter of debate. Fourth, the change from a predominantly community-based mindset to one dominated by individuality was well under way in the Roman era, but how it affected attitudes to one-on-one love and to the development of the self as a primary focus of identity will have varied greatly, by region, education and culture.

Finally, there is controversy in using the term 'Celt' to describe many of the peoples who lived in central and north-west Europe before and during Roman times, though it remains valid as a cultural rather than an ethnic classification.

Nevertheless, it is possible to outline the broad political and cultural context of *Beyond the Black Gate*, according to current scholarship.

THE BROADER CONTEXT: EXISTENTIAL POLITICAL AND CULTURAL THREATS

For 400 years from the time of Julius Caesar, the Roman Empire dominated all of the territories around the Mediterranean, as well as extensive hinterlands (including Britannia). However, by the early fifth century the classical political entity known as the West Roman Empire was in its death throes, due to internal disunity, cultural change and large-scale migrations from outside its borders.

The Empire had been definitively divided between Latin-speaking West and (the richer) Greek-speaking East in 395 on the death of the Emperor Theodosius I, who had struggled to maintain order. After Theodosius, disintegration accelerated, with migrating barbarian groups fostering anarchy and economic crisis, despite the fact that the aim of their leaders was not to destroy but to be accepted as part of the Empire.

It did not help that for 25 years after the death of Theodosius I, the Emperors of both the West and the East were incapable of leadership, due to age or feebleness of character. Theodosius's younger son, Honorius, was Emperor of the western half from 395 (when he was aged eleven) to 423, based (after 401) in the impregnable port of Ravenna, on the Adriatic coast of Italy. Honorius was weak and vacillating, and he fatally sapped what power he had by conniving at the overthrow and execution of his principal general, Stilicho, in

408. In the same year, Honorius's nephew, Theodosius II, aged seven, nominally took over from his father as eastern Emperor, based in Constantinople. Real power in the decades after 395 was exercised in both halves of the Empire by courtiers or military leaders, though always precariously.

In the year 409, the western Imperium or government faced three major military threats. First, from a very large and disparate host of 'barbarians' in Gaul: on the last day of the year 406 (though some historians plump for 407) a 'super-group' of Vandals, Alans and Suevi crossed the frozen Rhenus (the Rhine) at Moguntiacum (Mainz), pushing aside resistance from weak Roman military forces and thereafter laying waste much of north-eastern Gaul. Their invasion across the Rhenus was followed by that of Burgundians, Franks, Alemanni and many others over the following decades. These invaders were all Germanic except for the Alans, who were originally of nomadic Iranian stock. Unlike most previous incursions across the Rhine, this time the 'barbarians' wanted to settle permanently inside the Empire, and by 409 they were carving out territories across Gaul.

Second, in early 407, a junior Roman army commander in Britannia called Constantinus - unrelated to Constantine the Great, who died in 337 - declared himself co-Emperor of the West. He then promptly invaded Gaul, at least partly in order to combat the barbarian invaders. After many difficulties, Constantinus succeeded in making himself master of Britannia, Gaul and Hispania - the three territories which collectively formed the Praetorian Prefecture of Gaul. However, Constantinus was not in control of large parts of eastern Gaul where barbarian groups had (temporarily) settled, with whom he concluded peace treaties. Eventually, he was able to secure the Rhenus frontier and to garrison the passes that led from Gaul to Italy. In 408 he made the southern city of Arelate (Arles) his capital. In March 409, at the peak of his power, he was recognised as legitimate junior Emperor ('Caesar') by Honorius, becoming known to history as Constantinus the Third (hereafter called Constantinus III). His most effective general was the Romano-Briton, Gerontius. However, in the summer of 409 Gerontius, based in Hispania, revolted against Constantinus III, allied with various barbarian groups and sought a rapprochement with Emperor Honorius.

The third – and most dramatic - threat to the Empire in the West came from a large horde of Goths, who were allowed to settle - with their weapons and political independence - south of the Danube, inside the Empire, in 376. Soon after Generalissimo Stilicho's death in August 408, many of these Goths, led by their King Alaric, invaded Italy. Roman military reserves in Italy were too depleted to be able to confront the Goths, who roamed the Italian peninsular, seeking resources but also a settlement with Honorius. This Gothic menace is what principally preoccupied the Imperium and Honorius in 409. In 410 Alaric's Goths sacked Rome, though in a controlled manner, only lasting three days. Nevertheless, the blow to the prestige of the Empire was huge.

LOSS OF REVENUES TO PAY THE ARMY, AND THE IMPACT OF CHRISTIANITY

Arguably, as important as these military threats – and certainly more significant in the long term – the Western Roman Empire was falling apart due to the culmination of a long period of weakening loyalty to the idea of 'Empire' itself. Partly, this was because it was too large and too complex: it worked well while economic growth was steady, sufficient citizens joined the army, and most of the peoples on its borders were relatively primitive. But, by 400, large parts of the Empire were being devastated by civil war and by well-led barbarian invasions, both of which diminished the tax revenues which were crucial to paying for the army. This led to a vicious spiral of less money, less troops and more chaos. In any case, the army was dependent on Germanic 'barbarian' recruits (Stilicho was half-Vandal), which fostered suspicion and further division. Leadership at the top was poor, and there was a steady wilting of the ancient default of popular loyalty to the Empire, which had hitherto generally endured, despite many ineffective Emperors over the past four centuries.

At the same time as the late western Empire was politically disintegrating, a new spiritual and cultural force was on the rise: Christianity. This near-eastern religion transformed from being a sporadically-persecuted sect to becoming semi-official in 313, with the Edict of Milan. This was principally promulgated by the Emperor Constantine the Great, who gave great support to Christianity, which he saw as a unifying force. The new religion spread rapidly but was probably only practised sincerely by a minority of the Empire's subjects by 380-381, when Imperial edicts established Nicene Christianity - which regarded Jesus as divine and co-eternal with God the Father - as the official state religion. In 390-391, further edicts banned all pagan worship. However, continuing decrees against pagan practices demonstrated how difficult it was to root out ancient habits of superstition and sacrifice - not least in Rome itself, where many Patrician (aristocratic) families remained devoted to the old ways.

Christianity itself became divisive as many heresies arose in the fourth and fifth centuries (including one inspired by Pelagius, who came from Britannia). This did not stop it becoming the religion of the majority by the mid-fourth century, particularly in the African and eastern provinces of the Empire (the latter were already more homogenous, being dominated by Greek culture). Christian membership was essential to be able to progress in the Imperial bureaucracy or military. Saint Augustine of Hippo (354-430) was the dominant intellectual and theological figure of the age, profoundly influencing the Medieval European worldview and making major contributions not only to theology but also to human rights - for example, inveighing against slave trading - education and psychology. His *Confessions* was the western world's first interior autobiography, focused on the early development of his sense of selfhood as a prelude to Christian conversion.

More important than the necessity of conformity with state power, Christianity's fundamental attraction was that it was a source of personal meaning, consolation and mutual respect in an otherwise highly unequal society, where the old bedrocks of Imperial moral and political authority were crumbling. The revolutionary new cult of a monotheist God who became man helped to propel a seismic shift in cultural identity. Church leaders, especially bishops or charismatic figures such as St Martin of Tours (316-397), gradually became more important than the Emperor, though schisms complicated matters greatly.

Selfhood and individualism slowly became more emotionally and socially respectable and powerful: what mattered to a firm Christian was her/his personal relationship with the Trinitarian God, rather than ties to the secular, imperial community. Alongside this, the equality of all humans before God and the supremacy of the virtue of compassion began to compete with that of material power and duty to clan or state - at least in terms of prestige and aspiration for genuine Christians. However, in practice, then as now, these radically challenging values only found profound acceptance amongst a minority.

These transformations were piecemeal, varied across different regions, and were intersected or superseded at times by other political and cultural changes. Nevertheless, the fifth century was a pivotal point in the history of Europe, a time of great chaos, out of which eventually came an entirely different order in this part of the globe.

Technically, the Germanic leader Odoacer deposed the last west Roman Emperor in 476, though the Imperial centre had failed to exercise consistent control of much of the west since 395 (or earlier). In stark contrast, the Empire in the East endured as an intensely Christian entity for another 1,000 years, at least for the last bastion, until the fall of Constantinople to Muslim Ottoman forces in 1453. This gives the lie to the 18th century historian Gibbon's famous claim that Christianity was *the* major contributor to the fall of the Roman Empire, because (he said) it made its adherents 'servile and effeminate' and because much money that would have otherwise been used to promote the state was spent instead on Christian churches. However, it is widely accepted that Gibbon was right in asserting that Christianity weakened loyalty to the Emperor.

As mentioned above, the transformations and motivations sketched above are the subject of continuing controversy amongst historians – not least regarding why and how far the western Empire collapsed. However, the broad picture of major change in the west in the fifth century is generally accepted – with the most dramatic change and collapse being in Britannia.

Britannia was a backwater, threatened by Picts, Scotti and Saxons

In Britannia, the ruling classes had supported no less than four claimants to the Imperial throne during the fourth century, only one of whom was ultimately successful. This was the first usurper, Constantine the Great, who was proclaimed Emperor by his troops in 306 at Eburacum (York) and went on to defeat his rivals. The failure of the other three (later) usurpers led to fierce reprisals against their known adherents in Britannia. However, the province had not (generally) been ravaged by the frequent civil wars in the Roman Empire of the third and fourth centuries. Consequently, the south of Britannia experienced something of a minor economic revival in the fourth century. Nevertheless, from the 340s onwards, northern and eastern Britannia suffered from frequent slave and booty raids by Caledonii (also called Picts, from Scotland), Scotti (from Ireland) and Saxons (from north Holland and Germany). Until the early fifth century, these attacks did not usually affect the south-west and centre of Britannia, which were the wealthiest parts of the province and home to a majority of the large-scale Roman villas, particularly around Corinium (Cirencester) and Calleva (Silchester).

Britannia was a minor western Roman region in every sense; wealth and culture were much more advanced in

Gaul, especially in the warm south around Arelate (Arles), in the south-west around Burdigala (Bordeaux) and in the Rhineland border area around the major city of Treverorum (Trier). Indeed, for much of the fourth century Roman Emperors used Treverorum as their main base north of the Alps, in order better to control the army that was needed to contain Germanic threats from across the Rhenus (Rhine). Further afield, Italy, North Africa and the east of the Empire were far more populous, more agriculturally productive, richer and more culturally creative than Gaul, let alone remote and under-developed Britannia. In a near mirror-image of the current era, in the 4th century, the wealth and sophistication of the Roman Empire was generally located around the southern and eastern provinces abutting the Mediterranean.

The Britannic delegation, the Rescript of Honorius and what happened next

The historic background to *Beyond the Black Gate* is the journey in 409 of a delegation from Britannia to the Emperor Honorius in Ravenna, asking for troops to defend the province from barbarian attacks and for permission to raise local militia. This was, in effect, a request for Britannia to be reincorporated into the Roman Empire (a kind of reverse Brexit). The western Generalissimo Stilicho had withdrawn most troops from Britannia in about 400 and the usurper Constantinus III had taken the last significant Roman army forces across to Gaul in 407.

The request for military aid from Britannia to the Emperor is generally thought to have been an historic event, either in the form of a single messenger or in the form of a small delegation. The latter is more likely due to the importance and difficulty of getting Honorius to give an answer. However, the delegation and its members in this novel are fictitious. Because of the length of the journey, a departure from Britannia in the year 409 is probable, given that there was a response in the following year (or thereabouts).

What little is known is disputed. Nevertheless, according to the most plausible interpretation of brief mentions in two 6th century sources (Zosimus and Gildas), the Emperor Honorius sent a 'rescript' (a response to a specific question) to Britannia in 410. Zosimus wrote that Honorius 'sent letters to the cities in Britannia, bidding them to take precautions on their own behalf', implying that there would be no Roman troops coming to the rescue of Britannia.

It is not surprising that the Rescript was negative. The Emperor was preoccupied with the Goths ravaging Italy (under Alaric) and with a Romano-British usurper (Constantinus III – see above) in southern Gaul. He had too few troops for himself, let alone to consider sending any through war-torn Gaul to remote Britannia.

The fact that the rescript was addressed to the cities of Britannia, and not (which would be usual) to the local imperial officials, implies that by this time the central administration was no more and that the cities were the main authorities. This is why *Beyond the Black Gate* envisages delegates from the three main cities at the time – Londinium (London), Corinium (Cirencester) and Eburacum (York). Clearly, the delegation or messenger(s) did get through to the Emperor in Ravenna, since there was a Rescript, and, presumably, they were able to get back – a remarkable journey at this time, given the war-ravaged state of Italy and Gaul. A journey by ship is an alternative possibility, though sailing all the way from Britannia to the Mediterranean is relatively unlikely, given the widespread piracy and the paucity of suitable ships and related resources needed for such a major maritime journey.

Britannia never did rejoin the Empire. From the 410s, the island disintegrated into a series of feuding Romano-British petty kingdoms, which were gradually conquered (up to the Firth of Forth) by a relentless series of small-scale invasions by Angles and Saxons over the next two centuries, though most of Wales, Cornwall and Cumbria remained Celto-British. Every feature of the Roman Empire (except Christianity in Wales and Cornwall) disappeared more quickly and more profoundly in Britannia than anywhere else. Exactly what happened, and why, is obscured by the absence of all but the barest mentions in contemporary or even vaguely near-contemporary writers. The very few surviving sources in the sixth century (the best known being the Celto-British monk, Gildas) are more concerned with religious polemic than historic chronology.

Archaeology sheds some crucial but limited light. While there is academic debate about how violent the change was, there is archaeological evidence that between c400 and c600 the population of Britannia approximately halved, all cities and villas were abandoned, coinage disappeared, volume trade collapsed, mass pottery ceased and the average height of both humans and cattle dropped by 10-15%, indicating a massive decline in the quality of the diet. Unlike the more vibrant and transformational experiences of the rest of Europe, in Britannia the fifth and sixth centuries were truly grim for ruled and rulers alike.

GLOSSARY AND
HISTORICAL FIGURES

AGNUS DEI: Latin for 'Lamb of God', a Christian term for Jesus.

ALANS: an Iranian, semi-nomadic people, many of whom migrated into Europe in the 4th and 5th centuries, under pressure from the westwards-expanding Huns. The Alans were the main allies of the Vandals, who led a huge group of barbarians (warriors and their families) across the Rhine at the end of 406, looking for a better life.

ARELATE: present-day Arles (France), a major Roman port on the Mediterranean coast and seat of the Praetorian Prefecture of Gaul from c.401.

ARMORICA: the north-west Gallic region between the Seine and the Loire (ie Brittany, northern Loire and most of Normandy). After the legions left Britannia in 407, the Armoricans expelled the Imperial civilian authorities. Bacaudae (see below) took over in parts.

ATIR: an ancient British-Celtic word for 'Father'.

AVE: Latin for 'Hail' or 'Greetings'.

BACAUDAE OR BAGAUDAE: local or peasant insurgents, particularly in Armorica and northern Hispania.

BELGICA: Gallia Belgica was a Roman province that included modern-day Belgium and a chunk of north-east France.

Biarchus: non-commissioned officer in charge of a group of soldiers, approximately equivalent to a sergeant.

Black Gate ('Porta Nigra'): The Black Gate was one of four main gateways into Augusta Treverorum (Trier – see below), and was built at the end of the second century. The name 'Black Gate' was coined in the Middle Ages because of the darkened colour of its stone (and is therefore anachronistic in *Beyond the Black Gate*). The original Roman name is unknown.

Brigantes: a British tribe who lived before and during Roman times in northern England in a region that roughly corresponds to most of Yorkshire, Lancashire, Cheshire and Derbyshire.

Britannia: from around 300, the Imperial administrative Diocese of Britannia (England and Wales) was split into four provinces. The capital continued to be located at Londinium, the residence of the Vicar (governor), who was appointed by the Emperor to rule the Diocese. The second largest city was Corinium (Cirencester), capital of the province of Britannia Prima (south-west England plus Wales), which was the province least affected by the barbarian raids which erupted sporadically from the 340s. Britannia was always an extremely peripheral diocese, notable only for the unusual number of would-be imperial usurpers who started out there, until it ceased to be a part of the Empire from 410.

Burdigala: contemporary Bordeaux, in south-west France. It was the capital of the province of Aquitaine, within the diocese of Gaul, and was home to a wealthy and influential group of Honestiores.

CAESAR: title of the junior Emperor from the early fourth century, when both the western and eastern halves of the empire had a senior Emperor - the 'Augustus' - and a junior one - the 'Caesar'.

CALEDONIANS: tribes living in the highlands of Scotland. They were related to, or largely identical with, the Picts (the 'painted ones'). In the fourth and fifth centuries, they raided regularly through the lowlands and across Hadrian's Wall into Britannia.

CANIS MINOR: 'small dog', a constellation believed by devotees of Mithras to embody an ancillary spirit, part of the Mithras mystery cult (see below).

CATECHUMEN: one who is being instructed in Christian belief, prior to baptism.

CAUTOPATES: Cautes and Cautopates have been identified as torch-bearers attending the sun-god Mithras in the Roman cult of Mithraism (see below). In icons, Cautes holds his torch raised up (symbolising the rising sun) while Cautopates holds his torch pointed down (symbolising the setting sun or the night). Cautopates may also signify death, while Cautes is a harbinger of new life.

CELTO-BRITISH (PRE-CHRISTIAN) RELIGION: little is known about ancient religion in Britain, except that it was polytheistic, believing in many deities, some of which were venerated only in a particular area. The religion was probably animist, believing that objects, places and creatures possess a distinct spiritual essence; and that the material world inhabited by humans was unstable and liable to intrusion by spirits. There was a priestly caste known as the druids or elders, who may also have been shamans, able to move between the two worlds, perhaps through taking on the form of animals. Rites took place in temples, forest groves or at springs. There are references in Irish myths to Donn (the dark or the brown one) as the god of the dead and the underworld, standing apart from other gods.

CENTURION: senior non-commissioned Roman army officer, typically in charge of about 80 men.

CHI RHO: an early Christian monogram, formed by superimposing the first two letters, chi and rho (XP), of the Greek word "ΧΡΙΣΤΟΣ" (*Christ*):

CHRISTIANITY IN LATE ANTIQUITY: until the fourth century, Christianity was a minor and occasionally persecuted sect in the Roman Empire. In 313 there was a dramatic change when the Emperor Constantine the Great (ruled 306-337) legalised the religion by the Edict of Milan. This had many effects, one of which was to precipitate a crisis in the identity of Christianity, as multitudes converted and the Church ceased to be a relatively small and beleaguered group. Christianity's appeal was not simply that it was aligned with Imperial power. It brought membership of a vibrant and (generally) compassionate community, at a time of huge social dislocation and when traditional religions were losing their appeal. Beyond these sociological reasons, Christianity offered believers a personal route to incarnated reality and salvation, as well as equality in the eyes of God.

Meanwhile, under Constantine the Great, the Roman state in the person of the Emperor began to play a major role in Church politics and even theology. The Emperors wanted a clear religious orthodoxy to help maintain political unity–

and the church authorities were equally keen, though they disagreed about what was orthodox. During 380-381, the Emperor Theodosius I (ruled 379-395) and his co-emperors decreed that Nicene Christianity - which regarded Jesus as divine and co-eternal with God the Father - was the official and only religion of the empire. From the mid-380s anti-pagan and anti-heresy laws were promulgated, with severe penalties (which were sometimes enforced). This exacerbated a tendency to see the body and nature as inferior or antithetical to Godliness - though some were against this view (such as the minor historical figure of Vigilantius). Mainstream Christian beliefs became increasingly articulate, passionate and authoritarian. Nevertheless, the fact that laws decreeing Christian orthodoxy were issued repeatedly during the next century shows the strength of continuing pagan practice (especially in the countryside and amongst some of the old senatorial families of Rome), as well as the strength of a proliferating array of unorthodox Christian beliefs. However, with the Council of Chalcedon in 451 there was a shift in emphasis, as Jesus was now clearly seen as wholly divine *and* wholly human.

In terms of its geographic spread, Christianity reached southern Gaul (where it flourished) early in the second century. There were some Christians in Britannia by the third century - St Alban was probably martyred in the 3rd century - but Christianity was not a major presence in the island until the fourth century.

CITY COUNCILLOR OR CURIALIS (PL. CURIALES): an obligatory (male) local government post, dependent on a certain level of income, which carried massively more status and responsibility than the equivalent post today. As well as public order, the local courts, public baths, sanitation, building projects, festivities and the Imperial post, the Curia (city council) was responsible for levying all taxes - and the Curiales had to cover any shortfall out of their own pockets. A Curialis was usually a member of the local gentry, though the prestige of the post had declined considerably by the latter part of the fourth century due to the onerous financial burden.

COLONIA AGRIPPINA: contemporary Cologne in Germany, on the Rhine. It was the capital and military headquarters of the Roman province of *Germania Inferior*.

COLUD: Nehtan's (fictional) home village, two day's walk north of the east side of Hadrian's Wall (in contemporary Northumberland).

COMES OR COMITATUS: a senior Roman general commanding a field army (Comitatensis).

CONSTANTINUS III (HISTORICAL FIGURE) – not to be confused with Emperor Constantinus/Constantine I 'the Great' (lived 272-337). Constantinus III was a Roman army officer based in Britannia who declared himself west Roman Emperor (styled Constantinus the Third) in early 407, the third usurper from Britannia in a year. He invaded Gaul in the same year, to establish himself and to counteract the large-scale invasion of Germanic tribes who had crossed the Rhenus (Rhine) on the last day of 406 and who were laying northern Gaul to waste. Aided in particular by the Romano-Briton, Comes Gerontius (see below), Constantinus gained control of most of Gaul and Iberia. The Emperor Honorius recognised Constantinus as his junior Emperor (or Caesar) in March 409.

Military setbacks and collapsing support led to his abdication in 411, followed by his capture and summary execution.

Corinium: Corinium Dobunnorum, the contemporary Cirencester (in the south-west of England), was the second largest town in Britannia (after Londinium) and was the capital of the province of Britannia Prima. It was the centre of the Dobunni tribe.

Decurio (n): an officer commanding a cavalry detachment. (A Decurio was also one of the two main posts in the local city Curia, the other being local magistrate.).

Di Immortales! 'Immortal Gods' or 'Gods above!'

Donn: see Celto-British (pre-Christian) religion.

Durnovaria: town in southern Britannia, now called Dorchester (in Dorset), in the province of Britannia Prima.

Eburacum: York, the principal military garrison for the north of Britannia and the capital of the province of Britannia Secunda. The main tribe in the area was the Brigantes.

Edepol! 'By Pollux!' Mild oath.

Equestrian or Equites: in the highly structured society of the Roman Empire, the Equestrian rank (roughly equivalent to Knights) was based upon the military elite and the wealthy landowning aristocracy, with defined privileges and duties. Above the Equestrians was the order of Senators. Both these elite groups were Patricians (approximately equivalent to the aristocracy).

Federates: barbarian groups of warriors who were

incorporated into the Roman army in return for privileges granted to their tribes (usually, sanctioned settlement inside the Empire). By the 5th century, a major proportion of the Roman field army was composed of federates, from whose ranks many leading generals rose.

FILIUS DEI: Latin for 'Son of God', a Christian term for Jesus.

FREEDMAN OR FREEDWOMAN: an ex-slave, granted freedom by his/her master. This was in contrast to someone who was free-born, either as a Roman citizen or outside the Empire.

GAUL (LATIN, GALLIA): the Roman Diocese of Gaul included contemporary France, western Switzerland, Belgium, Germany west of the Rhine, and southern Netherlands. In the fourth and fifth centuries, the Praetorian Prefecture of Gaul additionally included the Dioceses of Hispania (Spain, Portugal and northern Morocco) and Britannia (England and Wales). Provinces were sub-regions of Dioceses, which in turn were sub-regions of Praetorian Prefectures.

GERMANIA: part of the diocese of Gaul and the Praetorian Prefecture of Gaul. The upper and lower provinces of Germania were both west of the Rhenus (Rhine) border.

GERONTIUS (HISTORICAL FIGURE): there are conflicting views about the details of his life, though it is generally agreed that he died in 411. He was probably a Romano-Briton by birth, and was appointed Comes (senior General) by Constantinus III in 407, to command half of his forces in Gaul. Gerontius did well, stabilising southern Gaul and then subduing Hispania. However, in the summer of 409 he revolted against Constantinus III, probably because he feared that he was about to be replaced by Constans, the son of Constantinus III, who had declared Constans his co-Emperor. Gerontius allied with various Vandals and Franks, and for the next year he battled with the troops of Constans, mostly in southern Gaul, while also trying to reconcile with the legitimate west Roman Emperor, Honorius. In 410 Gerontius abandoned his bid for recognition as a loyal leader by Honorius, and declared his associate Maximus as Emperor (whose power was slight, short and confined to Hispania). Gerontius eventually defeated and killed Constans in central Gaul in 410, from where he went on to besiege Constantinus III in Arelate in southern Gaul in the summer of 411. However, his siege was interrupted when the Emperor Honorius's new and highly effective general, Constantius (unfortunately with yet another similar name), arrived with a disciplined army. This led to the desertion of many of Gerontius's troops and the flight of Gerontius to his base in Hispania. He was surrounded in his house at Tarragona and committed suicide, after first killing his faithful Alan servant and his wife Nonnichia.

GOAR: (historical figure); a prince or chieftain of one of various tribes of Alans. He led his group across the Rhine at the end of 406, along with the Vandals, other Alans, and Suevi, but he split from them, deciding to seek federation and a homeland from the Emperor Honorius. Goar remained in Gaul, settling around Orléans. He played a part in subsequent Gaulish politics, in alliance with the Burgundians. Shanik Gochar is the (fictional) Alannic name for Prince Goar.

GOTHS: a major confederation of east Germanic peoples. The west Goths (or Visigoths) under King Alaric invaded Italy (for the second time) in 408 and eventually sacked Rome in 410 (fairly mildly), before being persuaded to move on to Gaul as a Roman federate ally and ultimately to Hispania, where they defeated the Vandals.

HADRIAN'S WALL OR 'THE WALL': this wood, stone and earth rampart ran from where Newcastle now is to Carlisle in northern England. It symbolised the northernmost border of the Roman Empire from its completion in c.128, though it did not strictly mark the boundary of the Empire, whose power and influence extended beyond.

HEIA! OR EIA! 'Good!' or 'Quick!'

HEU! 'Ugh!' or 'Alas!'

HIPPOSANDAL: the hipposandal was a device that protected the hoof of a horse. It was commonplace in the north-western countries of the Roman Empire and was a predecessor to the horseshoe. A game could be played with the metallic ring of old hipposandals, trying to throw them over a distant post.

HISPANIA: the Imperial Diocese of Hispania included the contemporary countries of Spain, Portugal and northern Morocco.

HONESTIOR: literally, a more honourable person (roughly equivalent to 'Gentlemen'), a legal and civic distinction in the Roman Empire, which meant that one was part of the ruling class (anyone from a Curialis up to the expanded Senatorial class of late antiquity). Honestiores could not be flogged or tortured and were part of the delegated system of Imperial power and taxation. Any Roman subject who was not an Honestior was an Humilior (a plebeian or member of the middle or lower classes, who were also citizens) or was a slave.

HONORIUS (HISTORICAL FIGURE, 384-423): the ruling Emperor in the western half of the Roman Empire from 395 to 423 was Flavius Honorius Augustus. Honorius gained power by virtue of succeeding his dynamic father, Theodosius, the last ruler of both halves of the Empire. In contrast, Honorius was young (25 in 409), inexperienced and vacillating. In 408 he connived in the murder of the powerful military Generalissimo and strongman, Stilicho, after which most of the west collapsed into a decade of anarchy. A year later, Honorius felt obliged by the dire political and military situation in Italy to recognise the usurper Constantinus III as junior Emperor in the West in 409 (see above). The rest of Honorius's reign was chaotic and by the time of his death in 423, Britannia, Hispania and most of Gaul had passed into barbarian control.

JUDAISM: was not actively suppressed at this time, though Jews were discriminated against and forbidden any official position or place of honour.

LEGION: by the 4th century, the Roman army had developed into mobile field armies (Comitantenses) alongside a large contingent of sedentary border guards (Limitanei). The massive legions of old, which included every type of specialist alongside a preponderance of infantry, were reduced to forces of about 1,000 infantry-men. Cavalry squadrons were separate, though some may have been permanently linked with particular legions.

LEMMA MAGNA: Matugenus's (fictional) main country estate and villa, south-east of Corinium.

LONDINIUM: London, the capital of the Imperial Diocese of Britannia.

MARE NOSTRUM: ('Our Sea') the colloquial Roman name for the Mediterranean Sea.

MARRIED CLERGY: at least up until the 6th century, continence was not universally expected of Christian clergy, and many priests were married. Even after the decree by Emperor Justinian I in 530 that all marriages contracted by clerics were null and void, within two centuries the law of celibacy was little observed in a great part of the Western Church.

MASSILIA: the contemporary Marseilles, an ancient port of the south coast of Gaul (France).

MEHERCLE! 'By Hercules!'

MERDA! 'Shit!'

MITHRAS: Mithraism was a mystery religion, centred on the 'unconquered' sun-god Mithras. It originated in Persia (or the Anatolian highlands), but in the Roman Empire it developed its own distinct identity. Mithraism was practiced in underground Temples, and attracted many Roman soldiers and bureaucrats during the 1st to the 3th century, though it never achieved official status and had to contend with a plethora of other Roman and near eastern cults. In the 4th century Mithraism, like all other non-Christian religions, was quickly superseded after Constantine I 'the Great' declared allegiance to the Christian God at the Edict of Milan in 313. The second half of the 4th century saw the widespread destruction of Mithraic temples and images by fanatic Christians, usually supported by the Imperial authorities. The most common subsidiary figure in Mithraic images is the dog – half-way between man and nature.

Mudebroth: 'By God's judgement' in ancient British.

Names: Roman naming is complex and changed over the centuries. In general, higher status individuals had three names: which names were used, and when, varied according to the formality of the context and the relationship between the addressee and the addressor. Low status people and slaves generally had only one name. For the sake of simplicity and easier identification, only one name is used for nearly everyone in *Beyond the Black Gate*.

Nymayr (or nyMayrey): an ancient British-Celtic (and Manx) word for 'Mother'.

Narbo: a significant Roman port on the south-west coast of Gaul. The contemporary city of Narbonne lies some kilometres from the sea due to the silting up of the river and marshlands.

Patrician: roughly equivalent to aristocrat (the upper echelon of the broader Honestior, or 'gentleman', legally-defined class). This included the Senatorial and Equestrian ranks.

Paulinus of Pella (historical figure): there are conflicting views about the details of his life. He was born in 377 at Pella in Macedonia (in contemporary Greece) but spent most of his life in Aquitania in south-west Gaul. He was an indolent, literary Patrician, and was married (his wife here is the fictional Clara). However, he was defrauded out of most of his estates (fictionally, by his brother) and was displaced by the Vandal-Alan invasion of Gaul in 407. He subsequently played a part in the complicated politics of southern Gaul, including a brief stint as the Administrator of the Imperial Finances of a Gothic-backed usurper in Gaul. Shortly after this, Paulinus was in a city besieged by Visigoths and Alans, and contacted the Alan chief (who may have been the historical Prince Goar), asking to be allowed to escape with his family. He was not permitted to do this but he did manage to persuade the Alans to desert the Goths in return for the promise of lands and on delivery of his wife and son as hostages. Hence, the Alans swapped sides and the Goths called off the siege. Towards the end of his very long life, Paulinus settled in Massilia (Marseilles), where he wrote a long, autobiographical (and not necessarily accurate) poem, *Eucharisticos*. He died some time after the year 461.

PICTS: see Caledonians.

PLEBEIAN: the 'plebs' or plebeians were the commoners or lower classes ('humiliores'), in the Roman Empire. All citizens who were not 'honestiores' (see above), were by definition plebeians.

PRESBYTER: literally 'elder', from the Greek. By the fourth century both presbyters and bishops had come to be thought of as 'priests', specially chosen to preside over the celebration of the Eucharist, though the term 'priest' was not widely used until later. Presbyters were frequently married at this time, though bishops were generally unmarried, or if married, were celibate. The relationship between the two was evolving. Jerome (347-420) wrote that 'presbyters may know that by the custom of the church they are subject to the one who has been placed over them; so also bishops may understand that they are greater than presbyters more by custom than by the veritable ordinance of the Lord'.

Ravenna: the major Roman port on the Adriatic coast of Italy. In c.401, the Imperial Court moved permanently to Ravenna, which was protected on the landward side by walls and extensive marshes. The city thus became the capital of the Western Empire. It was also the main base for the Imperial fleet.

Remorum: the contemporary Rheims, a significant Roman city in northern Gaul.

Rhenus, the Rhine, which was the eastern border of Roman Gaul, across which lived numerous Germanic tribes, many members of which had moved inside the Empire, notably as federate (auxiliary) troops.

Romanitas: aka civilitas ('civility'): 'the Roman way', meaning traditional Roman values and practices such as loyalty to the Empire, membership of a common political and cultural community, education in the classics, adherence to written law, self-control, public duty, and frequent bathing. Unlike virtually all other empires, Roman identity was not based on ethnicity. This term arose in the third century.

Sacramentum or Sacramenta: the early term for the Mass, the Christian sacrament of the Eucharist.

Saint Agnes: almost nothing is known of Agnes of Rome (c.291-c.304) except that she was very young when she was martyred. Legend has it that Agnes was a beautiful girl whom many young men wanted to marry. Among those she refused, one reported her to the authorities for being a Christian, which she refused to deny. This was during the time of the 'great persecution' of Christians under the Emperor Diocletian, and Agnes became one of its victims. Her age and martyrdom reportedly made a great impact at the time. In the Catholic Church, she is the patron saint of chastity, girls, engaged couples, rape survivors, virgins and gardeners.

SAINT PAULUS SERGIUS: Saint Paul of Narbonne was one of the "apostles to the Gauls", probably sent by Pope Fabian (236–250) to re-Christianize Gaul after the persecutions under Emperor Decius. Paul established the church at Narbonne as its first bishop and died peacefully. Later legend, in a bid to connect church relics directly with the apostles, identified Paul of Narbonne with the Roman proconsul Sergius Paulus, who was converted by Paul the Apostle according to Acts 13:6–13.

SAMHAIN: one of the four Celtic (pre-Christian) religious festivals, taking pace in early November. Samhain marked the beginning of winter and the onset of the darker half of the year, when the boundary between this world and the 'Otherworld' blurred and offerings were made to appease the gods - and dead kin – in order to ensure that the people and livestock survived the winter.

SARMATIANS: this loose confederacy of Iranian-related peoples roamed what is now eastern Ukraine in Roman times. They were part of a broader region north of the Black Sea known to the Greeks and Romans as Scythia (which covered much of Ukraine and southern Russia). In 175 the Emperor Marcus Aurelius defeated a tribe of Sarmatians and took many into the Roman army. Thousands were settled in the north of Britannia. The Alans (see above) were a major group that evolved from the Sarmatians.

SAXONS: the Saxons came from what is now north-west Germany, outside the Empire.

SCOTI: the Scoti (or Scotti) came from the northern end of Ireland, which the Romans called Hibernia.

SLAVERY: By AD c.400, slaves accounted for about 10% of the Empire's total population of perhaps 50 million, half owned by elite senatorial and Honestior households and half by middling urban and rural classes. Slavery was far more widespread in the Mediterranean littoral than in northern Europe. Natural reproduction was the main source of slaves, though slave raiding of vulnerable peoples (both inside and outside the borders) became increasingly significant from the late 4th century. The world of slaves and freedmen/women was highly complex, with many gradations, and there was a great difference between the life of a household slave as against that of an agricultural slave. A gifted and trusted household slave or freedman, if he had a powerful master, could well end up with considerable power and even wealth. But the vast majority of enslaved people lived at the mercy of exploitation and sexploitation by their master, with no rights.

SPATHA: the standard, three-foot long Roman army sword, in common military use in the fourth and fifth centuries. There was also a shorter version.

STUPRUM: a sex crime against an unmarried or widowed female or against a male citizen, generally equivalent to rape. Sexual crime was determined by the status of the female partner: 'adulterium' was violation of married women; 'stuprum' was violation of virgins, widows or men. In Roman law, the offence was defilement of the family honour. In late antiquity, stuprum was potentially punishable by death, depending on the status of the woman and her family. Like an animal, a slave was not a citizen and had no honour and so had no legal protection against rape. A slave owner whose slave was raped could sue for injury to his property.

TARRACO: contemporary Tarragona (on the Mediterranean coast, 100 km south-west of Barcelona). Tarraco was the oldest Roman city in Iberia and was the capital of the province of Tarraconensis, which was the largest of the Iberian provinces.

TOLOSA: contemporary Toulouse in south-west France. By the fourth century, Tolosa was one of the largest cities of the western empire. In 409, it was besieged by the Vandals, but under the leadership of its bishop, Saint Exuperius, the city resisted behind its strong walls. The Vandals lifted the siege and moved into Spain. In 413 Tolosa was captured by the Visigoths and later (in 418), after a peace agreement between the Emperor Honorius and the Visigoths, it became the capital of the (temporary) Gothic kingdom of Aquitania.

TREVERORUM: Augusta Treverorum, the present-day city of Trier in Germany. Treverorum was the capital of the Praetorian Prefecture of Gaul from 337 to around 401, after which the seat of the Prefecture moved to Arelate (Arles). For much of the fourth century the western Emperors held court for some of the time in Treverorum, in order better to be able to control their troops and the threatening Germanic tribes, alternating usually with Mediolanum (Milan) rather than Rome. Treverorum was the largest Roman city north of the Alps, with a population approaching 100,000 at its peak in the 4th century.

TRIBUNE: in late antiquity, a military rank corresponding roughly to a junior or mid-rank General.

VAE! 'No!' or 'Woe!' expressing strong dismay or pain.

VANDALS: a group of Germanic tribes who came to prominence after they led a massive barbarian incursion into the Roman Empire, across the Rhine on the last day of 406, devastating much of north-eastern and (later) southern Gaul. In late 409, with their Alan and Suevi allies, they crossed the Pyrenees into Hispania, where Roman-allied Visigoth forces eventually defeated one of the two major groups. In 429, a joint Vandal-Alan force crossed to North Africa. By 439, they had conquered the critical west Roman bread-basket of contemporary northern Algeria and Tunisia, sounding the death-knell of the western half of the Empire.

VICARIUS: the Vicarius was the civilian ruler or governor of a Diocese (a group of Roman provinces), appointed by the Emperor.

VIGILANTIUS: (HISTORICAL FIGURE): a Christian presbyter (priest) born in Aquitania (south-west Gaul) in the latter part of the 4th century. He was ordained under the learned Sulpicius Severus and went to Palestine in the 390s, where he stayed with the famous theologian and translator of the bible, Jerome. Vigilantius returned to Gaul, where he apparently spoke unfavourably of Jerome, with whom he disagreed strongly. Vigilantius wrote and preached against what he saw as pagan superstition and unbalanced asceticism. He attacked the growing cult of martyred relics (and associated claims for miracles), offering prayers for the dead, elaborate ceremonial, sending alms to Jerusalem (instead of giving them locally), clerical celibacy and the monastic flight from the company of women – all of which were gaining currency at this time, supported by Jerome and Augustine. Jerome rebutted Vigilantius in a splendidly furious and intemperate work,

Contra Vigilantius ('Against Vigilantius'), in 406, which is now the main source on Vigilantius. As well as reviling the 'perfidious poison' of Vigilantius, a 'monster who ought to be banished to the ends of the earth', Jerome accused him of playing 'the philosopher over his cups, soothing himself with the sweet strains of psalmody, while smacking his lips over his cheese-cakes'. The tide of history was against Vigilantius, who probably suffered a degree of official disapproval and banishment. He disappeared from recorded history after 406.

VOTADINI: a tribal federation whose territory (outside the Empire) in the fifth century was in south-east Scotland and north-east England, extending from the Firth of Forth down to Hadrian's Wall and the River Tyne.